MW01232569

Cold
Hearts
Burning

by

JOHN W. HUFFMAN

[handwritten] 12/16/2010

Acknowledgments

My deepest appreciation to my reader's circle for all their invaluable feedback and suggestions on the early drafts of this manuscript, with explicit appreciation to Charlotte Hillard, Whitney Brock, Jackie Jansen, Billy Sprouse, Anna Huffman, Jerry Nealy, and Sigrid Rosemarie Spangenberg.

I extend special recognition and gratitude to the very talented Whitney Brock for the striking cover design and the meticulous Fay Sprouse for the proof editing.

To my adorable wife, Misty, for the love, support, and encouragement that made this book a reality.

Chapter 1

Dean had no thoughts of love, murder, or mayhem as he parked his brother's ancient Ford in the drive on his side of the dilapidated apartment duplex. His central focus was the humiliation of sponging off his older sibling for basic transportation, a byproduct of his accident six weeks earlier that ended his career on the police force and compelled him to allow a friend to take up the payments on his practically new Camaro. He heaved his shoulder against the jammed door, wincing from the discomforting residue of his injuries, and limped to the street favoring his sore left ankle three days removed from a cast to retrieve the mail, grimacing as he stooped to pick up the newspaper from the lawn.

Normally not one to dwell within the realms of self-pity, regrets seemed his mainstay lately after spending weeks immobilized in a hospital encased in casts and tubes with nothing to do but dwell on his miscreant life. Foremost amongst his misgivings was that after eagerly leaving this backwaters town with its stagnant population vowing never to return, he was now back in this despised place licking his wounds in relative obscurity. Though the adverse circumstances surrounding his injuries prevented him from draw-ing medical compensation, he had no quarrel with that since some thought he deserved to be in jail. The fact that he was not was a direct tribute to his noble former boss, Captain Ingles, who used his considerable influence to allow him to resign in lieu of facing manslaughter charges, the only benefit culled from the ill-fated incident.

He gimped back up the drive to the old slab-sided house with its strips of peeling white paint searching through the stack of mail for his severance check. Not finding it, he set the electric bill on the kitchen counter, tossed the rest in the trashcan, and grabbed a six-pack of Bud from the refrigerator before hitching along back out to his half of the drooping front porch to settle down into the rickety old rocker. He propped his feet up on the rail, popped the top on his first of the day, and took a long draw as he shook open the newspaper, thinking his rotten luck had to change at some point. That notion quickly dissipated amid beer dribbling down his chin as he focused on Sharon Lucas staring wide-eyed back at him from the front page beneath the bold-faced headline:

LOCAL BEAUTY QUEEN PRIME MURDER SUSPECT

He carefully studied the grainy black and white image, remi-niscent of the hazel-green eyes set in an angelic face surrounded by silk-white hair, of the first girl he ever made out with, the first he ever loved with all of his youthful essence, and the first and only to ever break his heart.

He'd met Sharon the summer of their freshman year in high school when he went to work on her grandmother's farm bailing hay. She appeared out of the iridescent heat waves late one scorch-ing afternoon bearing a glass of iced tea, which she extended to him as the other workers watched spellbound. He stood trembling in near exhaustion, self-conscious of the rivulets of sweat cascading down his bare chest and the matted strands of fresh mowed grass covering his arms as her bewitching eyes searched his soul while he drank the cold liquid in thirst-quenching draughts. When he offered the glass back with a mute nod of gratification, she looked to a strand of weeping willows at the far end of the field.

"There's a spring-fed pond hidden in those trees." Her liquid green eyes sent shivers down his spine as she turned back to him and took the glass from his hand, her fingers cool against his skin. "I often swim there in the late evening to cool down a bit after a hot day like this."

He stood awestruck, breathing hard in the dizzying heat, his nucleus irretrievably hers for the taking, as she turned back to the big house in the distance and made her way through the field with unhurried care, watching after her until she faded back into the imprecise heat streamers.

His heart never recovered after she dumped him in their junior year, where she dreamed of becoming a super model when an opportunistic modeling coach convinced her she had all of the right equipment to get there. In that endeavor, she chose to ditch him in order to take up with the sleazebag twenty years her elder at her then tender age of seventeen. He stood aside watching in anguish as his nemesis sported her around in his Jaguar their senior year, and after a raw spell of wallowing in woeful sorrow, embarked on a tirade of womanizing to ease the pain. But the hurt never ceased. Her memory still brought an ache that left him weak at times … and bitter at others.

During his subsequent freewheeling two-year college misadventure and ensuing five years on the police force, he'd lost contact with her. No doubt, she had been through several coaches since then, and he regrettably through more women than he cared to remember, but none that ever captivated him as she had. He tried to steady his pulse and quell the stabbing pangs of remorse, recalling the taste and texture of her sensuous lips, as he dropped his feet from the rail and leaned forward to read the article.

> *Early this morning Sheriff Benny Parsons detained local beauty queen Sharon Lucas, age 25, as a prime suspect in the murder of Kenny Felton, age 29. Sheriff Parsons placed Miss Lucas in custody after Deputy Paul Miller responded to a call from a neighbor reporting the discharge of a firearm near midnight in the upscale Belmont Apartment complex off Lady Street, where Miss Lucas resides. Deputy Miller found Mr. Felton lying in the parking lot beside his car, where County Coroner Chris Higgins pronounced him dead at twelve thirty-five this morning from an apparent gunshot wound. Sources unrelated to the ongoing investigation report that Mr. Felton and Miss Lucas, formerly engaged to be married, had recently dissolved their marital commitments.*
>
> *Kenny Felton is the youngest of two sons of prominent First Citizen Bank President Robert C. Felton and his wife, Debra. Mr. and Mrs. Felton are reportedly vacationing out of the country and unavailable for comment.*
>
> *Sharon Lucas is the eldest granddaughter of Bernice Peters, who assumed custody of Miss Lucas and her younger sister Charlene after a tragic automobile accident took the lives of her daughter, Clarice, and son-in-law, John Lucas.*
>
> *Miss Lucas, an aspiring model, is a prior beauty queen for the annual Dogwood Festival and a former top ten finalist in the Miss Texas Beauty Pageant.*

Dean drained the beer from the can, crumpled it in his fist, tossed it onto the porch beside him, and reached for another as he propped his feet back up on the rail, his thoughts in disarray as a bright red Volkswagen Beetle clattered into the drive and parked behind his brother's Ford.

You will never be emotionally stable until you face your demons, echoed through Lisa's mind as she stared through the windshield at her demon. Although quite certain her therapist hadn't meant that in a literal way, she was here to do just that with the man before her now. A shiver of trepidation worked its erratic way through her as she watched his head turn quizzically in her direction attempting to discern her identity through the glare of the sun dancing off her windshield. *It's not too late to halt this foolish venture*, she thought tentatively. *I can back out of the drive and hurry away before he recognizes me. No, damn it, it's time to end it. I've been through enough brief liaisons with him eternally lingering in my psyche forcing me to compare his lustful embrace to others and inevitably find them lacking. The time has come to purge him from my soul. I despise him enough to do so, but my unquenchable draw to him is far stronger.* She took a deep breath and forced a smile as she stepped out of the car.

"Hi, Dean, welcome back home!" she called gaily.

Dean squelched an overpowering impulse to lift his near-crippled butt up from the rocker and run as the lithesome, blue-eyed brunette with dimples in her cheeks waved at him. If bad luck did indeed come grouped in threes, this was definitely the third whammy following his accident and the unfortunate news of Sharon's arrest for murder. *Surely bad luck can not pound me eternally, he thought furtively, there has to be a turn for the better somewhere in my dismal future!*

He hadn't seen Lisa since they graduated from high school. A slim cheerleader back then, with a reputation for being untouchable, she'd filled out into a fine looking woman now, he noted warily, eyeing her shapely bottom as she dipped into the backseat of the little car to emerge with a brown paper sack in her hand. During the period after Sharon and he broke up, when he was preoccupied with chasing skirts in his demented mindset, he dated Lisa for a short time near the end of their senior year to see if she really was impervious to his wildly galloping youthful hormones.

Unfortunately, she read more into their ensuing relationship than a casual fling and things thus ended on a rather dismal note, causing the mere sight of her now to throw a strong tremor of raw guilt pulsating through him.

"I brought a peace offering," she offered nervously, hefting a bottle of wine from the sack as she stepped up onto his porch. She paused abruptly, her stomach fluttering as his dazzling blue eyes appraised her from beneath his thick tangle of blond hair, finding the years had turned the slim, handsome teenage boy with the captivating, devil-may-care grin into a solid, raucously striking man with a sexy two-day growth of stubble on his chin. As he stood slowly with a bewildered look, she noted he was taller now—and his nearness decidedly more unsettling than anticipated. Unable to meet his intense stare, she glanced at the newspaper in his hand as she brushed by and entered his half of the duplex. "I see you're reading about the glamorous Sharon Lucas. Do you have wine glasses?"

"Uh, *no!*" he answered, hooking his six-pack with an index finger and hastening after her.

"*Pew-wee*, what a dump!" she observed piously, glancing at the bare walls and decrepit old sofa and easy chair crouched before the TV as she made her way to the kitchen to deposit the sack on the counter. "Why aren't you staying with your mother on the good side of town?"

"Are you lost?" he countered, placing his six-pack back in the refrigerator.

"I'm here to collect what you still owe me," she quipped as she took a corkscrew and wine glass from her sack, popped the cork, and poured. She lifted her glass, imagining his broad shoulders stretching a police uniform wide above his tantalizingly narrow hips and flat stomach. "So here's to … what … our magical time together?"

He tapped his can of beer against her glass scornfully. "*Ex-friends and former lovers*' works for me!" During a roaring pre-graduation party a few weeks after their brief liaison began, she'd caught him butt-naked in the backseat of his pal Glenn Barnes' Chevrolet with an equally bare-skinned Sandra Mae Thomas, who he'd heard had since progressed from designated slut in high school through local small-town harlot eminence to happily married mother of three. Caught up in the moment, Lisa punctuated her displeasure with their estranged state by placing the front bumper of her mother's new Cadillac Seville against the rear bumper of Glenn's unfortunate old Bel-Air and shoving it over an embankment into Duff's Creek at the end of Lilac Lane. A short time after the nefarious incident, he'd charged off to college on a partial academic scholarship determined to become one of the financial elites of the world, only to soon discover they didn't offer a degree in booze and broads. After losing his scholarship and flunking out in his second year, he'd then entered the police academy where he'd managed to hang around long enough to graduate at the bottom of his class.

"And *what* exactly do you think I still owe *you*?"

She lowered her glass, unwittingly focusing on his sensuous lips imagining them hotly consuming her own. "An apology, assuming you still don't find one beneath you!"

"Are you serious?" he demanded as another flash of annoying guilt worked its way through him, and then smiled complacently. "Okay, I'm really-really sorry things didn't work out between us years and years ago, so now you can just trot on back over to your good side of town!"

"A little sincerity would add a nice touch," she chastised testily.

"That's better than you deserve—Glenn is still *pissed* at me."

"He should be for wrecking his car!"

He jutted out his chin. "*I* wrecked his car?"

"As I recall, you were supposed to be my guy."

"As *I* recall, we never made any long-term commitments!"

She fought the urge to toss her wine in his smug face. "Do you recall all the *sweet nothings* you murmured in my ear while you were busily *deflowering me*?"

"*I recall* you were more than eager at the time!"

She glared as she sipped her wine, annoyed that he was theoretically right. She had consciously thrown herself at him anticipating the adoring affection he had lavished upon Sharon for the whole world to see in return—but her gift had meant virtually nothing to him, the bastard! "I'm surprised you recall at all since you couldn't seem to distinguish me from your other sleazy conquests at the time," she jeered, fury displacing the calm she had willed within before arriving.

He held up his index finger. "*One*, Blue Hole Lake."

She flushed remembering the sea of silver satin the moon wrapped them in on the blanket that night, her first nude in a man's arms. He had been gentle and patient, his roaming hands ardently stroking her body to a fever pitch of wanton abandon followed by sweet pain as he consumed her. With pulse racing and a searing heat rising in her abdomen, she recalled the joyful tears she shed afterwards clinging to him, her body weak and thrilled beyond wonder with newly awakened womanhood.

He held up his middle finger next to the index finger. "*Two*, the backseat of Glenn's Chevy at the drive-in movie."

"What was showing?" she demanded, forcing the tender reminiscence aside.

He scowled. "How the hell do I know, we were in the *backseat*, remember?"

"I can't believe you forgot what was showing!" she snipped in an attempt to thwart the budding pangs of desire seeping through her.

"*I* can't believe you remember the name of the stupid movie!" he argued as he waved three fingers aloft. "And *lastly*, in your bedroom while your parents were at the Country Club."

"You weren't even supposed to *be* there!"

"You didn't exactly slam the door in my face!"

"I *should* have!"

"It was *you* who suggested we go into your bedroom!"

"You had me *pinned* on my mother's crushed velvet sofa in the *living* room!"

She gulped at her wine to regain her equilibrium, exasperated at not having anticipated the keen appeal of his masculinity, the longing for the curl of his lips over hers, the lure of his enchanting eyes. *Damn you all to hell, I'm here to purge you from my system, not devour you!*

"Right after that, you dumped me in the creek," he concluded triumphantly.

"What about my front porch swing?" she demanded, searching for focus.

"That doesn't count—your mother turned on the damned porch light!" He took a deep breath. "Look, you got your apology, what more do you want?"

She appraised him aloofly over the rim of her glass. "Don't you find it stimulating to finally make amends now that you're back from sampling all the wicked pleasures of the world?"

"Make amends for what purpose?" he challenged.

She shrugged. "Perhaps to help me understand why you're such a lowlife jerk?"

What more could he say—that he was an immature, insensitive, self-indulgent, broken-hearted lout back then? "The past in past, Lisa, and best left there!"

Rage surged through her, stiffening her resolve. "You're so cynical, Dean! You'd think someone would've nursed you back into the human race by now!"

He focused on her inviting lips and leaned in close. "Nope, hasn't happened yet, but playing nurse with you is an intriguing prospect if you'd like to take on the task …"

She sidestepped him as her legs weakened and sank down in a chair at the table to put some distance between them. "Surely you're not suggesting we pick up where we left off?"

He seated himself across from her to get the weight off his ankle. "Of course not—we *left off* with me standing knee deep in a creek and you screaming I was an *asshole*, remember?"

She took a calming sip of her wine. "So, is there anyone significant in your life now?"

He crossed his arms. "Not that it's any of your damned business, but I tend to limit myself to the purely recreational types these days."

She bathed him in an acid stare. "I see nothing has changed in your warped outlook."

"I think of it as true insight born of hard experience honed to an exact science regulated to a strict discipline."

"Whatever *that* means!"

He smirked. "It means that basically I find women aren't worth the emotional investment and have very little intrinsic value outside of the bedroom and kitchen."

"You're still an egotistical jackass!" she declared, resisting the urge to throw the wine bottle at him. "I thought we could become friends!"

"*After* we've been lovers—what would be the point?"

She stiffened. "The point is you *still* need a strong dose of *reality* where women are concerned!"

He uncrossed his arms and leaned forward. "Frankly, I still have a problem with the reality of you ramming the ass-end of Glenn's car and knocking me over a cliff into a river!"

Her pupils dilated. "It was a *little* shove into a *shallow* creek which you *justly* deserved!"

"Furthermore, since *I* had to pay for the repairs to Glenn's wheels, *I* can't see us becoming *friends* until *you're* prostrate on the floor begging forgiveness!"

"In your *sweetest dreams!*" she spat furiously. The *gall* of the bastard! What had she been thinking in coming here?

They glared at each other for a long minute before he leaned back in his chair with a heavy sigh. "Look, fighting about the past is silly."

She nodded curtly. "I agree."

"Okay, I'll admit I didn't take things as seriously as you did back then if you'll agree to let the matter stand," he offered, thinking women were a hell of a lot more trouble than they were worth, especially ones who tended to harbor grudges.

She shrugged. "I suppose that's a start."

He reached for his beer. "So what have you done with yourself over the years?"

"After college, I worked as an administrative assistant with an investment firm in Beaumont," she replied, forcing a civil tone.

A stab of remorse shot through him at his own lack of initiative. "So how's the investment business these days?"

She lowered her eyes. "My position was recently eliminated due to downsizing."

"So now you're back with your parents?"

"Only until I find a place of my own," she admitted grudgingly.

"So what *really* brings you to my humble abode?"

"I told you, I mistakenly thought we could spend some quality time together healing old wounds."

"No one told you that was a dumb idea?"

She blinked her lashes diffidently. "My mother did." Actually, Mother essentially thought she was insane for wanting to confront him after all these years and even threatened to call her former therapist.

"Well, I'm delighted we could spend some quality time together healing old wounds. So what's next on your morbid little agenda?"

"Find a new job and get on with my life, of course."

"Have you considered applying for a position in a witch's coven? You certainly have the credentials and can list me as a reference if you'd like."

She glowered. "Oh, *fun-ny*."

"I suppose it depends on your perspective," he replied pleasantly. "So how's *your* love life?" When she pressed her lips together, he grinned and shifted his gaze across her ample breasts and down her shapely hips and long legs in a calculating manner. "What's the problem? You still seem to be packaged right."

"There's more to a relationship than sex, Dean," she chided. "But of course *you* wouldn't know anything about that!"

He snickered. "Maybe your lack of viable suitors has something to do with the vacuum between your ears?"

"I can't *believe* I was dumb enough to think we could finally resolve our unresolved issues together!"

"*I* don't have any *unresolved* issues to *resolve!*"

"You're *so* in denial, Mr. Macho-man!"

"*You're* the one looking to resolve unresolved issues!"

"I made a mistake coming here," she grated as angry tears glistened in her eyes.

He grimaced as his sympathy factor edged up the scale with the threat of her unleashing the waterworks. "Look, enough foolishness … *truce?*"

Her eyes narrowed. "*Truce.*"

"More wine?" He filled her glass.

She took a steadying sip. "So, why are you back?"

"I decided to go into business for myself," he lied. In the two weeks he'd been back, he had applied for and received his private investigator's license, posted bond, and received a permit to carry a concealed weapon.

She glanced around the drab room. "Yeah, I saw your ad in the newspaper." When her mother pointed it out over breakfast that morning, it sent her into an emotional tizzy, infuriating her even more that he could still have that effect on her. "So you're a gumshoe now, huh? I can see you're just rolling in the dough. But don't despair—I'm sure somebody's cat will come up missing before long."

He glowered. "I *thought* we called a truce?"

An evil grin teased her lips. "Sorry, the devil got me. Anyway, why would you want to go into that kind of business here in this little burg? Nothing ever happens around here worth investigating."

He snagged another beer from the refrigerator. "You'd be surprised at the secrets in a small town like this, and the need for discretion is much greater here than in a large city."

"I predict you'll starve to death."

"If things don't work out, it's no big deal," he allowed expansively. "I've got a standing offer from my old boss for an undercover job back in Houston." In reality, Captain Ingles had only *implied* such a position might be available when things had settled down politically back there, but that was nobody's damned business but his own. In the interim, he'd calculated his meager savings coupled with his pending severance check would tide him over for three or four months before he had to resort to finding a real job—or moving in with his mother, god forbid.

"You're still not a very adept liar—why did you *really* quit the police force?"

"It's *really* none of your damned business!" he replied belligerently, annoyed that she could see through his bullshit so easily.

"*Ouch*—did I hit a nerve?" she challenged gleefully.

"Let me be honest with you, Lisa: I don't think we can *ever* be friends!"

She pursed her lips. "Your go-to-hell attitude sure isn't helping any."

"What makes you think you know *anything* about *me* or my *attitude?*"

She poured more wine with an unsteady hand, unbalanced by his aggression. "Call it wisdom born of experience."

"I saw a sample of *your* wisdom when you nearly destroyed Glenn's car!"

She scowled. "Okay, let's go ahead and get that out of the way so we can quit fighting about it. Will you *please* forgive me? I'm soooo sorry for doing that. Now can we be friends?"

He calmed himself and leaned forward suggestively. "We could start out as lovers where we left off and work our way back down to friendship if you'd like?"

She pulled back. "Is a crude proposition all you have to offer?"

"Think of it more along the lines of an intriguing proposal."

"Didn't you figure out the first time around I'm not the *purely recreational* type?"

He stood and pulled her up into his arms. "Don't be so uptight, we can still be enemies in the morning, no strings attached. That's why you're really here, isn't it?"

She stumbled back unsteadily, his touch sending hot ripples through her. "I'm looking for something a little more substantial than a quick roll in the sheets, and we both know that's all *you* have to offer." She placed one palm to her forehead as a wave of nausea swept over her and grasped the back of a chair with the other for stability. "I don't feel well … I need to be going."

Dean glanced at the nearly empty wine bottle. "Under the circumstances, you'd be better off staying here tonight."

Dancing anger replaced the glaze in her eyes. "Is that another veiled proposition?"

"It's more the cop in me. You're too tipsy to be driving."

Her eyes narrowed. "I don't think that's a good idea."

"Being on the highway in your condition is a far worse one."

"Maybe I could just lie down on your sofa until my head quits spinning ..."

"Take the bedroom and I'll take the couch." When she hesitated, he grimaced. "Look, you can lock the damned door!"

"Okay," she mumbled as she turned and lurched unsteadily down the hall. "Are your sheets clean?"

"*Goodnight, Lisa!*"

She locked the bedroom door and plunged into the bathroom to bury her face in the toilet, heaving from all the wine and emotional turmoil of seeing him again. When she had emptied the bitter bile from her stomach, she washed her face and tumbled across his bed as waves of dizziness engulfed her, eventually succumbing to the gyrating darkness as self-loathing tears streamed down her cheeks.

Dean sat at the kitchen table in the dark amongst his ominous thoughts of his troubled past, taking care to add a neurotic ex-girlfriend to his growing list of regrets, and drank the remainder of the six-pack before plopping down on the couch to doze fitfully.

Chapter 2

Lisa lifted her throbbing head and looked around in perplexing confusion before remembering she was in Dean's bed. She stumbled to the bathroom to survey her smeared makeup and rumpled clothes in dismay before tiptoeing to the door to listen for the measured breathing coming from the living room signifying he was still asleep, eased down the hall, grabbed her purse, and slipped out.

Dean awoke with a start when the front door closed and hastened up from the couch to watch with some sense of relief as Lisa's Volkswagen backed out of the drive. He put the coffee on to perk, retrieved the paper from the front lawn, and scanned the professional section for his tiny listing as he made his way back to sit at the table to read the remainder without much interest other than the rehash of the ongoing murder investigation. Bored, he picked up the phone on his way out to ensure it was still working, surprised his mother for lunch, who in his opinion appeared to be the only person on earth still happy to see him, and covertly mowed her lawn as payment for the grub before drifting restlessly back to his apartment. That evening as he sat at the kitchen table with a Mickey Spillane novel the front door opened.

"Dean?" Lisa called.

He lifted his head in surprise. "In here."

She hurried into the kitchen with a suitcase in her hand and glanced at the book he was holding. "What are you doing—assessing the latest investigative techniques in your new profession?"

He smirked. "Actually, I'm boning up on how to woo beautiful, scantily clad babes. What are *you* doing?"

She set the suitcase on the floor. "I came over to fix you dinner for letting me stay last night when I got tipsy."

He glanced at her suitcase. "Did you pack the food in that?"

Her cheeks reddened as she gathered her courage. "I have a proposal for you." In reality, she considered it more a half-baked plan brought on by her dire circumstances, but nonetheless had rehearsed her presentation to put the best shine on it. "I was thinking we could pool our resources and share expenses."

His stomach clutched, thinking the woman crazy as a loon, no doubt about it. "Am I to assume there are unabridged fringe benefits associated with this proposal?"

Her eyes darkened. "Don't be uncouth, Dean."

"Think of it as refreshing candor—I'd hate to have any more misunderstandings between us—someone's car might get wrecked." When she winced, he sighed and put the book aside. "Sorry, that was a cheap shot."

"The deal *is,* I'll pay half the rent and do half the cooking and cleaning."

"Right, well, the *thing* is, I only have the one bed."

"We could alternate on the sofa."

He grinned. "Still won't work. People will think we're shacking up and I'm not interested in paying the toll unless I get the roll."

"Why do you have to be so crude, Dean?"

He sighed. "Lisa, in the spirit of being honest with each other, what do you really want from me?"

"To be friends. Why can't you accept that?" After last night's emotional fiasco, she had resolutely settled on a new course of action. She trusted friendship could kill love. There were many attractive men in her old work place she had become friends with, and later been repulsed by when they asked her out. She even knew of an acquaintance who complained about her fiancé spoiling the romance between them by becoming her best friend. It only made sense that placing Dean on another level would purge him from her heart.

"Friendships carry baggage and at the moment I'm carrying more baggage than I care to handle," he replied gruffly, staring her in the eye. "Now what's the *real* deal here?"

She turned to the sink, knowing that after all the prudent, thought-out reasoning she had failed to pull off the charade. "Mother and I had a tiff and I need a place to stay until I get myself sorted out." The simple truth sounded rather silly when weighed against all the practical reasons she had prepared beforehand to justify the somewhat unorthodox arrangement.

"What was the tiff about?"

"You." When she'd dragged herself home that morning looking like a harlot, her mother, distraught over her being with Dean all night, rushed to the phone to beg her former therapist for an emergency appointment, insisting she would drive Lisa over at once. When she refused to go, her mother threatened to call her father home to deal with the situation. Amid an angry barrage of tears, she'd packed her suitcase and hurried out, informing her mother she would be staying with a friend.

"That was dumb," Dean allowed uneasily.

"You and Mother think a lot alike. Look, I'm a good cook, and from the looks of this place, you could use the financial help."

He stared at her callously. "I like my privacy."

A sense of desperation closed around her. She couldn't go back to her mothers and fight endlessly in order to see this thing through. "Can I at least stay the night if I take the sofa?"

He grimaced. "I suppose … for tonight …"

Her heart sank as she hung her head miserably. "Thanks."

He heaved a sigh, folding in the face of her desperation, hating himself for doing so and knowing no good could possibly come of this situation. "Okay, if you want to be pals, fine, we'll be pals, and you're even welcome to crash on my couch for a couple of days while you look for a place of your own."

Relief washed through her. With time she was certain she could bring him around to her way of thinking. "Great! I'll get dinner started."

She prepared a decent pot of spaghetti supported by a good bottle of red wine, and was pleased when he politely praised her culinary skills. Over dinner, she chatted about old high school friends who mostly seemed pregnant or settled into dead-end jobs these days, and afterwards he volunteered to wash the dishes while she took her turn in the bathroom.

He drifted out of the kitchen to find her cuddled up in a sheet on the couch with the television on. "Last chance to share the bed," he offered solicitously. When she pointedly ignored his gracious offer, he drifted on down the hall to his bedroom to toss and turn fitfully half the night mystified by her seeming indifference to his substantial charisma. When he awoke the following morning she was gone, leaving the sheets folded on the couch.

He dressed and ran a few errands, again bummed lunch at his mothers, and made his way dejectedly back to his hole in the wall after washing her car, where he settled down at the kitchen table with his detective book. In late afternoon, the front door opened.

"Anyone home?" Lisa called.

"I didn't hear you knock," he advised as she hurried into the kitchen with a sack.

"I live here now too, remember?"

"Um, I thought you were a temporary house guest?" he clarified, thinking he seriously needed to clip this thing in the bud before it got out of hand.

Choosing evasion over confrontation, she set the sack on the counter. "I brought steak, potatoes, and some salad fixings. It's your turn to cook. I like my steak medium rare. Why don't you get started while I get a couple of boxes from my car?"

A caution light flashed in his mind as she turned to leave the kitchen. "Boxes?"

"I thought I'd hang some things while you fix dinner for us."

Alarm bells chimed in his head. "Hang what things?"

"This dump is so lifeless and barren I don't know how you stand it."

A full five-bell alarm blared. "I happen to *like* my lifeless and barren dump just the way it is, thank you very much!"

"Why are you getting so uptight about me hanging a few things in your little old monastery?" she tossed back as she hurried out.

"Aren't you being a little presumptuous?" he called after her.

"You *can* cook, can't you?" she called back.

"I happen to be an *excellent* cook!"

"Good. I'm starved!"

"I was *referring* to you hanging *junk* on my walls!" he yelled as she went out the front door. "And another thing, if I cook, *you* clean the kitchen!"

He baked the potatoes, marinated and grilled the steaks, tossed the salad, and opened the bottle of red wine she had brought.

27

"Dinner is served, Madame!" he called petulantly above the clamor of her busily hammering nails in his walls, observing she had replaced her modest skirt and blouse with jeans and a faded sweatshirt when she seated herself at the table.

"I put your clothes on the left side of the closet and mine on the right. Your stuff is on the left side of the bathroom cabinet and mine is on the right. I get the bed tonight." She sliced off a delicate bite of steak and placed it in her mouth. "*Umm*, you should be a chef."

He glared at her, thinking it time to put things back in perspective. "What part of our discussion did you not understand?"

She buttered her roll. "What are you referring to?"

"I agreed you could sleep on my couch for a few days until you find a place of your own. I *did not* agree to share my bed with you."

"Could have fooled me," she quipped diffidently. "You've propositioned me every night I've been here."

"Propositioning you means sharing my bed *with* you, not you kicking me out of it onto the couch."

"I'm honored, kind sir, but could you please clarify the rules again?"

"Sure thing—you're welcome to crawl in my bed anytime for purely recreational purposes."

"No wonder you're still a horny bachelor," she snipped. "You've been hanging around your disgusting little floozies too long and need to work on your technique a bit. A proper girl needs a tad more romancing than that."

"You're treading on my last ragged nerve here," he warned ominously.

"Your steak is getting cold." She forked another bite into her mouth and took a sip of her wine, eyes guarded. "Must we argue about every little thing, Dean?"

He picked up his knife and fork, sensing he had lost this round. "We were *arguing* about the *bed*. Forget it, we'll alternate nights while you're here. So, how was your day?"

She shrugged, pleased with wearing him down. "I went on two job interviews."

"And?"

"On the first, a creepy personnel manager stared at my chest the whole time. On the second, they wanted to know how many words a minute I could type."

He stared at her jersey pointedly. "Well, I'm sure you passed the boob test, so how many words a minute *can* you type?"

She glowered. "Don't be vulgar, Dean."

"Did either of them offer you a job?"

"One did."

"Which one?"

Her cheeks darkened. "I can't type."

He grinned.

"Jackass!" She stormed out of the room, thinking him the most exasperating man alive and wondering if she had lost all of her common sense.

As the hammering in the living room resumed, he dumped the scraps in the trash, set the plates in the sink to soak, and poured Lisa's virtually untouched glass of wine into his own. When she placed a pillow and sheets on the couch and went to bed, he turned off the lights and sat at the table to polish off the bottle, his thoughts as deep as the darkness around him.

✲ ✲ ✲

Sometime later, her dark form materialized in the doorway, startling him. "I thought you were in my bed with the door locked tight," he growled.

She slipped into a chair concerned by whatever was troubling him so deeply. "Why are you sitting in the dark brooding?"

He forced the despondency aside in favor of lightening his mood. "It's where I do my best brooding."

"So what are you brooding about?"

"That you were supposed to clean the kitchen."

"I never agreed to that."

"This is not a democracy, I own the lease, remember?"

"Your overbearing attempts at male domination are becoming tedious."

He grinned, enjoying the banter. "That sounds suspiciously like irrational female logic to me. Why are you skulking around in the dark spying on me?"

"I wanted a drink of water."

"Liar."

Perhaps the direct approach would work, she decided. "Okay, I was worried about you sitting here in the dark all alone with your morose thoughts. Is that such a big deal? So talk to me, I'm a good listener."

"I don't need a confidant," he advised coldly.

She flinched at the rebuke. "I ... heard you were in an awful wreck in your police car and in the hospital for over a month. Is that why you quit?" She waited through a strained silence. "Why won't you let anyone near you, Dean?"

"You want to live with me, but not have a relationship," he replied irritably, the fun of baiting her slipping away. "I'd say you're about as near as you can get under the circumstances."

"There's more to a relationship than the physical side, Dean," she urged, sensing him withdrawing and determined to reach him on a basic level. "Why do you insist on being so *distant* from the rest of the world?"

"We split on something less than amicable terms years ago—what do you expect from me now, roses?"

She stiffened in resentment. "That was one of the most significant periods of my life, how can you just shrug it off?"

He fought the queasiness, realizing he had callously blundered onto sensitive ground, but his surly mood not allowing him to back off. "Isn't that a little melodramatic? What's holding you back from hopping in the sack with me now if it was all that great?"

"It wasn't something that just happened between us, you idiot," she bristled. "Don't you realize that by now?"

"I naturally assumed my irascible charm seduced you," he chided.

She placed the tips of her fingers to her eyes to stench the welling tears. Why couldn't he love her the way he loved Sharon back then? Why did he find her so lacking in comparison? Even now, she felt like she was poaching on hallowed ground at the mere mention of Sharon's name. "Why can't you put Sharon behind you, Dean?"

"She *is* behind me, damn it!" he lied like the cur dog he was, swallowing the constriction in his throat as painful visions of Sharon flowed uninvited into his mind.

"Do you plan to see her now that you're back?"

"Beyond the fact she's in jail for murder, what would be the point?"

She placed her hand over his on the table. "I think you're still in love with her, Dean, and you can't effectively deal with that issue until you acknowledge it."

"That's crazy!" He jerked his hand from hers as waves of longing engulfed him. "It was years ago … we were only kids! You're wasting your time with this-this *psychoanalysis* babble!"

"It may help us both get over things," she urged gently.

He grimaced, thankful for the darkness. "I don't need any help getting over *anything*! You're certifiably loony tunes!"

She swallowed back a sob. "What I once felt with you was genuine, Dean. I want that feeling again with someone someday."

Memories of Sharon darted at him. He wanted that feeling again someday too. "Then I hope you find it again with someone someday, Lisa!" A great hollowness grew in him as the familiar pangs of anguish descended over him like a heavy cloak. He silently renewed his vow that no woman would ever make him feel that way again. *Ever!*

"Dean, there's more to me being here than needing a place to stay for a few days," she whispered.

"Do tell," he sneered from the darkness. "But don't you think there are far too many bad memories for us to overcome?"

She sighed. "You're such an egotistical jackass. I suppose that's part of your *irascible charm* as you put it. I'm not here to reconcile with you—in fact, nothing could be the worse for either of us."

"Then please enlighten me as to exactly why you *are* here, Lisa!"

She took a deep breath sensing honesty would be the best policy to heal their individual wounds. "Closure, Dean. I desperately want closure. You see I ... I nearly suffered a nervous breakdown after finding you with that ... little slut. My parents put me in therapy because they were concerned I ... I might ... harm myself. I still find it hard to trust men or have a meaningful relationship."

Remorse slammed his gut like a sledgehammer. "So you plan to make me as miserable as you are in order to get your closure thing?"

She wiped at her cheeks, unable to contain the tears any longer. "Oh, Dean, I don't wish you evil. I admit I once did, but not now. The point of all this is, my therapist said I'd never be emotionally stable until I face my emotions head on. Seeing you again might help me do that. The truth is I want us to be friends so I can get on with my life. Does that make sense?"

He sighed, wondering how he got himself into these crazy situations. "Lisa, I've got my own problems to deal with. I don't know what you expect from me, or have a clue of how to help you find this closure thing."

She stood, resisting the urge to move to him, to comfort him, realizing for the first time he was as tormented over Sharon as she was by him. "I don't expect you to do anything, Dean, except be yourself. We each have to come to grips with things on our own terms. Are you going to bed soon?"

"Soon," he answered weakly.

She turned to the bedroom as he sat wishing with all of his heart he could feel something for her other than raw guilt or lustful desire—belatedly realizing they were both crippled souls because he had ostensibly done to her exactly what Sharon had done to him. Would being friends with her be so terrible if it ultimately helped her get a grip on reality? He supposed he owed her that much.

"Lisa…" She paused with her back to him. "I … I'll try to be your friend, if that's what you need. But I'm me, and sometimes … I'm not much of a friend to anyone … even myself."

She smiled, knowing he was speaking his heart. "That's more than enough for me, Dean, and I'm very grateful. Good night." She slipped down the hall elated.

Later when Dean eased onto the couch, he noticed she had left the bedroom door open. He lay back as Sharon's warm memories clutched at him painfully, insistently, from the deep pungent gloom of his soul.

Chapter 3

Dean snatched the phone off its cradle next to the raggedy old easy chair in his living room as he sorted through the horde of junk mail looking for his severance check.

"Dean Davis, Private Investigations."

"Mr. Davis? This is Bernice Peters."

"Mrs. Peters ... how are you?" he stuttered as Lisa paused in the midst of fixing lunch and tuned in vigilantly.

"Not well, I'm afraid. I guess you've heard about Sharon?"

"Yes, Ma'am ... I read about it in the newspaper."

"*I saw your ad there as well. Could you come by then?*"

"Uh, well—"

"*I'll be expecting you.*"

When the line went dead he hung up the receiver and turned to Lisa, who stood poised in the doorway with a knife in one hand and a tomato in the other.

"Mrs. Peters, Sharon's grandmother?" she asked, her heart skipping a beat.

Butterflies pummeled his stomach. "She saw my ad in the paper and wants me to come by this afternoon."

"Why does she want to see you?"

He grinned. "Possibly one of her cats has come up missing?"

"Jackass."

"Well, whatever she wants, I can't imagine her springing for fifty bucks a day and expenses for my services."

"Why do you say that?"

"I used to work on her farm in the summer bailing hay for a dollar a day. She's as tight with her money as an old Baptist spinster is with her cleavage."

She turned to the counter as a cold chill washed down her spine and efficiently sliced the tomato. "I'm sure you and Sharon had a great time romping around in her haystacks together."

He scowled. "Of course we did—why else would I be willing to work for a dollar a day?"

She flushed. "That was trite of me."

"Indeed it was," he agreed cheerfully.

"Would you like me to drive you over to meet with her?"

"I'd like no such thing!"

"Why not?"

"I don't need a loopy ex-girlfriend mucking around in my livelihood."

She turned to him, eyes narrowed, knife poised. "Do *not* refer to me as an *ex*-girlfriend!"

He smirked. "How would you prefer I refer to you then?"

She turned back to the counter. "Merely as a friend will suffice."

"You're still on probation in that department," he countered as he turned to the door.

"Just call me an associate then!" she offered as she quickly wrapped her sandwich in a napkin and swept the refuse in the garbage before hurrying out after him. "Are you sure you wouldn't rather me drive you?"

He paused at his brother's car. "Now why would I want you to do that?"

She nodded at the relic contemptuously. "That old thing is a piece of junk. The seats are covered with dog hair and have holes in them, the windshield is cracked in two places, the fenders and doors are banged up, it hasn't been washed in five years, and the tires are bald. I wouldn't be caught dead in it."

"It's my brother's *hunting* car," he explained, pained. "And there's little risk of you ever being caught dead in it."

"No self-respecting private eye in the world would be caught dead in it either."

"No self-respecting private eye in the world would be caught dead being chauffeured around in a *Volkswagen* either!" He jerked open the jammed door, climbed in, and hit the starter. The engine made two half-hearted attempts and then ground to a mournful halt.

She bit into her sandwich to hide her smirk as he climbed out, slammed the door, and stalked to the passenger side of her Volkswagen.

"I'm not sure you're doing the right thing here," Lisa whispered as he knocked on Mrs. Peters' door.

"You just keep your trap closed and let me do the talking."

"Sure thing, Sherlock."

A diminutive woman in her mid-sixties, with sun-browned skin beneath a flowery dress and starched apron strapped down the front, the effect giving one the impression of a dried out raisin topped with frizzy white hair, opened the door.

"Good afternoon, Ma'am," Dean gushed, noticing she hadn't changed much in seven years as her inquiring gaze shifted to Lisa. "Uh, this is my associate, Miss Lisa Bryant."

Mrs. Peters' forehead creased. "Are you Mildred's child, by chance?"

"Yes, Ma'am," Lisa acknowledged.

"Mildred is a fine, God-fearing woman and a credit to our community."

Lisa smiled. "Thank you, Ma'am. She speaks highly of you as well."

Mrs. Peters peered up at Dean. "I hardly recognize you, you've grown so. I've had trouble getting good help since you went off."

He flashed a modest grin. "That's kind of you to say, Ma'am."

"Please have a seat on the veranda." She indicated the swing and a cluster of wooden chairs at the end of the porch. "I'll prepare some tea."

Dean ushered Lisa to the swing as Mrs. Peters disappeared off inside the house, soon to reappear with a tray containing four glasses of iced tea and a small saucer of cupcakes. She served them and took one of the two remaining glasses before seating herself in a rocking chair.

"It's going to be another hot one," she observed by way of opening conversation.

"You've got a beautiful farm, Ma'am," Lisa replied graciously as she appraised the cattle grazing in the meadow.

Dean glanced out across the green fields recalling the hot summer days of grime and sweat, of aching backs and blistered hands, as he inhaled the sweet fragrance of fresh cut hay on the thin summer breeze. A shudder of nostalgia rippled through him with the reminiscence of the delightful shock of the spring fed pond in the grove of trees at the head of the meadow where he once plunged his tired body at the end of a long, grueling day. Rapturous memories flooded him anew as he imagined Sharon slipping out in the obscurity of late evening to spend a blissful hour with him there kissing and groping in the shade of the weeping willows in that youthful, carefree era, his essence filling with longing as the old familiar burning sensation expanded into the cavity of his chest.

Mrs. Peters beamed. "Why, thank you, dear. I've tried hard to keep the place up since my poor Albert passed on to his reward some twenty years ago now." She studied Dean as he sipped at his tea. "You've filled out into a handsome young man, Mr. Davis."

He swallowed to ease the ache. "Thank you, Ma'am."

"Charlene will join us shortly."

Dismay waffled through him. "It'll be nice to see her again," he allowed with little sincerity.

Mrs. Peters smiled. "She seems quite excited about seeing you as well."

"I haven't seen her in years," Lisa said.

Mrs. Peters shifted her gaze to the meadow. "Yes, she's only recently returned home."

"Dean! It's so good to see you again!" Charlene swept out onto the porch with a flourish and hugged him as he stood. "You're even more handsome than I remember!"

"It's good to see you again, Charlene," he mumbled as he disengaged himself, vaguely aware that she had evolved from a thin, awkward girl into an attractive young woman with a striking resemblance to Sharon, though taller, with eyes a lighter green and hair a darker hue.

She fixed Lisa with an inquisitive stare. "So you two are back together again?"

"We're just … associates!" Dean corrected as Lisa blushed and gulped her tea. He focused on Mrs. Peters. "Ma'am, would you prefer to meet with me in private?"

"I have no objections to your associate being present, Mr. Davis."

"So you're still on the market after all these years?" Charlene observed, seating herself in a rocker across from him, eyes mischievous. "I'm surprised some lucky girl hasn't run you to the ground by now."

"I'm sure you remember what a tease Charlene is, Mr. Davis?" Mrs. Peters soothed.

Dean faked a smile. "Uh, the matter you wanted to see me about, Ma'am?"

Mrs. Peters fixed him with a penetrating stare. "Do you believe my granddaughter murdered Kenny Felton, Mr. Davis?"

His mind froze. "I ... can honestly say I find it difficult to believe."

Her features softened. "Then I want you to prove her innocent of the crime."

"Prove her innocent, Ma'am?"

"I would like to employ you on her behalf."

Dean choked on the swelling apprehension. "I-I'm not sure I—"

"I assume you to be experienced in criminal matters due to your police training of course, but foremost in my reasoning is that I know first loves are forever things. I expect you will bring a measure of passion to this undertaking that others would not."

"Er, proving someone innocent of a crime is more about factual evidence than bringing, uh, *passion*, to the, uh, undertaking, Ma'am."

"The evidence is all circumstantial, Mr. Davis. I'm confident you'll find sufficient grounds to prove her blameless in this unpleasant matter."

Dean swallowed his trepidation. "Ma'am, I was a simple police officer. Homicide was not something I—"

"Sharon is *innocent*, Mr. Davis. She needs your help to prove it. Will you deny her in her time of need?"

"Our normal fee is one hundred dollars a day and expenses," Lisa offered as excitement built around a vague plan taking shape in her mind.

Dean nearly dropped his glass of tea, thinking that kind of money ludicrous, especially since he was a novice at this detective business and almost certain he couldn't do anything to help Sharon in any case.

Mrs. Peters nodded. "I find the terms acceptable."

Dean set his glass on the table with care. "Ma'am, the district attorney is reviewing the merits of the case, and as such, and I think it would be premature at this point to hire—"

"I can't bear seeing my granddaughter in that awful place." She drew an envelope from the pocket of her apron and extended it to him. "I've prepared a check for a thousand dollars as a retainer for your services."

Dean shuddered as a spasm brought on by his dire financial circumstances shot through him. "Uh, you'll get my best effort, Ma'am."

"I expect as much, Mr. Davis. Moreover, I will add a five thousand dollar bonus if you and your associate here clear this matter up within the week. I will arrange through her lawyer, Mr. Fields, for you to visit with her in the morning. You'll want to meet with him beforehand to familiarize yourself with the case, I'm sure." She sat back in her chair and clasped her hands in her lap as moisture gathered in her faded blue eyes above her weathered cheeks.

Charlene stood. "I'll walk you to the car, Dean." She slipped her arm through his and led him off the porch as Lisa trailed after them. "I've been saving this all these years." She placed a nickel in his palm. "So consider it used."

"Uh, goodbye, Charlene," he mumbled as he slid into the passenger seat.

"Let's do dinner soon!" she called as Lisa lurched off.

"What do we do now?" Lisa asked, filled with anticipation as she mentally worked the angles of her new strategy.

Dean scowled at her. "*We?*"

"I'm working with you on this, right?"

"Says who?"

"You did."

"I did no such thing!"

"You said I was your associate."

"That's what you *told* me to call you!" he protested.

"She specifically offered us *both* that bonus if we solved the case within a week. I'll be your sidekick, like Doctor Watson was with Sherlock Holmes."

"I don't want a sidekick, thank you. Besides, you're not qualified."

"How am I not qualified?"

"You're not a doctor."

"I'm *serious*, Dean. Two heads are better than one and you said yourself you don't have any experience in homicide investigations."

"Being my sidekick won't pay your rent or buy your groceries."

"Being your partner will," she reasoned, animated by the prospect of working on an actual case for gads of money, as well as providing the perfect excuse to stay close to him until she got herself sorted out.

He gaped at her. "My *partner?*"

"It's not like I've got anything else to do at the moment," she reasoned.

"Are you nuts?"

"You're just being stubborn!"

He shrugged, amused, thinking *what the hell, this isn't like a for real case or anything, so where's the harm in playing along with her delusions of grandeur, and it just might provide an opportunity to check out that terrific body she's packaged in these days*. "Okay, suit yourself, you can be my associate on this case."

She beamed. "Really? Great!"

He turned his head to the window to hide his smirk. "You do realize associates do all the dirty work, right?"

She frowned. "That's not very flattering."

"That's the price you pay to sit at the feet of a craftsman and learn his trade."

"Exactly what dirty work do you have in mind?"

"Oh, you know, answer the phone, take messages, run errands, chauffeur me around, handle whatever is called for that may infringe on my valuable time."

"How much do associates get paid?"

"Starting out, just room and board, but perhaps a small subsidy could be worked out if you also agree to cook, clean, and warm my bed at night," he replied, warming to the jousting.

"That sounds suspiciously like being a kept woman."

"Heavens *no*, with associates one isn't required to deal with expensive restaurants or diamonds and furs and such."

"That doesn't sound like much of a deal to me. As partners, I'd get half the profits."

"*Half?* You don't know the first thing about the detective business, how do you figure you'd be worth half?"

"Because I'm willing to do half the work, and I'll probably end up doing *all* the thinking," she vowed. "Besides, I doubled your fees, so I'm already earning my way."

"As a point of future reference, associates don't go around giving their masters a lot of lip," he advised sagely. "They're very subservient, so start learning your place."

"Have you always been delusional, Dean, or is this just an unfortunate byproduct of your recent accident?" she demanded.

As she drove seething with hostility, he mulled over the commitment he'd made to help Sharon with a tug of contrition. Getting involved with her again, regardless of his questionable qualifications for clearing her of a murder rap, was unsettling. Nevertheless, he had taken Mrs. Peters' money, so he had forfeited the choice.

"It's your turn to fix dinner," Lisa advised in the strained silence.

He pushed his vexing thoughts aside. "So?"

"I thought you might take me out to dinner instead."

"I make it a point to only wine and dine women who're willing to put out afterwards."

"Fine, you can cook then," she retaliated frostily. "I just thought you might want to celebrate our first case."

"Pull into the Dairy Queen and I'll spring for cheeseburgers."

"You're a selfish, self-centered jackass!"

He smirked. "Many think that's one of my more adorable traits."

"Are you going to take Charlene to the Dairy Queen when you take her out to dinner?" she probed, troubled by the prospect.

He blinked, stunned. "I don't intend to take Charlene out *anywhere* to dinner!"

"Why not? She was hitting on you big time back there."

"It's a long story."

After placing their orders with the carhop, she turned to him. "So entertain me with the story on Charlene while we dine."

He grimaced. "The crux of it is she was always a big pain in my ass."

She batted her lashes. "*Goodness*, all women seem to have that effect on you. Do I detect a disturbing trend here?"

"Not *all* women!"

"At the risk of flattering you, she seems to have a big time crush on you."

He scowled. "She was a total brat who made my life a living hell."

"How so?"

"Like sneaking around behind Sharon and me and snitching on us to old Mrs. Peters every chance she got."

"It sounds like she was jealous," she observed as the carhop brought their order.

"Of what?"

"Of you and Sharon," she explained as she handed him a burger.

"Whatever. I'm also certain she vandalized Glenn's car once when I borrowed it to pick up Sharon. Somebody scraped the side of it with a sharp object and the little bitch was suspiciously smug afterwards."

"Maybe she was trying to get your attention. Were you encouraging her?"

"Why would I encourage her to vandalize Glenn's car?" he scoffed. "It cost me almost fifty bucks to have the damned scratches polished out!"

"I'm referring to you being an unbearable tease and a flagrant flirt where women are concerned."

"She was like *thirteen* at the time, Lisa! I was *not* flirting with her!"

"Girls don't need much encouragement at that age. What was the deal with the nickel?"

"After Sharon and I split she followed me around annoying the hell out of me, so I handed her a nickel and told her to call me when she grew up."

"There you have it. Sounds like a case of whatever Sharon had, she wanted, and after you two split, she saw an opportunity. I mean, Sharon was always the beautiful swan in the limelight. I can only imagine what it was like for her to be hidden in her gorgeous big sister's shadow."

"Do I get to recline on a couch or something for all this psycho-analysis bullshit?" he demanded irritably. "Frankly, I really don't give a damn *what* her problem was."

"And you don't find her attractive now?"

He shrugged. "She seems a bit more charming, but I really don't give a hoot in hell about her, then *or* now."

"So what's next?" she prodded, delighted with his response.

"I'll go see Sharon in the morning and hear her side of the story."

"What time are we going?"

"*We're* not."

She busied herself with her burger and fries to hide her annoyance. "This is going to be hard on you, Dean. You're going to need my support to deal with it. Plus, we need to move fast if we're going to earn that bonus. You need my help whether you're willing to admit it or not."

He grimaced, hating women's so-called intuition. "The chances of me finding anything of value to help Sharon are slim to none. This is basically a wild goose chase."

She glanced at him slyly. "Are you scared of seeing Sharon again?"

Ice water settled in his veins. "You're giving me heartburn. Do you mind if I finish my burger in peace?"

"You're *such* a Neanderthal, and totally incapable of addressing your true emotions on *any* level, Dean!"

"How do I get into these stupid discussions with you anyway?" he demanded crossly. "You're giving me a headache."

"You may need me to help you pick up the pieces," she continued.

"What pieces?"

"Of your heart."

"Will you *please* give the Sharon thing a rest, damn it!"

"It's obviously a waste of time since you can't deal with it," she snipped happily.

"This is simply a case of me nosing around, finding nothing of value, pocketing the retainer, and waiting for the whole thing to blow over," he reasoned.

She started the VW and drove them home in speculative silence. When they entered the apartment, she turned back to face him, her emotions running rampant.

"Dean, please be very careful with this situation."

He paused, his senses teased by the musk she wore. "You know, I think we get too much pleasure out of making each other miserable. We both need to lighten up a bit." He pulled her close as she stiffened. "What do I need to be careful of, anyway?"

She ignored the tremors pulsating through her body pressed against his. "You're not very bright when it comes to women. Regardless of how you think you feel about Sharon now, you're still mesmerized by her whether you're willing to admit it or not."

"*Mesmerized?* Where do you get this crap from?"

"You're still emotionally lost. If you get tangled up with her again you may never find your way back."

"Find my way back where?" he demanded in exasperation. "Look, I'll leave my favorite shirt here as a guarantee I'll find my way back."

"Don't be so banal about this, Dean!" she insisted as the anger rose in her.

"It's dirty anyway. Maybe you could wash it while I'm gone?"

She flung his arms away. "You're *such* an ass!"

"A jackass, as I recall, now go take a shower and quit being silly. I'm tired and it's your night for the couch."

"You're a *certified* jackass," she called as she stormed off down the hallway.

"*Finally* something we can *both* agree on!" he yelled after her.

Chapter 4

Lisa glided into the living room with a towel wrapped around her body and another wound turban-style about her head. Dean studied her as she proceeded to make up the couch, thinking women draped in damp towels were intriguing—one little tug and . . .

She glanced in his direction. "The bathroom is all yours. Sleep well."

After considering the stimulating possibilities and analyzing the potential consequences, he reluctantly headed for a cold shower—which he found didn't help much. Finding the lure of her too enticing, he slipped on his pajama bottoms and a t-shirt and padded back to the living room where she sat on her freshly made-up couch dressed in a white flowing nightgown sipping a glass of wine backlit by wickedly flickering candlelight.

He took the easy chair across from her and nodded at the arrangement. "Nice. What's the occasion?"

"Just unwinding," she answered cautiously, eyes narrowing. "Why are you in my bedroom?"

"Um, can we talk?" he asked, deciding to apply cool logic to their illogical situation.

"About what?"

"I'm thinking I might need a better reason to come back than a dirty shirt."

She suppressed a smile. Toying with him would provide a little lighthearted entertainment to offset the frustrations she was experiencing in trying to form a professional relationship with him. "I thought it was your favorite shirt?"

"It's actually kind of threadbare."

"Mm, I can see your dilemma."

"We really weren't that bad together back in high school, were we?"

Her body flushed with heat. "I suppose that depends on your point of view."

"I mean, except for that one small incident, we had fun together, didn't we?"

She nodded hesitantly, growing resentment replacing the sensuous memories and affording her a degree of security. "I suppose we did ... until that *one small* incident."

"So I was thinking maybe we should give things another shot," he reasoned. "I mean, are you really happy with our current arrangement?"

"It's what we agreed on."

"Well, yeah, but only as a temporary setup for a couple of days until you could find a place of your own. Now that we've evolved into something a bit more permanent, maybe we should relax the rules a bit. It only makes sense, right?"

She experienced a covert thrill at the suggestion that something more enduring was developing between them. "Where is this leading?"

"I mean, we're obviously still attracted to each other after all these years, right? Why deny ourselves when a good time is waiting?"

"Goodnight, Dean," she replied frigidly as a stark blast of artic air shot through her.

"You're not even willing to discuss the issue?"

She watched him steadily. "To my way of thinking, things should have meaning in the light of day, so I really can't see this leading anywhere constructive since you're still a selfish, self-centered jerk whose sole interest is in rekindling merely a physical relationship."

He shifted his gaze to the throbbing vein at the base of her throat absorbing the tantalizing scent of her perfume, his mind growing feverish. "It could lead to a wonderful night together."

"Are you overly anxious to repair more cars?"

"I thought we agreed to let that go?" He took her wine from her hand, set it on the table, and pulled her up into his arms. "To hell with tomorrow, Lisa, what matters is tonight."

"The light of day always follows the dark of night," she whispered as he brushed her lips.

He sank down on the sofa and pulled her into his lap, the heady desire making his head spin. "Do we need to discuss meanings?"

She quivered as he nuzzled her neck. "I think it best if we do."

"I want you now," he murmured against the hollow of her throat. "Isn't that meaning enough?"

As his lips teased her, she sensed her resolve slipping away, the heat rising in her, hunger overcoming caution, her body eagerly yielding, even as a far vestige of her mind warned it was only temporary insanity. "To hell with being friends," she whispered, relinquishing all control as her lips sought his in reckless swirls.

As the full impact of her meaning sank in, swift anxiety chilled raging desire as fearful tremors raced through him. He pulled back and reached for her wine with an unsteady hand.

"What's wrong?" she whispered as she sagged against his chest in a molten heap.

The tantalizing flavor of her lips fought his growing apprehension. "I guess I'm suddenly hung up on the light of day thing."

She shifted out of his lap and snatched her wine glass from his hand. "Do you want to *wear* this? You're *ruining* the moment!"

"Maybe it's best if we don't have a moment." A shudder worked its way through him as rabid fear edged out waning desire. She was far more vulnerable than he remembered, not discounting the fact that he was even beginning to like her somewhat now—which brought the damned friendship thing into the equation. "I'm just trying to think things through—I mean, let's face it, we did this before for the wrong reasons and I ended up in a creek."

"*Stop* it with the *creek* thing!" she insisted, yearning for his touch.

"Sorry—guess I'm still traumatized."

"What about your need for a stronger reason to come back than a dirty, threadbare shirt?"

"Upon further reflection, I realize I'd *never* leave that shirt behind."

"You're *such* an ass, Dean!"

He sighed. "Lisa, I can't define what tonight would mean tomorrow. It would be what it is, nothing more. But I do know friendship is a forever thing."

"Damn you! How can you go from being the world's biggest Romeo to such a puritan in just a few short years?"

"I hurt you once, and that's not something I'm especially proud of. Why don't we just take it slow and easy until we get a grip on things?"

"You're driving me nuts, Dean! You don't have a *clue* as to what you want, do you?"

"I know I don't want this for all the wrong reasons … and I don't want to jeopardize us being friends afterwards."

"Then what's the point of us alternating nights on this lumpy old sofa?" She grabbed the pillows up, stalked back to the bedroom, and arranged them down the center of the bed. "You can have the right side."

His pulse increased tempo knowing he could *never* pass this test! "That won't work. I'd be facing you. I might scoot over and snuggle you in my sleep."

"You're such a spineless coward, Dean!"

"Okay, I'll take the left side, with my back to you."

She flounced back to the living room to blow out the candles as he slipped in between the sheets filled with misgivings. When she returned and slid in on her side, he lay silent for a few moments sensing her near warmth and inhaling her tantalizing fragrance. When his give-a-shit meter pegged upward into a quivering mass of lustful desire, he sighed in defeat.

"This isn't working."

"What's wrong now?" she demanded from the darkness.

"I can't sleep without a pillow."

"Well get one from between us!"

"Then we won't have a barrier."

"Maybe you need to go sleep on the sofa."

"It's *my* turn for the bed! *You're* the intruder!"

"*I'm* fine, it's *you* who has the problem."

He reached back and snatched one of the pillows. "Goodnight, Lisa!"

"Night, Dean," she cooed as he stomped off down the hallway to the lumpy old couch, where he tossed and turned the whole night through bothered by her closeness just down the hall in his bed and the stupid friendship barrier she had inadvertently placed between them.

✵ ✵ ✵

He awoke the next morning feeling prickly and stumbled to the bathroom to find Lisa standing at the counter with a towel wrapped around her putting on her makeup. He leaned against the door jam in drowsy lassitude enjoying her morning freshness and natural beauty, fighting the pangs of desire. The thought of drawing her back into the bed was tempting, but the price was more than he was willing to pay. Still, he had this *thing* with attractive women wrapped in towels …

"I need the bathroom, if you don't mind," he advised irritably. "Why are you getting all dolled up?"

She brushed by him in a soft, feminine wave. "Would you prefer I look dowdy when we meet with Sharon?"

"Well save yourself the effort then, because you're not going with me."

"Yes I am."

"We discussed this last night," he reminded her as he closed the door.

"We did, so there's no need to rehash it this morning," she called. "Do you want some toast before we meet with the lawyer?"

"You're not going with me, and that's final!" he yelled back.

"Do you plan to walk?" she threatened as she disappeared down the hall. "Your car won't start, remember?"

"Damn it, Lisa!"

"Do you want to drive?" she asked as she led him out.

"*You're* the associate," he snarled.

"Sounds like you need to go back to bed and get up on the opposite side, Mr. Cranky."

"*I* don't seem to *have* a bed anymore," he groused as he clumped around to the passenger side and got in. "Look, we'll compromise.

You can accompany me to meet with the lawyer and then wait in the car while I meet with Sharon."

She drove them to Mr. Field's office, where his secretary ushered them into a richly wood-paneled office after a tedious twenty-minute wait. Dean glanced at the diplomas lining the walls amongst pictures of distinguished friends and clients as they coldly shook hands.

Mr. Fields eyed Lisa cynically as he indicated the matching red leather wing chairs before his desk and the secretary hurriedly placed cups of coffee on a table between them before departing, and then settled in behind his tidy desk clasping his hands before him.

"So, Mr. Davis, Mrs. Peters informs me you're working for us now. I'd like to state up-front I'm opposed to this."

"Why?"

"I don't like outsiders meddling in my cases."

"Is that how you view my pending investigation?"

Mr. Fields leaned forward. "May I inquire as to your experience in this kind of undertaking? My understanding is you've only recently acquired your license and opened shop here. Have you ever been involved in a murder case before—or any other type of case, for that matter?"

Dean held his stare as he picked up his coffee and took a sip. "Let's get something straight, Mr. Fields. I'm not here for a job interview. Mrs. Peters retained me to investigate Kenny Felton's murder as it pertains to her granddaughter. Per her instructions, you are to fill me in on the charges pending against Miss Lucas and the evidence that supports those charges."

Mr. Fields frowned. "And Miss Bryant is?"

"My associate," Dean answered.

"Is she a licensed investigator?"

"Does it matter?"

"Indeed it does, Mr. Davis. Unless she is licensed and bonded, it would be difficult to hold her to the same high moral standards of client confidentiality as you—professionally speaking, of course."

"I take full responsibility for her confidentiality. You may speak freely in front of her."

They stared at each for a full minute before Mr. Fields sat back in his chair. "Miss Lucas is being held under suspicion of murder. The police found the murder weapon outside her front door. They also have an eyewitness who saw her fleeing the scene of the crime. My client claims she is innocent, of course." He picked up some papers and shuffled them. "Now, if you will excuse me?"

Dean stood and started for the door. "You've been an enormous help."

"Please keep me informed, Mr. Davis," Mr. Fields directed.

"You'll need to rely on Mrs. Peters for that," Dean tossed over his shoulder as Lisa scrambled after him.

"That was fun," she quipped as they made their way to her car. "What's his problem?"

"He'll lose his huge defense fee if we prove Sharon innocent before the trial."

"How do I get licensed and bonded?"

"You don't."

"He seemed to think it necessary."

"He's an idiot."

"He had a point about the confidentiality thing," she insisted. "I mean, if we're going to be partners, maybe it's the right thing to do."

"For the last time, we are *not* partners, damn it!"

"Why not?"

"Because I said so: Now take me to see Sharon."

"That's not a proper justification!" she argued as she fired up the VW. "It doesn't even make sense."

"It does to me," he insisted, grabbing the dash as she careened through a caution light and turned hard left without slowing down.

"You're really, *really* making me mad," she swore.

"That light was *red,* damn it!"

"*Do you want to drive?*"

Chapter 5

Dean lurched forward as Lisa slammed on the brakes with a screech of rubber in front of a gray stone, two-story affair that had seen better days.

"I assume you've considered the questions we need to ask her?" she snipped as she got out on the driver's side.

"No, I'm a moron, can't you tell?" he snapped as he got out on the passenger side. "Now wait in the car, because there ain't no *we* in this."

"It's too hot out here and I can't assist you by waiting in the car," she replied, nonplused.

"I'm awestruck by your deductive reasoning, Doctor Watson. You can wait in the lobby then where it's cooler."

She hurried along beside him in the shimmering humidity to the cool interior of the county jail, which smelled of urine, vomit, and sweat, crinkling her nose in distaste as they drew up to the battered counter where a middle-aged, heavy-set deputy sat on a stool writing on a clipboard.

"Can I help you?" he inquired without looking up.

"I'm here to see Sharon Lucas," Dean replied to the top of his head.

"Your name?" the deputy asked as he scribbled on his clipboard.

"Dean Davis."

"Are you a relative?"

"No."

"What is the purpose of your visit with inmate Lucas?"

"To lay the groundwork for her escape."

The deputy glanced up, laid his clipboard aside, opened a folder, looked down a sheet, and frowned when he found Dean's name. He glanced at Lisa. "And you are?"

"The woman who will be waiting out here with you while I visit with *inmate* Lucas," Dean advised.

Lisa smiled sweetly. "I'm Lisa Bryant, and I'll be accompanying him in to see Miss Lucas."

The deputy glanced from one of them to the other. "You'll be notified when the detainee is ready to be brought to the visitor's room."

Dean took Lisa by the elbow and steered her to a bench set against the back wall. "Every decision I make is not open to debate," he reasoned as they plopped down.

"It is if I don't agree with it," she defended as the deputy left the room. "Besides, I might pick up on something you miss."

"Do tell? I *never* miss *anything*," he insisted.

The deputy returned. "Place all of your personal items in the basket before we go back," he instructed as he set two trays on the counter.

"*You* wait *here*," Dean directed.

"*I'm* going *with* you," Lisa insisted.

"*No* you're *not*!"

"*Yes* I *am*!"

"Would you two prefer to come back when you've worked this out?" the deputy asked.

Lisa flushed as she glanced at the deputy and leaned closer to Dean. "You're not completely objective where she's concerned. You need me!"

"Like I need fleas!" he retorted.

"Are you two coming or not?" the deputy demanded as he opened the door leading back into the jail.

Lisa nudged Dean aside and tossed her purse into the tray. "Sorry! We're just having a little professional disagreement here." The deputy held the door for her as Dean emptied his pockets into the tray and hurried after them.

"The last door on the right is the visitor's room. You have thirty minutes from the time inmate Lucas arrives," the deputy advised, ushering them into the room and closing the door.

Dean paced in nervous anticipation around the worn green tile floor of the small room as Lisa settled into one of the four metal folding chairs at the metal table, the only furnishings in the airless place containing one small observation window in the door and a dim fluorescent bulb overhead encased in wire mesh.

"This associate thing isn't going to work out if you continue to argue over every little thing I tell you to do," Dean grumbled. "Not to mention you stealing my bed."

"The sofa was *your* doing!" she insisted.

"I can't sleep without a damned pillow!"

She smirked at him. "I think you're more concerned about being close to me!"

"I'm just particular about who I sleep with."

"Since when?"

"Since …"

"*Yeah, right!*" she supplied airily.

After several deafening minutes of silence, the door opened and Sharon demurely entered wearing a gray one-piece jail uniform three sizes too large for her, sending Dean's heart hammering as their eyes met.

"Dean!" She rushed into his arms, her perfectly proportioned body soft and warm against him, bringing a familiar flash of keen desire.

Out of sorts, he shuffled back from her in acute discomfort, wanting to crush her hard against him instead of releasing her, finding her silky hair as fine as ever and if anything the intervening years having made her even more beautiful and desirable. She wore no makeup, but neither that nor the jail garb detracted from her voluptuous figure or clear-skinned beauty. Worry filled her green eyes, replacing the teasing glimmer he remembered so well, but they melted his core nevertheless, as they always had. She seemed smaller and more delicate, and he longed to protect her from all the evils of the world as he dizzily realized he wasn't breathing and forced his chest to expand and fill with oxygen.

She wiped a tear from her eye. "Oh, Dean, it's so good to see you!" she sobbed as she embraced him again. "You're even more handsome than I remember. I know I look a sight! They won't allow me to use makeup or even brush my hair after my morning shower."

Dean swallowed to loosen his vocal cords. "You look … wonderful."

She focused on Lisa sitting at the table and frowned. "Lisa? I haven't seen you in ages. Why are you here?"

"We *do* tend to travel in different social circles," Lisa agreed tritely amid the swelling resentment. "I'm Dean's partner now."

Sharon turned to Dean. "Oh, really?"

He steered her around to the opposite side of the table, still faint from her nearness, and pulled out a chair for her. She took his hands as he sat across from her next to Lisa.

"When I heard you were a private investigator, I knew I could depend on you to help me. I can't believe I've gotten myself into such an awful mess."

"Your grandmother hired us to prove you innocent of the murder of your former fiancé," Lisa injected coldly. "So naturally the question has to be addressed ... *are* you innocent?"

Sharon released Dean's hands, her eyes lethal daggers as the air between them charged with static electricity. "Do you think I'm capable of such a thing?" She turned to Dean, her eyes softening. "*You* know I couldn't kill anyone, don't you?" She glanced back at Lisa with open hostility. "I would think *everyone* would know that."

"Uh, can you tell us what happened, Sharon?" Dean suggested as the two women glared at each other in the hanging silence.

Sharon's enchanting green eyes turned back to him, again sending his heart racing. "There's not much to tell. Kenny came by my apartment late. We got into an argument. The police say someone shot him in the parking lot when he left. I can't believe they think I did it. You have to help me, Dean. This is all so crazy!"

"What was the argument about?" Lisa asked.

"I've been grilled on this as much as I care to be," Sharon answered in a frigid tone. "Dean, I would prefer to meet with you alone, if you don't mind?"

"We can't help you if we don't have the facts," Lisa snipped.

"Grandmother said you were meeting with my attorney this morning to get the basic facts. I don't want to waste the little time I have with Dean talking about things I've already answered with him and the police a hundred times. Will you please excuse us?"

When Lisa stalked out of the room, Sharon again took Dean's hands across the table as her eyes devoured him. "The worst mistake I ever made in my life was letting you slip away!"

You didn't let me slip away—you dumped me for your old fogy modeling coach with the little red sports car, he lamented mutely as the heat from her touch rose up through his arms into his chest. "Sharon, I can't help you unless I hear your side of the story, and I want to hear it from you directly, not from your attorney or the police. I'm sorry, but it really is necessary."

Her eyes grew moist. "I didn't kill Kenny. Do you believe me?"

"I accept that at face value or I wouldn't be here," he reassured her. "Now please give me the particulars of what happened that night."

She lowered her eyes. "I broke off our engagement three weeks ago. Kenny came by because I wouldn't take his calls. He became angry when I insisted he leave. He got loud and then rough. He slapped me, called me names, and threw me against the wall and choked me before storming out of the apartment. I was still on the floor crying when I heard the gunshot. I've told the police this over and over."

"What did you do when you heard the shot?"

"I went to the window and looked out. I saw Kenny's car, but I couldn't see him. I didn't know until the police arrived that he was ..."

"Did you see anyone else?"

She hesitated. "No."

He sensed she was lying. "Did you see *anything* out of the ordinary?"

She frowned. "I was very upset at the time, so I wasn't thinking clearly. I was afraid Kenny would come back to my apartment when I saw his car still in the parking lot."

"Go on," he encouraged.

She bit her bottom lip. "Kenny kept a pistol in his glove compartment. When I heard the shot, I thought he was just acting crazy and trying to scare me. I swear I did *not* kill him. I don't even know how to *use* a gun."

"How many shots were fired?"

"Just one."

"How long after he left before you heard the shot?"

"Only a minute or so. Will you hold me, Dean?" she pleaded, rising. "I'm so terrified. My whole life is ruined. Please hold me. Please help me."

He stood as she came around the table and molded into his arms. As she sobbed, his heart drummed with tender desire. "I'll ... do what I can ..."

She relaxed in his arms as her weeping subsided. "Lisa is very attractive," she whispered. "Are you seeing her again?"

He tensed. "She showed up at my door a few days ago with some silly notion of us becoming partners."

She tightened her hold on him. "I've never gotten over you, Dean. Do you know that?" She lifted her head from his chest and brushed her lips against his, sending electric currents down to his toes, leaving him shaken and confused.

"Sharon ... we need to keep this on a professional basis," he stammered, pulling back from her. "If I'm going to be of any help to you, I need to remain objective."

"Oh, Dean, I know I hurt you badly," she whispered, embracing his ridged body. "I'm so sorry for that. I was so silly back then. Danny convinced me I could be a top model. I believed him. All I could think of was my career. He used me. I'm so ashamed. Will you ever forgive me?"

He disengaged himself from her embrace, guided her back to her chair, and sat down opposite her as he tried to gather his scattered emotions. "Sharon, why did you break off your engagement with Felton?"

She lowered her lashes. "Does it really matter now?"

"It might."

"We just weren't right for each other. I'd prefer to leave it at that."

"Do you know of anyone who would want to harm him?"

She took his hand. "Not directly."

"Do you know of anyone who threatened him, or that he considered as a threat to him?"

She wiped her eyes. "He was very arrogant and self centered. Lots of people didn't like him, but I don't know of anyone who would want to kill him."

"What kind of business was he in?"

"He inherited money from his grandmother when he turned twenty-five. All I know is he consulted with various stockbrokers." She stood and turned her back to him. "Dean, you've got to believe me—I didn't kill Kenny!"

"Did you two have a physical altercation when you broke up three weeks ago like the night he was killed?"

"No … I simply gave him his ring back." He sensed she was lying, again, as she turned back to him. "This is all so humiliating! *Please*, I don't even want to *think* about him anymore!"

A knock at the door produced the deputy. "Time's up. Please follow me, Mr. Davis."

She gazed at him wistfully as he stood, her forlorn eyes tugging at his frayed emotions, and then embraced him tightly. "When will I see you again?"

"Soon," he promised.

"Please get me out of here, Dean!"

He pried her arms from around him and followed the deputy back to the front desk to retrieve his personal effects, where Lisa waited by the door. "I'd like to speak with Sheriff Parsons and Deputy Miller."

"The Sheriff will be back in an hour," the deputy replied. "You'll have to clear it with him to talk to Deputy Miller."

Dean ushered a grim Lisa out to the car.

"The heat between you two was suffocating," she accused as she got into the driver's side of her Volkswagen. "I thought there was going to be a meltdown in there."

"Your imagination is running wild," he muttered as he slammed the door.

"*Oh, Dean, you're even more handsome than I remember,*" she mimicked. "*I look a sight, they won't allow me to use makeup or brush my hair.*"

He calmed his jangling emotions. "Quit acting like an insecure little jealous bitch, Lisa."

"Don't flatter yourself!" She sat back in the seat and drew a deep, composing breath, knowing she couldn't do this. She thought she could, but she couldn't. Last night proved she was still vulnerable to him. She drew another deep, composing breath. "After seeing you and Sharon together I realize I'm not strong enough to—my intentions were to get you *out* of my system, not to—*damn it*, I'll have my things out by tonight!"

His pulse jumped, startling him. "Where will you go?"

"I don't know—back to my parents."

With disquieting clarity, he realized that as aggravating as she was he honestly did not want her to go—but *be-damned* if he could find it in himself to ask her to stay.

"Why the sudden hurry to leave?"

She blinked back the tears welling in her eyes. "What do you care?"

"I'm ... getting attached to that picture you hung on my living room wall."

"Which one?"

"The fuzzy one of the naked chick with the big boobs."

"That's *art*, Dean!"

"I most certainly agree. We've got an hour to kill before the sheriff returns. I'll buy you a cup of coffee and a doughnut while we discuss the merits of that picture."

John W. Huffman

"It's a *painting*, Dean."

"Whatever. I don't suppose you'd be willing to trade it for your half of the rent?"

"I thought part of our arrangement was free room and board?"

"Do you know who the model is, by chance?"

She sighed in exasperation. "Most people would want to know who the *artist* is."

"It doesn't take much talent to paint a set of knockers like that model has."

"I'd *rather* hear what Sharon had to say than try to educate you on the fine points of modern art!"

"We can work our way around to that subject as well," he promised.

Chapter 6

Over coffee, Dean filled Lisa in on the salient points he and Sharon had discussed, deliberately skipping the more intimate details that transpired between them, and spent the remainder of the hour sparring over the fuzzy nude without bringing up the subject of her moving out—the foremost issue on his mind. When Lisa pulled into the visitor's parking lot next to the jail, he nodded at the sheriff's cruiser in its reserved spot.

"Looks like Sheriff Benny-the-Weenie's back. Better let me do the talking."

"What if I have a question?" she demanded.

"Ask away. We're probably not going to get any answers from the jerk anyway."

"I've always found Sheriff Parsons to be a good man," she insisted. "What don't you like about him?"

"He and I had a brief run-in when I was a teenager."

"He's been the sheriff for over twenty years and as far as I know is highly thought of around here. I voted for him in the last election and even worked as a volunteer in his campaign."

"Have you ever looked him in the eye?"

She frowned. "What do you mean?"

"If you have, you're the first skirt with long legs and big boobs that has. He's a lecherous old coot."

"You're awful!"

"You're confusing me. I thought I was an impossible, certified jackass."

"That too," she quipped as she followed him inside.

The deputy glanced up at them. "I'll notify the Sheriff you're here." He reappeared a moment later and motioned them back.

"Quick, show some cleavage," Dean whispered. "We need all the help we can get."

Lisa punched him in the ribs as the deputy led them back to the sheriff's office, knocked on the door, and ushered them in. Sheriff Parsons, over six feet tall, in his mid-fifties, with graying, short hair, sat behind his desk reading a report. Dean took in his white Stetson hanging on a hat rack with his western style leather holster and six-shooter on the peg below it as they stood in front of his desk in silence.

"Sit down, Davis," he grumbled without looking up when Dean finally cleared his throat impatiently.

"Good to see you again too, Sheriff," Dean replied as Lisa and he settled into the chairs in front of his desk.

"The last time I saw you, Davis, you were in your neighbor's yard around midnight squatting beside his car with a piece of garden hose stuck in your mouth and a five gallon gas can between your knees."

Dean chuckled. "What can I say, Sheriff? I was on empty in my friend's car after a hot date. My dad was able to work things out with Old Man Johnson, so no harm, no foul."

Sheriff Parsons scowled, still intent on his report. "My understanding is you were required to mow his yard the whole summer for free. You got off light. If I'd had my way—"

"*Right*, well, sorry to spoil your fun and all, but—"

"I reviewed your application a few weeks back for your investigator's license and your permit to carry a concealed weapon. For the record, I was against issuing either."

"Can we cut to the chase here, Sheriff? Your sign out in your parking lot said one-hour maximum. I'd hate to get towed."

He scowled and flipped a page in his report. "It's your dime, Davis."

"I've been retained by Mrs. Peters on behalf of her granddaughter, Sharon Lucas. I'd like to review the evidence against her."

He licked his finger and turned another page. "You can read about it in the newspaper like all the other good citizens."

"Actually, I'm entitled to the same information as her lawyer, Sheriff, which is full disclosure and a detailed review of any and all evidence you've gathered to support the charges pending against her. You know that."

His cold brown eyes shifted from the report to Lisa's bosom. "Don't tell me what I know or don't know, Davis. You can request a copy of the incident report and any other information held by this department from the clerk of court. You can then schedule a convenient time with the deputy out front to view the evidence."

"I'd hoped we could expedite the process since it's a foregone conclusion it will be provided to me anyway."

His eyes shifted from Lisa's bosom back to his report. "Why do you assume you merit special consideration?"

"Miss Lucas is in your jail on suspicion of murder. If she is in fact innocent of that crime, I'd think you'd be motivated to set her free in the shortest time possible."

His lips curled into the semblance of a sneer. "And you're going to set us straight by finding the *real* culprit for us, boy?"

"I haven't been a *boy* since I graduated from high school, Sheriff," Dean advised. "I'm led to believe the evidence against her

71

is circumstantial. Based on that, I intend to review the facts surrounding the case and hopefully provide your office with an alternate suspect."

The sheriff tossed the report on his desk. "Uh huh. I see you're still as cheeky as you were as a teenager. I did some checking on you, Davis. It seems you left the Houston Police Department on less than amicable terms."

Dean's stomach clutched. "I made a mistake, Sheriff. I accept full responsibility for that even if I was cleared in the ensuing investigation."

"Cleared? It's my understanding you received a career-ending letter of reprimand and the prosecutor agreed not to indict you on charges of manslaughter if you in turn agreed to resign from the force and get out of town. That's some distance from a clearance, in my opinion."

Dean flinched, his words rekindling the overwhelming grief still haunting him. "Even if your opinion had merit, Sheriff, what does that have to do with the Sharon Lucas case?"

"Your partner in Houston and a little ten year old girl died for your *mistake*, Davis. You're damned lucky you're not in jail for negligent homicide. In my view, you made another mistake in coming back here to set up shop. As a professional courtesy, I suggest you take your long-range cameras and slimy occupation to another town to chase after cheating husbands and wayward wives."

"I would think as long as it's not *your* bare backside I'm focusing my long-range lens on you wouldn't have a problem with how I earn a living as long as it's within the legal guidelines of the law, Sheriff," Dean countered.

The sheriff's eyes narrowed. "There are no *guidelines* to the law, Davis. There is only black and white. You keep that in mind and watch your p's and q's while you're in my jurisdiction, you hear? Now, is there anything else I can help you with?"

"I'd like to talk to Deputy Miller."

"For what purpose?"

"I understand he was the first officer on the scene at the Felton murder."

"Denied."

"Why?"

He snatched up the report from his desk and resumed his review of it. "Department policy, all information will be provided by me exclusively until the case is closed."

Dean stood. "Okay, Sheriff, we'll do this the hard way. I'll have Miss Lucas' lawyer file a grievance with the court and schedule a formal meeting with you, Deputy Miller, and the eyewitness you profess to have to take legal depositions from each of you. I will also have him subpoena copies of all documentation concerning the case. In the interim, I will advise Miss Lucas that if it in fact turns out she is innocent, she may have a strong case for denial of her due process, as well as false arrest and imprisonment."

Sheriff Parsons tossed the report back on his desk and rose to his feet. "Are you threatening me, Davis?"

Dean locked eyes with him. "I prefer the operative word here of *forewarning*, Sheriff."

Sheriff Parsons placed his knuckles on the desk and leaned forward. "If I catch you tampering with my staff, the eyewitness, or any of the evidence in this case, I *guarantee* you'll be in a cell beside your client. Do I make myself clear?"

Dean turned to the door. "Is that *threatening* or simply *forewarning*, Sheriff?"

"Sheriff Parsons, our sole interest is to ensure the correct person is brought to justice," Lisa observed cautiously. "Doesn't that put us on your side?"

He stiffened and glared past her to Dean. "I assume *his* sole interest is to muddle up the scene as much as possible. I'll not tolerate anyone trying to make a fool of my department."

Dean stopped at the door. "If you in fact have a witness to the murder, then I would think you acted prudently in arresting my client. I'd have done the same under the circumstances. However, you and I both know eyewitnesses don't always hold up in court. I have no desire to embarrass you or your department. I give you my word if I find anything noteworthy, I'll contact you immediately."

"Sure you will—a day *after* the media gets the information," he scoffed.

Dean walked back to his desk. "I'll make it a point not to talk to the media about this case until it's closed. You also have my word on that."

He studied Dean with cold eyes before turning to Lisa. "Miss Bryant, isn't it?"

"Yes, I worked as a volunteer on your re-election campaign a few years back putting out posters and signs, and attended your re-election party with my parents afterwards."

He nodded. "What is your interest in this case?"

"I'm Dean's partner."

"*Associate*," Dean corrected.

"I will also give you my word that if we find anything that will help clear Sharon Lucas we will come to you first," she continued.

His eyes shifted to her bosom. "Dispatch got a call at 11:54 p.m. from Mrs. Jean Sanders in apartment 110, directly across from Miss Lucas' apartment. She stated she heard a gunshot and that when she looked out her window she saw a man lying on the pavement. Deputy Miller arrived on the scene at 12:05 a.m. He found an unidentified male lying in a pool of blood. He secured the area and called for an ambulance and backup. Deputy Cartwright and the ambulance arrived together at approximately 12:25 a.m. The Coroner arrived at 12:35 and pronounced the victim dead at the scene from an apparent gunshot wound. Documentation on the victim identified him as Kenny Felton. I and two other deputies arrived at 12:55 a.m. I took charge of the investigation at that time.

"Upon further questioning, Mrs. Sanders stated she saw Miss Lucas running from the scene towards her apartment immediately after the shot was fired.

"Miss Lucas appeared disoriented and distraught. She accompanied me to the crime scene and identified the victim as Kenny Felton. She further stated Mr. Felton was her former fiancée and that he came by her apartment unannounced and threatened and beat her. She had marks on her cheeks and neck consistent with someone slapping and choking her. A search of the area produced a .38 caliber snub-nosed revolver found hidden in the bushes beside Miss Lucas' apartment door. The chamber held one expended casing and four intact rounds.

"Miss Lucas insisted she was in her apartment when she heard the shot fired that killed her ex-boyfriend. I offered her the opportunity to take a lie detector test, which she refused after consulting with her attorney. I subsequently placed Miss Lucas in custody on suspicion of murder in the death of Kenny Felton.

"The pistol was later identified as belonging to the victim, Kenny Felton. A lab analyst confirmed the slug taken from the victim's body came from that weapon. According to the autopsy, the determining cause of death was a bullet fired at close range entering the victim's body from the lower abdomen and traveling upward at a sharp angle entering his heart. Mrs. Sanders picked Miss Lucas' picture out of a line-up later that day.

"The county prosecutor is reviewing the evidence from my investigation and expects to file formal charges sometime tomorrow. I will arrange for copies of the statements and the investigative report to be delivered to you this afternoon."

Dean's mind raced, absorbing the facts, none of which looked positive for Sharon. "I appreciate your assistance, Sheriff."

Sheriff Parsons fixed him with a cold stare. "I'm going to take you and your … er, *associate* here, at your word, Davis. If either of you attempt to embarrass my department in this matter, or interfere with the proper investigation of this crime in any disparaging way, I'll make you wish you were back in Houston facing manslaughter charges."

Dean met his stare. "Do you have a problem with us visiting the crime scene or talking with Mrs. Sanders?"

"I've made my position clear on this issue. Don't cross the line."

Dean offered his hand. "Thank you for your cooperation, Sheriff."

The sheriff looked at his extended hand and picked up his report. "Good day."

Dean held the door open for Lisa and followed her out. "That went better than expected."

Her cheeks flushed. "I felt like he was undressing me in there. I never noticed that about him before."

"That's why I'm a detective and you're an associate. Let's go visit the crime scene."

"What happened in Houston, Dean?" she asked as they got into her car. "What did he mean about you facing manslaughter charges?"

Hot flashes swept through him. "Let's not go there."

"Why? You said you were cleared in the ensuing investigation."

"As he said, my partner and a little girl died because of my stupidity. Let's leave it at that."

"There should be no secrets between us if we're going to work together."

"*Are* we going to work together?" he demanded. "I thought you were moving out today."

"Is that what you want me to do?"

His stomach did the strange clutching thing again. "That's your decision."

"Tell me about the little girl and your partner, Dean."

He took a deep breath assuming her decision to stay or go hinged on this moment, on him being honest with her. He had never discussed the accident with anyone outside of Captain Ingles and the internal affairs investigator. There was no point in rehashing the tragic event.

She placed her hand on his arm. "Dean, please don't freeze me out. It's important for me to know you trust me."

A vise gripped his heart and squeezed the breath out of him as he stared straight ahead, seeing the past, reliving that day with all of the ensuing anguish. "My partner and I were on patrol. It was late afternoon. Our shift was nearly over. We got a call over the radio. There was a robbery in progress at a convenience store near us. I was driving. I flipped on the lights and siren while he informed dispatch we were responding to the call.

"We were on the loop. Dispatch alerted us to shots fired at the location. I cut through a residential neighborhood to save time. It is against department policy to exceed the posted speed limit in a residential neighborhood, even when in pursuit or responding to a call for assistance. I should have … I was *required* to slow down to the posted speed limit. I didn't. My partner cut the siren when we were close to the location so as not to alert the perpetrators. I turned down a side street to approach the location from the rear. A little girl rode her bicycle out of her driveway in front of a plumber's truck parked on the street. I swerved and hit the back of the truck head on. When I came to in the hospital, they said a piece of pipe hanging out of the back of the truck came through the windshield in the collision and pierced my partner's chest. They said our patrol car spun and hit the little girl on the bicycle." He drew a deep, ragged breath and let it out. "So now you know. And now that you do know—what difference does it make?"

Lisa eased the car into gear and pulled out into the street. "I'm so sorry, Dean."

"Yeah, me too," he replied bitterly.

Chapter 7

"Better let me handle this," Dean advised as he rang the doorbell to apartment 110, flashing his winning smile when a middle-aged, well-dressed woman opened the door. "Mrs. Sanders?"

"Yes?"

He held up his private investigator's license. "I'm Dean Davis. This is my associate, Lisa Bryant. We'd like to ask you a few questions concerning the recent murder that occurred here, if you have a moment?"

She hesitated. "I've told the police everything I know."

"We'd like to go over the statement you gave to Sheriff Parsons."

"Wait here." She closed the door in their face.

"*Smooooooth*," Lisa praised. "You're a real charmer, Sherlock. You better let me handle her the next time around."

"Go for it, Watson," he allowed snidely.

The door reopened. "Sheriff Parsons says I don't have to talk to you if I don't want to."

"No, Ma'am, you don't," Lisa replied. "But it would be a big help to us since you were a witness to the event."

Mrs. Sanders lifted her hand to her throat. "I never said I witnessed the murder!"

A faint ray of hope sprang up within Dean. "Ma'am, may we come inside?"

Mrs. Sanders hesitated. "I was just on my way out to a luncheon appointment."

"We won't take but a minute of your time, Ma'am," he urged.

She reluctantly led them inside, where she settled down on the edge of an overstuffed chair in her living room as they sat together on her sofa amid small glass figurines cluttering every available space on her tables and shelves in a pristine setting.

"Ma'am, would you please describe what you saw that night?" Dean opened.

"Well ... I'm a light sleeper. A rather sharp sound woke me up around midnight. I lay in bed for a moment, and then got up and looked out my bedroom window. Initially I saw a woman running from the parking lot to the front door of apartment 220 across the way. Then I saw a man lying in the parking lot. I immediately went to the phone and called the police."

"Did you recognize the woman?" Lisa asked.

Mrs. Sanders' hands fidgeted in her lap. "The street lamp on the corner cast some light over the area, so it wasn't completely dark. It looked like Miss Lucas."

"Did you see this woman go into apartment 220?" Dean asked.

She shook her head. "Well, no, I didn't actually see her go *into* the apartment. I called the police as soon as I saw the man lying in the parking lot."

"Can you describe this woman and how she was dressed?" Lisa asked.

Mrs. Sanders frowned. "She had light hair. I think she was wearing ... a white skirt and a dark blouse ... yes, I'm sure of it, a white skirt and a dark blouse."

"And based on the person you saw, you picked Miss Lucas out of a picture line up Sheriff Parsons presented to you?" Dean prompted.

"He brought by several photographs and asked me if I could identify Miss Lucas."

Dean held her eye. "How certain are you that the woman you saw was Miss Lucas?"

Mrs. Sanders twisted her hands in her lap as her eyes shifted. "I . . . *think* it was her. It looked like her from the back in the faint light. At the time, I *assumed* it was Miss Lucas."

"But you never saw her face or saw her go into the apartment?" he pressed.

Her eyes clouded. "No. I never actually saw her face or saw her go into her apartment. As I said, I rushed to the telephone to call the police when I saw the man lying in the street."

"Did you see anyone else in the parking lot other than the woman?" he asked.

She frowned. "I saw no one else that I recall. I was only at the window for a minute."

"Would you take us to the window?" he asked.

She led them upstairs to her tidy bedroom and pointed to the window, which provided a clear, unobstructed view of the parking lot and apartment 220 directly across the street.

Dean turned back to Mrs. Sanders. "Which telephone did you use to call the police?"

She pointed to the nightstand beside her bed. "That one."

"Did you turn on the light to dial the police?"

"No. The keypad lights when the receiver lifts."

"How long were you on the phone with the police?"

"Maybe three minutes, at the most," she replied as she sat down on the edge of the bed.

"During this period did you hear any sounds from out in the parking lot?"

She frowned. "Well … come to think of it, I did hear a car start up and drive off. It seemed in a hurry from the way the engine raced."

"What did you do when you hung up the phone after talking to the police?" Lisa asked.

"I went back to the window and watched until the police arrived. Then I went downstairs. The officer who responded informed me to stay on my porch, so I did as instructed."

"When you went back to the window after calling the police did you see or hear anything you would consider out of the ordinary?"

"I do seem to recall Mr. Jenkins standing at his window."

"Mr. Jenkins?" Dean asked.

"He lives in the apartment building facing us at the end of the parking lot, unit 330."

"Are you positive it was Mr. Jenkins?" Lisa asked.

She hesitated. "There was a lamp on behind him. I'm … certain of it."

"Is there anything else you can tell us about that night?" Dean asked as she looked at her wristwatch anxiously and stood.

"No, I'm sorry, but I'm running late for my luncheon appointment."

Dean wrote his number on a pad and handed it to her. "If you should think of anything else that comes to you later, anything at all, no matter how trivial it may seem, please call me."

She took the slip of paper. "I'm sorry I can't be of more help to you, Mr. Davis."

"You've been a big help to us, Ma'am, and again, we appreciate your time," he assured her as she led them down the stairs and opened the front door. "Have a nice day."

"Yes, goodbye." She closed the door behind them.

Lisa followed Dean across the street, where he paused at the edge of the parking lot to stare down at the black stain on the asphalt where Kenny Felton's body had lain.

She wrinkled her nose. "This is gruesome. They should at least clean up the blood."

She trailed after him to the small front porch stoop of apartment 220 as he studied the low-lying shrubbery on each side of the narrow walkway and reached into the recessed alcove to turn the door handle, surprising himself when it opened.

"I can't believe they left the door unlocked," he mused as he entered.

She followed him inside cautiously. "Is this legal, Dean?"

He paused in the living room. "It's not exactly breaking and entering since the door was unlocked and we've been hired by Sharon's grandmother to investigate the case."

She followed him surveying the dark cherry tables and light blue sofa and easy chair adorning the room with matching curtains on the windows, the large entertainment center on one wall holding a television and stereo, strewn cushions and record albums littering the floor, and half-filled glasses of diluted drinks standing on the tables among overflowing ashtrays. She eased into the kitchen after him, noting with revulsion the liquor bottles lining the counter top with the tops scattered about amidst half-filled drink glasses and spills marring the kitchen counter and dishes cluttering the sink in soiled disarray. She followed him down a short hallway and paused in the bedroom, where discarded clothing littered the floor, a set of men's cotton briefs rested in a corner, a shredded, flimsy nightgown hung from one of the bedposts, a comforter hung half off the mattress with soiled sheets tangled beneath, and a dressing table held spilled cosmetics. She paused at the bathroom door noting crumpled towels on the floor, a tub with a ring around it and matted hair over the drain, dried toothpaste plastering the bottom of the sink, eyeliners, creams, spray cans, and prescription bottles dotting the counter top, a trashcan overflowing with assorted grubby waste, and a pink housecoat hanging from the doorknob.

She turned back and paused beside Dean who stood before a large ornate frame hanging on the wall holding a ménage of cut up pictures jumbled together in a myriad of people and poses. In one, Sharon and he reposed languidly in bathing suits on the trunk of Glenn's old Chevy with their backs against the rear window, their lips locked in lavish bliss. Another had them backed against a tree with his arms wrapped around her waist and his chin resting on her shoulder as they smiled at the camera. Yet another was of them at the state fair with her lugging a huge teddy bear and him wearing a silly hat with a long purple feather fluttering from the band. At least a dozen other men beamed out at her as they clutched Sharon in one fashion or another.

"Are you looking for clues?" she asked spitefully, fighting a surge of resentment as he studied the kaleidoscope of images with a faraway look in his eyes.

He sighed. "No, just walking down memory lane, if that's okay with you?"

"Don't trip," she chirped as she turned to survey the disheveled bed and discarded underwear. "She wasn't much of a housekeeper. Let's get out of here before we catch a social disease in all this filth."

When they exited the apartment, a police cruiser pulled in beside Lisa's Volkswagen and a deputy climbed out with a brass nametag pinned to his right breast pocket reading *P. Miller*.

He extended a manila envelope to Dean. "Mr. Davis, dispatch thought you might be out this way and asked me to drop off the incident report to you."

"I understand you were the first officer on the scene that night?" Dean queried as he took the envelope.

"That's correct. I was dispatched out here just before midnight."

"Would you mind describing what you found?"

"Sheriff Parsons is the point of contact for all information related to this case, Mr. Davis. I assume he informed you of that when you met with him earlier?"

"Yes he did, and we're not trying to put you on the spot," Lisa assured him, fluttering her long lashes as she smiled engagingly. "I'm Lisa Bryant, Mr. Davis' partner."

"Associate," Dean corrected.

"We would appreciate a firsthand report on what you observed," she cooed. "Dean here was a police officer himself. Of course, we'll keep anything you say strictly confidential."

Deputy Miller blushed under her coy gaze before shifting to Dean. "One cop to another, off the record, right?"

"One cop to another, off the record," Dean reassured him.

"I found the body right off, lying over there beside his Corvette. The driver's door was open. The interior light was on illuminating him as he lay on the ground on his back. His stomach was soaked in blood—sorry, Ma'am," he apologized as Lisa grimaced, for which she graced him with a sweet, indulgent smile. "I checked for a pulse and found none. I could see a bullet hole in his shirt on the left side below his ribcage. I called for backup, an ambulance, the coroner, and then secured the area."

"Could you tell if there were powder burns on his shirt?" Dean asked.

"Not as far as I could tell. It appeared to be a clean puncture."

"Did you see or talk to anyone while you waited for the emergency team to arrive?"

"Mrs. Sanders came out to inform me she made the call. I told her to please stay on her porch, that someone would be over to talk to her soon."

"Did you observe anyone else?"

"I had my blue lights flashing, which always draws onlookers, so there were several people at their windows and on their porches trying to see what was happening."

"Did you question anyone after your backup arrived?"

"No. Sheriff Parsons took charge of the crime scene when he arrived and I was assigned to search the area."

"Who found the murder weapon?"

"I did, in the bushes right up there beside Miss Lucas' front door. I saw a glint of metal when I shined my flashlight in there or I might have missed it."

"Did you see Miss Lucas?"

"I saw her when Sheriff Parsons brought her out to identify the body. She seemed pretty upset at the time."

"How was she dressed?" Lisa asked.

"Umm … in a nightgown, I believe, with a pink bathrobe and some fluffy slippers on her feet, like bunny rabbits, with ears that flopped around when she walked."

"Did you go inside Miss Lucas' apartment?"

"No. After I found the murder weapon, Sheriff Parsons dispatched me back to the jail to have it fingerprinted and logged into the evidence room in order to preserve the chain of custody. The next day I transported it to the lab to have ballistics test the bullets with the one the coroner took from the body. Ballistics confirmed they matched. Later that afternoon I traced the serial number of the weapon to Mr. Felton, who purchased it the previous year."

"Were any prints found on the weapon?"

"No, it was wiped clean."

"Cop to cop, what do you think happened?" Dean asked.

He shrugged. "Looks to me like her ex-boyfriend came by, they got in an argument, and she ended up shooting him with his own gun. As a former cop, you know domestic arguments are the most dangerous situation we face."

"Was his glove compartment open in his car?" Dean asked.

"Uh ... no. Only the driver's door was open. Look, I have to get back to my rounds. Don't go getting the sheriff all riled up about us talking, right?"

"Have we talked?" Dean asked.

Deputy Miller smiled and tipped the brim of his hat politely to Lisa before turning back to his car.

"Did you lock the door to Sharon's apartment?" Lisa asked as he drove off.

"No. Why?"

"I don't recall seeing a white skirt in Sharon's bedroom."

"By the way, you did a marvelous job of seducing that poor deputy with your little eyelash act," Dean complimented dourly as he followed her up the narrow walkway.

"He's cute, don't you think?"

"Not really my type," he groused as she lead him back into Sharon's bedroom.

She walked around the littered clothes and inspected the closet, pulled one hanger off the rack with a thin plastic covering, and hung it on the doorknob. She went into the bathroom, came back out into the bedroom, and got down on her knees to check under the bed.

"Only one white skirt, which was hanging in the closet, still in its dry-cleaning bag, with cleaning label attached," she advised. She poked a finger at the ripped nightgown hanging on the bedpost. "If she was wearing this when she fought with Kenny, it would explain why it's torn. She was still wearing it when the sheriff brought her out to identify the body. The bunny shoes are under the bed and the pink bathrobe is hanging on the bathroom door. I don't think she's the woman Mrs. Sanders saw running to the door that night."

"I'm impressed," Dean praised agreeably. "And it appears the sheriff's eyewitness report has more holes in it than Felton does."

"That's gross," she chided.

"There are other things that puzzle me," he continued. "The driver's door was open, which would indicate he was in the process of leaving, but the glove compartment was closed."

"So?"

"Sharon said Felton kept his pistol in the glove compartment. Anyone snatching a pistol out in the heat of an argument would likely leave the glove compartment open. I also think the odds of Sharon taking Felton's pistol from him and shooting him with it are slim. And if she *was* running away in panic after shooting him, she probably wouldn't have been thinking clearly enough to wipe the prints off of the gun before tossing it in the shrubbery beside her door either."

"You're saying it doesn't add up?"

"So far it doesn't," he affirmed as he led her out of the apartment. "Let's go talk to Mr. Jenkins. This thing is shaping up into a pretty shoddy investigation so far."

"We promised not to embarrass the sheriff or his department," she reminded him.

"Another thing that bothers me is that whoever shot Felton had to press the muzzle of the gun against his stomach at an extreme angle in order for the bullet to travel up and hit him in the heart. Why not shoot him directly in the heart to begin with, which would fit the prototype of someone in a fit of rage?"

"And who was the woman in the white skirt and dark blouse if it wasn't Sharon?" Lisa added as she followed him across the street to unit 330.

Dean pressed the doorbell. "Maybe Mr. Jenkins can tell us."

After a short pause, a heavyset woman in her fifties opened the door. "Yes?"

"Ma'am, I'm Dean Davis. This is my associate, Miss Lisa Bryant." He flashed his PI identification. "We're investigating the recent murder that occurred here. Is Mr. Jenkins home?"

"He's out of town."

"When will he return?"

"Not for several days."

"Has he mentioned anything about what he may have seen that night?" Dean asked.

She shook her head. "No, he hasn't. I was in bed asleep and don't want to get involved." She closed the door.

Lisa grinned. "You're just a silver-tongued devil with the ladies, aren't you?"

Dean scowled. "It's hard to lay on the charm when they're old enough to be my mother. I guess we'll come back when he returns from his trip."

"We don't have the time to spare if we want that bonus," Lisa advised as she punched the doorbell. "Better let me handle this, Romeo, since you seem to be batting zero with the women these days."

Lisa smiled pleasantly when the door reopened. "We're sorry to bother you again, but do you have a number we can reach Mr. Jenkins at while he's away?"

"No, he's traveling and stays at different places every night."

Lisa wrote Dean's phone number on a sheet of paper. "If you should hear from him, I'd appreciate you having him call us at his earliest convenience. It's very important that we talk to him."

The woman took the note and closed the door.

Dean turned back to the car. "Nice move, Watson."

"Was that *praise* yet again?" she gushed.

"Don't let it go to your head."

"A nice dinner out would be a suitable reward for my invaluable assistance to the team today," she suggested.

"Sounds good to me," he agreed, relieved that she seemed to have forgotten her earlier threat to have her things out of his apartment by evening.

Her eyes widened in mock wonder. "In a real *sit-down* type of restaurant?"

"I'll even pull your chair out for you," he offered grandly.

Her eyes narrowed. "So what's the occasion?"

Apparently you're not packing and leaving, but I'm not going to come right out and admit it, he thought haughtily. "Does there have to be an occasion?"

"With you I never know. I need to get my hair done and run a few errands first."

"Drop me off at the apartment and I'll go over these reports the sheriff gave us while you're doing your girly stuff."

"You're not just teasing me?"

"You can even pick the restaurant if you'd like."

Her eyes grew wishful. "There's a new steakhouse on the south side, but it's expensive."

"Since you're getting your hair done, you can wear that snazzy low cut black dress hanging in the closet," he suggested amiably.

Her eyes narrowed. "Why are you being so nice to me?"

He shrugged. "Damned if I know. Maybe you're beginning to grow on me, heaven forbid."

"Are you setting me up for something?"

"You're a suspicious little wench, aren't you?"

"*You're* the one being so civil."

He scowled. "You're really pushing it—in fact you're working your way back down to the Dairy Queen!"

"*I'll be good!*" she promised as she hurried before him to the car.

Chapter 8

"The steak and service were superb," Dean admitted as he casually surveyed the cozy couples filling the tables around them in the dimly lit room with soft music playing in the background, furtively admiring Lisa's enchanting appeal in her black dress with just the right touch of jewelry and sapphire-blue eyes mirroring a tantalizing touch of vulnerability. Precisely what she had done to her hair when she was out that afternoon escaped him, but he liked it. Even her captivating perfume led his senses on an erotic excursion, leaving him wondering idly if she had panties on underneath the dress or merely the fishnet hose that clung to her legs and disappeared in an alluring fashion up under the hem, the whole effect drawing him to her in a way he had never experienced before.

Lisa waited patiently as the waiter cleared their table, poured them coffee, and handed Dean a small dessert menu, troubled by his benign mood and appraising glances. When the waiter departed, he stared at her with that perplexed look yet again.

"Why do you keep doing that, Dean?" she inquired cautiously.

"Doing what?"

"You keep looking at me oddly."

"Um, you seem different tonight all made up in that outfit."

She smiled, pleased he approved of her attire. "You're not bad yourself. You should wear a suit more often."

He resisted the urge to reach up to his collar and loosen the chokehold around his neck, hating suits period, and ties even worse. The outfit was the only real dress-up rags he owned, which he'd bought for a friend's funeral a couple of years back and not worn since, but when Lisa swept into the room dressed to the hilt for their evening out, he'd slunk back into the bedroom and grudgingly slipped the ensemble on.

"You should let me pick out a professional wardrobe for you, some nice jackets and ties," she offered, thinking he looked invitingly urbane, if somewhat uncomfortable. "People judge you by how you dress, professionally speaking."

Gag and double gag, he thought peevishly. "People's judgment of me is the least of my concerns. Your lipstick looks enticingly spicy."

"I could lend you some if you'd like?" she taunted.

"An excellent idea," he agreed, watching her eyes widen as he half stood and leaned across the table to kiss her, the warmth of her lips sending his pulse pounding as the tease turned into something more sensual than he had anticipated.

"Dean! There are people all around!" she exclaimed, mortified.

"*Umm*, it *is* good," he praised, licking his tingling lips in an evil fashion. "And your eyes are different, too."

Slow down, Tiger, get a grip, the voice of reason cautioned. *Don't lose your perspective here.*

The devil hopped up on his shoulder with a scornful snicker. *Go for it big boy, she's putty in your hands. Look at those eyes. They're chock-full of desire. She wants you. She's yours for the taking.*

Lisa flushed at his compliment. "I only wear this particular eyeliner on special occasions. You're very observant tonight. In fact, you've made this whole evening a pleasant experience. What's gotten into you all of a sudden?"

You threatening to pack up and leave today, he thought morosely. *Why else would I be sitting here in this monkey suit eating a meal that costs more than a week's worth of groceries acting like some dumb-assed kid out on his first date?* "I'm glad you enjoyed it. We should do this more often."

"What's brought on all of this charming attention?" she asked uneasily, mystified by his amiable mood.

He leered. "Obviously I'm trying to seduce you. Is it working?"

She met his eyes as the heat grew within her, thinking it was definitely working, which made her the more uneasy, especially after his hasty withdrawal from her the night before. "Do you mean that, Dean? Do you honestly want me?"

He felt his leer slip to a crooked grin. "The thought has crossed my mind on occasion."

"Why do you suddenly want me *now?*"

The silence grew heavy between them as he sensed his crooked grin sliding away. He wanted her now because she looked so ... so *accessible* ... and *gorgeous* ... and *wickedly tempting* ...

She watched him intently, finding his troubled stare compelling, wanting to devour his lips, to feel his arms tenderly squeezing her to him. "Tell me *why,* Dean."

Why do I want you? he mused to himself, growing weak and disoriented. *Because I simply have this overpowering urge to take you in my arms, to become lost in your divine aroma, to crush your softness against my chest, to devour you selfishly, completely, utterly, until you helplessly beg for mercy!*

"Dean?" she prompted, confused by his silence.

"Uh … because I find you so, uh … so very … uh …" he mumbled, irritated at sounding like the village idiot as he searched for a concise thought.

She tilted her head, pleased to have him off balance. "So very *what?*"

Careful now, Tiger, she's searching for more than just a word here, she's looking for a significant meaning, the voice of reason warned. *Don't fall into the trap. You'll hate yourself in the morning.*

He looked appraisingly at her as she waited, finding her one beautiful woman he could easily care for if he'd only give himself half a chance. Would that be so bad? Every woman wasn't a Sharon who would play basketball with his heart. Was he such a coward he couldn't admit that someday he might be able to care for her in a meaningful way?

"Dean, are you still here with me?" she asked impatiently.

"Uh, sorry." He cleared his throat nervously as he pulled his thoughts back. "What were you saying?"

"I asked why you want me, and you said because you found me so very—and then you got tongue-tied. What were you going to say?"

Careful now! the voice of reason whispered in alarm. *You've hurt her enough in your callous, self-serving rambunctious past.*

Don't listen! the devil urged. *Go on, say it! Just one asinine, meaningless word and you can have your way with her.*

He swallowed the suffocating constriction in his throat. "I-I … think I … could … someday …"

Look at her! the devil sneered. *Look at how mouth-watering delectable she is in that dress. Imagine her without it! You know you want her. Go on, take her! What are you waiting for? One dumb word is all she needs to leap into your arms in a cloud of vaporous rapture!*

Don't do it! the voice of reason urged. *You know where this could lead! How can you even* think *what you're thinking?*

Say it! the devil fought back. *Say it and she's yours. Take her!*

Lisa frowned, alarmed by the fading sparkle in his eyes. "Are you alright, Dean? You look like you're going to be sick."

He fought the surging panic. "I-I'm fine. I-I just lost my train of thought there." He gulped at his coffee, scalding his tongue. "What were we talking about?" he gasped.

"I asked why you wanted me," she replied irritably. "But you can't seem to come up with an answer."

He took a deep breath to regain his perspective. *What is going on here? Get a grip*! He gulped some more hot coffee as his heart hammered, his hands trembling so badly the coffee sloshed over the side of the cup when he set it back in its saucer.

"Why wouldn't I want you?" he wheezed. "You're a beautiful, sexy woman."

She lowered her lashes in bitter disappointment. "I'd like to think it had more relevance than that."

The soaring flames of desire within him slowly surrendered to the familiar dousing of damp fear, which he embraced like a drowning man clutching a limb in a raging river, gaining strength and courage as he backed away from the abyss. "Are you fishing for a symbolic commitment of some kind, per chance?"

Resentment flashed through her. "Would that be so bad?"

He scowled. "There are too many loose ends in my life for commitments at the moment."

Close call, but you've got it back together now, the voice of reason soothed.

You're making a big mistake here, the devil sulked. *Don't listen to him*!

Get thee behind him, Satan! the voice of reason gloated.

"Dean, people face adversity together," she reasoned, desire skirmishing with her growing exasperation. "That's what a commitment is all about isn't it—being there for each other through the tough times?"

He ducked behind the dessert menu. "We could split the *Tira Misu* …"

She snatched up her small purse from the edge of the table as irate disappointment swept through her and weaved her way through the crowded tables to hide her tears for having been susceptible to him yet again, *the bastard*!

Pangs of apprehension darted at him as he noted other men watching her passage with a calculating gleam in their eye, some turning their heads to follow her in open admiration. He had lost the moment. No, he had *destroyed* the moment.

What a fool! the devil chastised despairingly.

You did the right thing! the voice of reason consoled.

Both of you go to hell, he mumbled as he motioned for the tab, which he found enormous, but left an over-generous tip anyway under the bleak circumstances.

Later, back in the apartment, while Lisa was in the bathroom, he slipped into his pajama bottoms and t-shirt and crawled into bed. She came out dressed in a black silk ensemble that left little to the imagination, instantly re-fanning tantalizing waves of receding desire within him.

"What is that slinky black thing you're wearing?" he demanded.

"My new nightgown," she replied. "Do you like it?"

"You look like you're auditioning for a job in a bordello."

"I thought you liked me in black. Would you prefer I wear something different?"

"Yes, something less ... *enticing*, if you don't mind."

She flounced over to his dresser shaking with fury, dug amongst his clothes, snatched one of his t-shirts from the drawer, and rushed into the bathroom. When she emerged, the t-shirt hung down to her knees.

"Is this better, my Lord?" she demanded.

It wasn't. He could see her nipples protruding through the fabric and for some strange reason the shapeless garment made her even more alluring—but he decided it best not to push it further and turned onto his side with his back to her.

"Much better, thank you."

Boiling with rage, she turned off the light and stormed down the hall in search of the sofa.

The next morning after he made coffee, he sat in the easy chair staring at Lisa's troubled frown as she slept on the couch, his eyes tracing one long bare leg jutting out from under the sheet up to the alluring bottom of her t-shirt, imagining the patch of heaven just beyond.

She stirred without opening her eyes. "Why are you staring at me?"

"Early morning is the best delineation of a woman's true attractiveness," he quipped.

"Jackass," she grumped, and jerked the sheet over her head.

Later, as they sat at the kitchen table drinking coffee and studying the incident report together, which offered no useful information beyond what they already knew, the phone rang.

"You get it," he directed.

"Why me?"

He smirked. "Because *you're* my associate and I *told* you to do so. Oh, and if it's my mother wanting me to come to dinner, tell her I'm busy."

"Won't your mother wonder why a strange woman is answering your phone so early in the morning?"

"She'll naturally assume I picked you up in some sleazy bar last night."

She glared at him as she hurried into the living room to pick up the receiver. "Hello?"

After a pause. "Yes, it is, how may we help you?"

Another pause. "Mr. Davis is unavailable at the moment, but I can take the information down for him."

Another pause. "Actually, I'm not his secretary, I'm his partner. We just recently merged into the D&B Detective Agency."

Dean lifted his head alertly.

"I see. What is the nature of this information?"

After a pause. "Yes, I'm sure he would be interested in discussing that possibility. When can he meet with you?"

Another pause ensued. "I see. This evening at six, then. Thank you for calling." She came back, sat down at the table, picked up her coffee, and resumed her study of the incident report.

"Who was that?"

"A female who wouldn't identify herself."

"What did she want?"

"To discuss the Kenny Felton murder."

"Why is she calling me instead of the police?"

"She heard you were hired to clear Sharon Lucas of the murder and wanted to know if you were willing to pay for information that might help you."

"And?"

"You meet with her at six this evening at the Traveler's Rest Lounge to work out the details. You're to sit alone in the back booth."

"What is the D&B Detective Agency?"

"It stands for Davis and Bryant. Do you like it?"

"No."

"I put your initial first."

"We're not partners."

"We can be."

"You're not even a detective."

"I'm as much of a detective as you are."

"You don't know the first thing about being a detective."

"Sure I do. You gather clues and follow leads until they pan out. That's not very complicated."

"You aren't even licensed."

She went into the living room, returned with three sheets of paper, and laid them on the table. "When I sign these forms and post a bond I will be. I've already filled them out. We can drop them off this morning when we pick up our new business cards."

"Business cards?" he stammered.

"It's not professional to scribble your name and number on a piece of paper. I ordered five hundred for each of us."

He glowered at her. "So *that's* what you were doing yesterday when you had a few errands to run?"

"I also got my hair done and bought that slinky black nightgown you hate so much. Do you realize you're incapable of making a commitment on *any* level?"

He blinked. "I can make a commitment."

"Okay, sign here." She slid one of the forms over to him.

He picked up the paper and reviewed the application for a business license in the name of the D&B Detective Agency. "You're truly nuts, do you know that?"

"We can rethink the agreement after this case is over," she counseled. "If we're not happy with the arrangement, we'll dissolve the partnership. Does that take some of the terror out of making a commitment for you?"

He scowled, trapped. "Are you willing to accept I'm the boss if I agree to this?"

"Sure, I can accept you're the boss." She watched attentively as he signed the paper, and then snatched it from his hands and ran. "*When pigs fly!*"

"*Come back here!*" he yelled.

✿ ✿ ✿

"Where are we going?" Lisa asked as he came out of the bedroom buttoning his shirt.

"Back to the crime scene. Something is still not right in my mind. I want to try and reconstruct the murder."

Lisa grabbed her purse and followed him out to her Volkswagen. He waited impatiently while she dropped off her paperwork for her bond, the application for their new business license, her application for her private investigator's license, and then stopped by the printers for their business cards.

"You owe me six hundred dollars," she advised as she handed one box to him.

"*Six hundred dollars*! For what?"

"The application, our business cards, and my bond. Here are the receipts."

"I didn't pre-approve this!"

"It's the cost of doing business," she advised as she pulled away from the curb.

When she parked near Sharon's apartment, he walked over to the bloodstained pavement and stared at it in puzzlement.

"What's bothering you, Dean?" she asked as he walked around the spot where Kenny Felton had fallen.

"It doesn't make sense. If he were getting in his car to leave, as suggested by his open car door, it would seem someone jammed his own pistol up under his ribs and shot him without leaving a powder burn on his shirt. If Sharon was the killer, how did she get his pistol out of the glove compartment in the first place?"

"Maybe he had it on him when he went into her apartment."

"If that's the case, why did he feel the need to be armed? In any case, I think it highly implausible she followed him to the car, tussled with him, somehow got his gun from his pocket or the glove compartment, and shot him with it."

She shrugged. "I admit it seems improbable, and the fact that Sharon didn't have a worn white skirt would lead me to believe some other woman was waiting for him out here. If so, she could have taken the pistol out of the glove compartment before he came out."

"But if some other woman was waiting for him in the parking lot to shoot him, we have to assume she ran to Sharon's apartment afterwards, wiped the gun clean, and ditched it in the shrubbery beside her door. Why?"

"To frame her for the murder?"

"I suppose that's possible," he conceded. "But she took a big chance on being seen by Sharon and identified."

"What if Sharon knew her?" she offered. "What if the woman actually ran to her after killing Kenny?"

"Why would she do that?"

"Maybe she ran to Sharon for protection."

"If Sharon knows who the killer is, why would she be willing to face a murder rap instead of turning her in?"

"Maybe the woman has something on her," Lisa reasoned. "Why else would Sharon protect her if she herself is being charged with Kenny's murder?"

He scowled. "You're saying some mystery woman followed Felton here and killed him when he tried to reconcile with Sharon and then ran to Sharon to blackmail her for protection because she has something on her? That's ridiculous! What could be worse than a murder rap? You need to keep to the facts and quit inventing dumb-assed theories."

"Do you have a better theory, Mr. Expert?"

He shook his head bleakly. "Well, no."

"And try this on for size," she continued. "What if when Kenny came out, they got in an argument and he shoved her to the ground before she shot him? That would explain the angle of the bullet and the absence of a powder burn on his shirt, wouldn't it?"

He nodded grudgingly. "Okay, I can buy some of it. It's possible this mystery woman knew Felton kept a gun in his glove compartment, and may have followed him here to Sharon's apartment in a jealous rage, got the gun, waited until he came out, and shot him from her position on the ground after he shoved her down. She may have even thrown the gun in the bushes to try to frame Sharon for the murder. But I'm not buying her blackmailing Sharon. Let's go visit the sheriff."

Sheriff Parsons impatiently watched Dean examine the .38 caliber snub-nosed revolver the deputy brought in from the evidence room and then offer it to Lisa, who declined to take it.

"Where do you suppose these came from?" Dean asked, pointing to abrasions on the rear of the grip and the hammer as he returned the weapon to him.

The sheriff examined the indentations. "From being thrown in the shrubbery, I assume."

"You said all the chambers were filled with bullets?"

"Four intact, one fired, which matched the bullet in Felton's heart," he affirmed.

"Were there any indications from the lab of a powder burn on his shirt?"

"There was no report of such. Are you going to half-step around here, Davis, or do you have something specific in mind?"

"Do you recall how Miss Lucas was dressed when you questioned her, Sheriff?"

"In a nightgown and a robe, Davis, what's your point?"

"Mrs. Sanders claims she saw someone who admittedly favors Miss Lucas running from the murder scene, but only from the rear in dim light, and is positive the woman was wearing a white skirt and a dark blouse. The only white skirt in Miss Lucas' residence is still in its dry cleaning wrap with the cleaning label attached. Also, the open door on Felton's automobile would indicate someone was waiting for him in the parking lot and confronted him when he came out of the apartment. I'm suggesting that another woman may have removed Felton's pistol from his glove box while he was in Miss Lucas' apartment and shot him with it, possibly after being shoved to the ground, which would account for the extreme angle of the trajectory of the bullet and the absence of powder burns on his shirt."

"That's all pretty subjective, Davis."

Dean shrugged. "No more subjective than the circumstantial evidence indicating Sharon Lucas committed the murder."

Sheriff Parsons sat forward in his chair. "Have you shared your harebrained hypothesis with anyone else, such as the press?"

"I gave you my word I wouldn't talk to the press as long as your investigation is active. I just think this case bears a closer look."

Sheriff Parsons sat back in his chair. "The DA plans to formally arraign Miss Lucas on murder charges today. Frankly, I haven't heard anything here that would warrant him holding back from charging her with the crime."

Dean stood. "That's the DA's decision, Sheriff. I'll keep you informed."

Sheriff Parsons nodded in dismissal. "You do that, Davis—*when* you have substantial facts to back up your wild-assed theories."

Lisa pulled out of the parking lot. "He sure doesn't seem very appreciative of our help."

"I just insinuated he did a half-assed investigation."

"He thought about as much of my theories as you did."

"Let's head to the Traveler's Rest Lounge, I need a drink."

"Your wish is my command."

"*That's* certainly an intriguing offer."

"In your wildest fantasy, you pervert!"

Chapter 9

Dean escorted Lisa through the door of the Traveler's Rest Lounge thirty minutes before his scheduled meeting with the anonymous female.

"Why don't you sit at the bar and have a cocktail while I assess the situation," he suggested.

"Okay, Sherlock, I've got your back," she agreed, taking a seat at the corner of the bar where she could observe without being obvious.

"That's of immense comfort to me," he allowed, settling into the back booth.

An attractive cocktail waitress decked out in a white blouse, short black skirt, and black stockings sauntered up to the booth flashing dimples. "Hi, handsome, what can I do you for?"

He grinned up at her. "We might get arrested in here for that, so just bring this ole redneck a long-neck instead."

She returned with a beer and placed it before him. "I haven't seen you in here before, sugar, just passing through?"

"I'm from here, but just moved back a few weeks ago."

"Where have you been off to?"

"Houston."

"Big city."

"It is that."

"You married or anything like that?"

"No, nothing like that, how about you?"

Lisa swiveled around on her barstool, eyes narrowing, irritation building.

"Me either," the waitress allowed, flashing a saucy smile. "I can't believe some lucky girl ain't already snapped you up yet."

"Me either, darling, but I'm always open for proposals."

She laughed. "Sugar, you don't strike me as the *proposing* kind."

He looked her up and down. "Long legs can be very persuasive."

She flashed a wicked grin. "Honey, there ain't *nothing* about me you wouldn't find real persuasive."

"I'm Dean Davis."

"I'm Grace Albright, Dean. I get off at eleven. If you happen to be in the neighborhood, I might let you buy me a drink and tell me your life story."

"That could take awhile."

She winked. "Sugar, if it's entertaining enough, I've got *aaaalllll* night long."

"Sorry, but he won't be in the *neighborhood*," Lisa interrupted as she slipped off her barstool and glared at them.

Grace sized her up. "*Excuse me*, honey—I didn't see the ring through his nose."

Lisa locked eyes with her. "We're here on business, *honey*, and he doesn't have the *time* to tell you his *life story*."

"Maybe some other time?" Dean offered meekly as Grace sashayed off, hips swinging.

"*Maybe some other time?*" Lisa demanded irritably.

"We were just kidding around—"

"I can't *imagine* you *really* wanting to *make it* with that *cow*!"

"Cow?"

"Damn, you're so dumb, Dean, I don't know why I waste my time!" She plopped back down on her barstool and took a calming draught of her wine.

Dean nursed his beer, idly trying to figure women out, before glumly deciding *that* was definitely an endless loop. An attractive brunette in her mid twenties with a nice figure encased in a tight fitting skirt and an even tighter cleft-revealing blouse entered, paused to look around, fixed shop-worn eyes that belied hard miles in short years on him, and headed for his booth.

"Mr. Davis?"

"Call me Dean. Please have a seat."

She slid in across from him. "You're younger than I expected."

"Can I order you a drink, Miss …?"

"Everyone calls me Kitty. I'll take a Scotch and water."

He motioned a frigid Grace over and placed her order. "I understand you have some information that might help clear Sharon Lucas of the Felton murder?"

Slyness crept into her eyes. "What's information like that worth?"

"Depends on the information."

"I could use a hundred bucks. My rent's due and I'm a month late on my 'lectric bill."

"What do you have to offer?"

"Shouldn't I see the money first?"

He took out his wallet and placed five twenties before him. "Start with your full name, Kitty."

She shifted evasively. "Is that necessary? I really don't want to get caught up in all this."

"That will depend on the nature of the information." He smiled at Grace as she set Kitty's drink down and cut him a spiteful glance before flouncing off. *Women aren't worth it*, he decided, turning his attention back to Kitty. "I'll keep it as confidential as I can, but I can't give you any guarantees until I hear what you have to say."

"Kenny was a real jerk." She sipped her scotch, watching him over the rim of her glass.

"So far that's not worth the price of your drink," he advised.

Kitty toyed with her napkin. "My name is Katherine Moore. I've known Kenny for years."

"In what manner did you know him?"

"He and I've done some partying together off and on, if that's what you mean." She took a sip of her drink as her eyes flashed up to his and away again. "But we were never serious or anything, we just, like, partied together, is all."

"Were you seeing Felton when he was engaged to Sharon?"

"Yeah, I partied with him and Sharon several times."

"Could you clarify *partying*?"

She lowered her eyes. "Kenny liked to spice things up sometimes."

"I see." Dean took a sip of his beer to mask the impact. Sharon had been bold and daring from the first day he met her, but he'd never considered her the type to go for the *ménage* type of thing. He cleared his throat and refocused on Kitty. "Did he pay you for partying with him?"

"He helped me out with my rent sometimes, but it ain't like I'm a hooker or anything. He didn't always give me money. Sometimes it was other things."

"Other things like what?"

Her features tightened and she just stared at him by way of answering.

"Was Sharon … *agreeable* to this arrangement?" he pressed, realizing the question was more personal than professional and mutely cautioning himself to stay emotionally detached.

"Sharon was cool about it."

"Cool? As in *okay* with it?" *What the hell was he fishing for here?*

"When she got high she enjoyed being far out. Do you know what I mean?"

"High?" he asked. "You mean drugs?"

"They enhance your awareness," she answered.

He took a sip of his beer to quell the growing cavity in his stomach. "Did Felton and Sharon get *far out* with others beside you?"

"Sometimes."

"Were there other men involved as well?"

"Kenny was way too macho to go for that."

"Did Felton see other women without Sharon knowing about it?"

She laughed. "Kenny wasn't the type to ever limit himself to one woman."

"But he and Sharon were engaged to be married, right?"

"Everyone knew Kenny wasn't exactly the marrying kind, you know?"

"Do you know of any particular woman he was seeing other than Sharon?"

She shrugged. "What does all of this have to do with anything? I thought we were here to talk about who killed him."

Dean cleared his throat to mask his embarrassment. "What can you tell me about his death?"

"I don't think Sharon killed him."

"Who do you think did?"

"I think Al Roberts did."

"Al Roberts?"

She sipped her drink as her eyes darted around. "I wish you wouldn't use my name in this. I have a two-year-old kid. If something should happen to me she wouldn't have nobody to take care of her."

"Do you feel threatened by this Al Roberts?"

"Wouldn't you?"

"Are you married?"

She fixed him with an insolent stare. "If I was, I wouldn't be partying around with people like Kenny and Sharon, now would I? I ain't like that!"

"Sorry, I didn't mean to infer otherwise," he soothed. "Who is Al Roberts and why would he want to kill Felton?"

"Al is married to Becky. Kenny and Becky go way back. When she started hanging around Kenny again, Al showed up one night threatening to kill him."

"How do you know this?"

"I was there. Al was crazy mad at the time. Kenny had him beaten up over it."

"Felton had this Al fellow beaten up in front of his wife, who he was fooling around with?"

"Not in *front* of her, he showed up looking for her right after she left."

"How did Al know she was seeing Felton again?"

"I don't know *everything*, Mr. Detective, I just know somebody *told* him. Is it all that important anyway?"

He sensed she was telling the truth. "When did this event happen?"

"About a week before Kenny got killed."

"Was there anyone other than you there at the time?"

"Just Little Joe and Bear—they're the ones who beat Al up for Kenny."

"Who is Little Joe and Bear?"

"Kenny's friends."

"So you think this Al Roberts killed Felton because he was fooling around with his wife. Other than hearing Al threaten him, do you have anything else to indicate he *did* kill him?"

"Well, the main thing is, Becky called me the night Kenny got killed crying and begging me to come get her. She said Al beat her up and took her car keys after accusing her of being with Kenny that afternoon, and then left with his gun to go find him."

"Did you pick Becky up that night?"

"No. My car is broke down so I had no way to get there. She said for me not to worry about it then, she'd get someone else to bring her over to my place. But she never showed up. She called me the next morning still scared to death and ask if I had heard about Kenny getting killed. She said Al didn't come home until early that morning and she thought he was the one that killed Kenny. She said he might kill her next and wanted me to borrow my neighbor's car and come get her before he came home from work."

"Did you go get her?"

"'Course not. I figured Al might kill me too if he found out I helped her. So I told her I'd borrow my neighbor's car and go shopping for her instead."

"Go shopping for her?"

"To get some steak."

"Some steak?"

"I told her to fix his favorite meal of chicken fried steak and smashed potatoes and cream gravy when he got home, and after she fed him, to say she was sorry he didn't trust her and then screw his eyeballs out. I figured there was no way he'd stay mad at her then."

"Um, did it work?" Dean asked, intrigued.

She smiled slyly. "He ain't killed her yet, has he?"

"Was Becky in love with Felton?"

"'Course not, she just liked the candy he gave her."

"You mean the drugs?"

She lifted her eyebrows knowingly. "The candy helped her escape from being married to Al. I told her one time I didn't know why she ever married him in the first place and she said she didn't know why either."

"Where did Felton get his, uh, *candy*?"

She leaned forward. "From Little Joe and Bear, of course, where do you think? You sure don't know much for a detective, do you?"

"Was Felton seeing other women besides you, Becky, and Sharon?"

She shrugged. "They came and went."

"Can you give me the names of some of the others he was, uh, *partying* with?"

She leaned back in the booth eyeing him carefully. "I don't think they would appreciate that since some of them are married, like Becky. The married ones came and went as the mood hit them or when they could sneak away from their husbands."

"How about just the ones he was seeing in the last few weeks?" Dean coached, diddling with the stack of twenties with his fingertips.

Her eyes dropped to the money. "Am I getting that hundred for all this?"

"You're doing a good job of earning it so far," he encouraged.

"Well, in the last month there was me, Becky, Sharon, Linda Thompson, Allison Neely, and Janice Murray."

He managed not to gulp. "Were all of Felton's women into drugs?"

"Some of them were just looking for thrills. A couple of them thought they could actually hook him, like Sharon. Look, I've told you everything I know. Do I get the money now? My baby's home all alone and I got my neighbor's car borrowed."

He pushed the five twenties over to her. "How can I reach you if I need additional information?"

She scooped up the bills and stuffed them in her purse. "Do I get paid for that too?"

"If the information has value, I'm sure we can work something out." He pulled one of his fancy new business cards from his pocket and handed it to her. "You know how to get up with me if you think of anything else that might be important, right?"

"Just try to keep me out of this mess, okay? I got all the trouble I need." She placed his card in her purse, extracted a pad and pen, wrote her name, address and phone number on it, and slid it across to him, eyes locked to his. "Look, I think you're a nice guy. You can come by and party with me sometime if you want to. It won't cost you nothing unless you want to give me something on your own. I ain't no hooker or nothing, you know?"

"I'll keep that in mind. By the way, where do Al and Becky live?"

"Unit 112 in the old Briargate Apartments, off Sweet Creek Road, but you didn't hear that from me, okay? I gotta go now. See you later. That is, if you want to, you know?"

"Goodbye, Kitty."

As Kitty hurried off Lisa slid in across from him with her glass of wine. "I heard most of it. What do you think?"

"I think we've got a strong suspect in this Al Roberts."

"Drugs and sex," Lisa mused. "That's a lethal mix, and your sweet little Sharon was right in the middle of it all."

"Is it really necessary to put this on a personal level?"

She tasted her wine thoughtfully. "If you think this Al character is such a strong suspect, how do you explain the witness who saw a woman running from the body?"

He stood. "Eyewitnesses are not always reliable. Sometimes they get confused about what they saw and when they saw it. Let's go talk to Al and see what his story is. He certainly seems to have a strong motive for doing Felton in if everything Kitty said is true."

"If you think there's a chance this Al character killed Kenny, shouldn't we notify Sheriff Parsons?"

"Let's make sure Kitty's story checks out first, otherwise we'll look like the amateurs we are. The sheriff would love that."

Dean knocked on the torn screen door of unit 112 in the run-down apartment complex at dusk. A TV blared inside. A large man in his late twenties wearing a soiled t-shirt, faded dirty blue jeans, a yellow baseball cap with a bold CAT logo on the crown and a confrontational frown appeared on the other side of the sagging screen.

"Yeah?"

"Al Roberts?" he inquired.

"Yeah. What d'ya want?" He glanced beyond them to a green Ford F-150 pickup with a rifle rack hanging over the rear window. "I'm sending a payment in Friday when I get paid. Honest."

"I'm Dean Davis. This is my associate, Lisa Bryant. We're not bank Re-Po agents, we're private investigators hired to look into the murder of Kenny Felton. Can we have a minute of your time?"

Roberts cut his eyes over his shoulder, opened the screen door, stepped out onto the front stoop, and pulled the battered wooden door closed behind him. "I don't know nothin' 'bout that. Why ya wantin' to talk to me 'bout that?"

"We were informed you made threats against Mr. Felton's life," Lisa replied.

"That's a *damned lie*!" Roberts shouted, puffing out his chest aggressively. "Who told ya that shit anyway?"

"Where were you around midnight on the night Felton was murdered?" Dean pressed.

Roberts balled his fists in a menacing fashion. "I don't have to tell ya a damned thing! Get off my porch, ya hear?"

Dean took Lisa's arm and turned to the street. "Okay, Al, we'll let the sheriff handle it."

"The sheriff?" Roberts demanded, starting after them. "Handle what? I don't know nothin' 'bout it, I tell ya!"

"I'll bet the sheriff arrests him on suspicion of murder when he hears what we've heard," Lisa added as Roberts trailed after them.

"Hey, wait a minute!" Roberts shouted. "I ain't done nothin'!"

"You and your attorney can sort that out with the sheriff," Lisa tossed over her shoulder.

"Wait a minute now! I ain't got no attorney. You don't need to be talkin' to the sheriff 'bout me. Ya hear? Hey, wait a minute. I guess I'll talk to ya if it's goin' to be a big deal!" He shoved his hands in the pockets of his dirty jeans and hunched his shoulders. "What is it ya wantin' to know 'bout, anyways?"

"Why you threatened to kill Felton, for starters," Dean replied, turning back to him.

Roberts stiffened. "H-He was tryin' to mess around with my ol' lady. I warned him to steer clear of her. That's in my rights, ain't it? But I ain't gone and killed him over it or nothin'!"

"Lisa, go have a word with Mrs. Roberts while Al and I talk out here," Dean suggested.

"Now hold on here. She ain't got nothin' to say! Ya said ya wanted to talk to me. I'm talkin', so just leave Becky outta this!"

"Al, you and your wife can talk to us, or you can talk to the sheriff after we give him the information we have," Dean threatened. "We can clear this up between us, or you can clear it up with him, but one way or the other, this issue needs to be resolved. It's your call."

"Damn it all to hell, who told ya 'bout me havin' a problem with Kenny anyways? They got no right involvin' me and Becky in this thing."

Dean watched Lisa return to the apartment and knock, a petite dishwater blonde open the door, and after a moment's hesitation, invite her in. "Al, this will go a lot smoother if you give me the straight scoop. Where were you around midnight when Felton was murdered?"

Roberts ducked his head and kicked at a tuft of grass. "Ridin' around. Ain't no crime in that, is there?"

"Riding around where?"

He looked away. "Okay, I was sittin' outside Kenny's house waitin' for him to come back home, but he never did, and that's the honest-to-god truth."

"Why were you waiting for him?"

"I done told ya—he was tryin' to mess around with my wife. I was gonna tell him off. Maybe scare him a little."

"Were you armed?"

He glanced at his green truck where a rifle and a shotgun lay in the double rack. "Hell, I always got a gun or two around. Don't mean nothin'."

"Other than you, do you know who else may have wanted Felton dead?"

"Me and about a dozen other people. He was nothin' but a rich asshole. I done told him once to stay away from my Becky."

"I understand he had Little Joe and Bear give you a beating for that."

"That's a damned lie too! We had a little scuffle is all. Who's tellin' ya all that shit?"

"Did you see Felton on the night he was murdered?"

"No I didn't! I sat outside his house 'til nearly two in the mornin' waitin' on the asshole. Then I went on back home myself since I had to go to work at six. I didn't even know 'til the next day the bastard got killed by somebody."

"Who are some of the other people you mentioned that might want to see Felton dead?"

"Hell, 'bout anybody that knew him. I can't give ya no name's in particular. I don't know many folks who liked him, is all."

"You're not being very helpful. You admit you had a grudge against him. You admit you went looking for him on the night he was murdered, and you admit you were armed. You don't have an alibi for the time he was killed. You admit he had a couple of his buddies rough you up the week before when you warned him to stay away from your wife. That's a long list of grievances against the man—or reasons to make you a prime suspect in his murder. You need to give me something solid to go on or the sheriff will need to pursue this matter further."

"I don't know nothin', I tell ya! I didn't like the bastard, but I didn't kill him. Ya barkin' up the wrong tree with me."

"How did Felton know your wife?"

"From a long time ago, but Becky wouldn't have nothin' to do with him, no matter how much money he had. She told me so herself."

"Exactly what did Felton do to upset you on the day you went to his house?"

Roberts' face flushed. "It don't matter none now, does it? He's dead, so it's done with as far as I'm concerned."

"It was important enough for you to go hunting him armed to the teeth."

"Damn it all to hell! Don't a man have any privacy anymore? There's some things don't need spreading around."

"We're talking murder here, Al. I'm trying to clear you, but you're not being much help."

"He had a *thing* for Becky from a long time ago, is all there was to it, I'm tellin' ya."

"So he called her?"

"He saw her downtown. Becky's sort of dumb where men are concerned. She got in his car and drove aroun' with him. They talked and that was all there was to it."

"How did you find out about it?"

"A friend of mine saw her ridin' in his car."

"Who was the friend?"

"Damn, ya ask a lot of questions. Why's that important?"

"I have to confirm the facts. You *do* want me to help clear you in this mess, don't you?"

He scowled and ducked his head. "My friend's name is Clyde Hawkins. He works over at the saw mill with me."

"Was he with you the night you sat outside Felton's house waiting for him?"

"Clyde was with me 'til about eleven 'o clock, then he went on back home 'cause he had to get up early, too."

Lisa opened the door and exited the apartment as Becky stood in the doorway.

"Okay, Al, I'll do what I can to confirm your story," Dean said, handing him one of his business cards. "If you think of anything else to help me, give me a call."

Roberts took the card. "I'd sure appreciate ya not involvin' the sheriff in all this."

"You have a nice day, Al." He opened the passenger door to Lisa's Volkswagen as she slid in behind the wheel.

"That there little VW's a good disguise for a private eye," Roberts advised. "Nobody would ever think to look for a silly little car like that if they was bein' tailed."

Dean winked at him. "That's the idea, Al. See you." He sighed as Lisa backed out and pulled away. "Damn it, the first thing I'm going to do if I earn that bonus is get me a real car."

"He just complimented you on how smart you were for being in this one."

"Did you get anything useful from Becky?"

"Buy me dinner and we'll exchange notes."

"I bought you dinner *last* night! Besides, it's *your* turn to cook."

"Let's go to that barbeque place out on the north highway. They've got great ribs."

"Do you ever listen to anything I say?"

"Only when it makes sense. I'll spring for the tab if you'll give me an advance."

"An advance on what? Associates don't make the payroll until they've completed *years* of apprenticeship."

"I've got a business license that says differently, *partner!*"

"*Damn!*" he swore.

Chapter 10

"I don't think Al Roberts is smart enough to kill anybody and get away with it," Dean offered as he inhaled the spicy aroma of charbroiled pit barbeque in anticipation while awaiting their order in the crowded dining room.

"So you're ruling him out as a suspect?" Lisa asked.

He shrugged. "Not totally. He does have a three-hour gap in his alibi since he didn't get home until sometime around two that morning after his buddy left him outside Felton's house around eleven that night. He could have easily driven to Sharon's house in less than twenty minutes, saw Felton's car, found the pistol in the glove box, and waited for him to come out around midnight. He's even big enough to have taken the pistol away from Felton if he had it on him."

"And he'd also have time to slip on a white skirt and dark blouse in the process," Lisa speculated dryly.

Dean grinned. "I *do* think that'd be asking a bit much of him. He's dumber than a rock, but it doesn't take a great deal of intelligence to pull a trigger."

"He's even dumber if he thinks little Mrs. Roberts wasn't doing more than riding around in Kenny's car," Lisa added. "That woman has rather loose morals."

"What's the scoop on her?"

"She claims she started sleeping with Kenny when she was fifteen, and has been with him off and on the whole three years she's been married to Al. The last time she was in his bed was the afternoon Kenny was killed."

"How did you get all that out of her so quickly?"

"She bragged about it, actually."

"She sort of fits the description of the woman seen by Mrs. Sanders running from the murder scene," he allowed. "Do you think we should consider her a suspect?"

Lisa forked ribs onto her plate as the server placed a heaping platter of meat and side dishes before them. "Not really. I think she's bored with married life and into the drug thing, like Kitty said."

"Did she admit to sleeping with both Sharon and Felton?" He squelched a flutter, not really wanting to hear the answer.

"She was pretty frank about it, even to the point of freely admitting she enjoys 'going both ways,' which sort of diminishes a motive to kill both her lover and her source."

"Did she hit on you?" He arched his eyebrows and grinned when she blushed. "So she thought you were a hot dish, huh? Remember, partners share equally."

"You *wish*."

"I'm speaking theoretically, of course."

"Sure you are you depraved voyeur. But back to the point, after admitting to being part of Sharon and Kenny's sick little love triangle, she also mentioned a boyfriend on the side named Clyde, but I didn't get the impression she was interested in anyone in particular. She seems more the free spirit type."

"Clyde Hawkins?"

"She just referred to him as Clyde. Why?"

"Roberts says a gent by the name of Clyde Hawkins is his best friend and the one who told him about seeing Becky in Felton's car. Hawkins also sat outside Felton's house with Roberts for a few hours the night of Felton's murder. Becky sounds like a real nymphomaniac. I'm surprised she can keep all of her exterior sexual activities secret from her hubby."

"She was quite smug about him believing everything she tells him."

"Did she give any indication as to who she thought may have killed Felton?"

"She said she thought her husband did at first, but now she thinks Sharon did it. She thinks Sharon was infatuated with his money and figures she was distraught when they broke up. She says Sharon called his house three times the afternoon he was killed."

"How does she know that?"

"She claims she was in bed with him at the time, but that Kenny wouldn't answer his phone."

"How does she know it was Sharon calling?"

Lisa set a bare rib bone down and delicately licked the ends of her fingers before snatching up another. "She left messages on his recorder crying and begging him to call her."

"Sharon told me Felton came by unannounced because *she* wouldn't take *his* calls. Did you get anything else out of her?"

Lisa rolled her eyes. "She thinks you're a hunk and wanted to know how you were between the sheets."

"The woman has *exquisite* taste!"

"I informed her that unfortunately a recent traumatic event on the police force left you completely impotent."

"I assume she was devastated?"

Lisa licked the sauce from the tips of her fingers and snatched another rib. "Actually, she was very sympathetic and advised me not to waste my time on dysfunctional men."

"Hell, now *I'm* devastated!" He stared at her jaw as she reached for the last rib. "You've got sauce on your chin," he advised, and speared the rib as she snatched a napkin up to her face.

"*Hey*!"

"Lick your lips," he suggested as he bit into the juicy chunk. "You've got enough sauce around them for a second course."

"Jackass!"

✲ ✲ ✲

Lisa emerged from the bathroom with his old t-shirt on and glanced disapprovingly at her image in the mirror over the dresser. "I look like Hilda the wash woman in this getup!"

"You can always slip into your slinky black thing," he offered as he gathered up the sheets and a pillow lying on the foot of the bed. "I don't have a problem with you looking like a working girl in a cat house if you don't mind acting like one."

She snapped off the lamp. "One of these days, Dean," she swore in the darkness as she slid into bed and adjusted the sheet around her.

Dean trudged down the hall to the couch swearing at himself.

✲ ✲ ✲

"Wake up, sleepyhead, we've only got five days left to earn that bonus," Lisa cajoled as she slid a cup of coffee under Dean's nose to tantalize his sluggish senses.

"Coffee in bed?" he approved as he sat up amid the tangled remnants of his bed on the couch. "*Now* you're getting the hang of things."

She shook her head grimly. "You just can't let well enough alone, can you? What's on the agenda for today, Sherlock?"

"We gather and analyze more clues, Doctor Watson."

"That's really innovative," she complained as she sank down on the couch beside him.

Dean focused on the twin peaks jutting out of his old t-shirt wondering why she was always so appealing in the morning with her makeup-free face and tousled hair. In idle curiosity, he curled a finger into the bottom of the t-shirt and tugged it upward to see what was underneath.

She slapped his hand without even spilling her coffee. "Where do we gather new clues?"

"I'd like to confront Sharon with a few of the facts we've uncovered. Maybe we can get some new leads from her."

"Such as?"

"Such as why she broke off her engagement with Felton. After all we've heard, that's a real mystery to me. Later, we can run down some of the other women Kitty mentioned."

"Are we going to fight about me going in to see her with you this time?"

"Absolutely not, I find it entertaining as hell to watch you two hiss at each other like alley cats."

Her eyes narrowed as distinctive glints of anger danced about them in a fashion he'd come to admire.

Sharon rushed into Dean's arms when she entered the visitor's room. He breathed in her fresh soap scent, finding it more tantalizing than perfume in the dank interior of the visitor's room as he absorbed the sensuous softness of her body through her prison clothes, subtly realizing what he did *not* feel was the frantic thudding of his heart or a wave of heady desire overwhelming him. The cold and distant sensation he now experienced was somewhat exhilarating as she stepped back and glanced at Lisa.

"Does *she* have to be here?"

He steered her around to her seat across the table. "Lisa is my partner now."

Sharon arched her eyebrows. "Oh really? I suppose congratulations are in order. Does the working arrangement extend to the bedroom as well?"

Lisa smiled coolly. "We're still negotiating the fringe benefits."

Dean cleared his throat half-expecting sparks to flash between them. "Sharon, did you end your relationship with Felton over another woman?"

Sharon looked away. "I told you, it doesn't matter why we broke up."

"Why are you so reluctant to talk about it?"

She diverted her eyes. "I'd just prefer not to discuss it."

He tipped her chin up and forced her to make eye contact. "You could be facing the death penalty. I need your help if I'm going to find the real killer."

She stood and turned her back to them. "The reason I broke off our engagement has nothing to do with this mess, Dean, you're just going to have to trust me on that."

"I've met with Kitty Moore and Al and Becky Roberts."

She whirled back to him. "They're liars! Whatever they told you is a pure, bald-faced lie! I don't like you snooping around in my life like that!"

"I have to snoop around if I'm going to help you, especially if you won't help me."

"You're fired! Now please leave!"

"You can't fire us," Lisa injected. "Your grandmother hired us. Besides, as long as we work for her, we're required to exercise discretion in disclosing what we discover. Firing us could relieve us of that responsibility."

Sharon sank down in her chair. "Are you going to repeat those lies to my grandmother? It would hurt her deeply to hear such things."

"We haven't told you what they said yet," Lisa reminded her pointedly.

Sharon glared at her. "I can imagine what they had to say. I know those people. They're trash and don't like me. Why would you believe anything they tell you?"

"Kitty and Becky say they've been intimate with both you and Kenny," Lisa accused.

"You see—they're *lying*!" Sharon shouted, rising abruptly. "You better not repeat that rubbish to my grandmother! I mean it! I'll sue you and them for slander!"

"That's only possible if it's not true," Lisa countered. "Can you imagine the headlines if they're called to testify at your trial?"

Sharon clutched the edge of the table. "Please, you don't understand ... Dean, you can't let them do this to me ... *you've got to help me*!"

"Did you know Felton was seeing them on the side as well?" he asked lamely, avoiding her eyes.

"*No!* I don't believe that. They're *lying*!"

"You said Felton stopped by unannounced the night he was killed when you wouldn't take his calls," he continued. "Becky says she was in bed with him that afternoon and heard you leave three messages on his recorder demanding he call you."

Sharon began pacing. "That's not true! She's lying!"

"Why would she lie about such a thing?" Lisa asked. "She's a married woman with a lot at stake if this becomes public."

"She'd like to see me get convicted of killing Kenny. She hates me!"

"Sharon, you've got to tell me everything so I can help you," Dean urged. "Let's go back to the night of the murder. When you heard the gunshot, exactly what did you do?"

"I *told* you! I went to the window and looked out."

"How long after you heard the shot did it take you to get to the window?"

She paused. "I sat there on the floor at first. I was scared. Then I got up and went to the window. A minute or so, what does it matter?"

"A witness saw a woman running up the sidewalk to your front door," Dean replied. "The witness also heard a car start up and drive off shortly after that. If it only took a minute or so to get to your front window, surely you saw or heard *something*?"

"I didn't hear or see anything!"

"Did you let anyone into your apartment after you heard the shot?" Lisa asked.

"No! I did not *hear* or *see* anything, and I *did not* let anyone into my apartment! Whose side are you on anyway?"

Lisa's eyes narrowed. "Are you sure, Sharon?"

Sharon's nostrils flared as she sank down in her chair. "You don't believe me! You think I had something to do with Kenny's death, don't you?"

Dean placed his hands on her arms in an effort to soothe her, knowing in his heart she was lying through her teeth. "Sharon, we're only trying to piece this thing together so we can clear you of the murder, but you've *got* to tell us what you know. If we can find these things out, so can the police. This thing is not going away. Don't you understand that?"

"*I did not kill Kenny*!" she shouted, jerking away from him.

"We'll try to keep as much of your past as confidential as possible," he promised. "But it's imperative we get to the bottom of this quickly. The longer this investigation drags on the more things are going to come out."

"You need to help us, Sharon," Lisa urged. "We're bound by client confidentiality the same as your lawyer. Whatever you tell us will stay with us."

She buried her face in her hands and sobbed. "I'm … *so ashamed*! I can't believe I was so *stupid*."

"Were Kitty and Becky telling the truth?" Lisa asked gently.

Sharon nodded. "Kenny … liked things like that. He would give us drugs. Don't you understand that's the only way I could have done something like that? Please don't tell my grandmother! It would *kill* her to know how *awful* I've been!"

Bricks settled in Dean's stomach as cold remorse swept through him. "Why did you break off your engagement with Felton, Sharon?"

"It … doesn't matter … why," she gasped. "Please go now."

He stood, a growing sadness replacing whatever he had once felt for her, wondering where the beautiful, carefree girl he had once known, so full of ambition and life, had gone over the years. "I'll check back in a day or two."

Sharon laid her head on her arms on the table and wept as Lisa and he departed.

"That wasn't as much fun as I'd anticipated," Lisa observed after they picked up their personal things from the deputy and made their way to her car.

"She's still not telling us the truth about that night," Dean insisted. "She's holding something back that could be the key to all this."

Lisa opened her door. "She was scared, but I didn't sense she was as much afraid *of* someone as she was *for* someone."

"What the hell does that mean?"

"She's protecting someone for some reason. We need to find out who and why, but where do we start?" She turned to a phone booth on the corner next to the car. "Let's check out Felton's apartment. After that, we can go down the list of the other women Kitty mentioned and keep digging until we find something."

Dean sighed. "And exactly what are we digging for?"

She took a pen and pad from her purse and carefully copied Felton's address from the phone book. "A motive for someone wanting to see Felton dead, of course, and a suspect other than Sharon."

"Brilliant, my dear Watson, *brilliant*!" he praised despondently as he followed her to the car.

Lisa pulled into the circular driveway in the secluded section of town and parked behind a well-manicured hedge blocking the street from view. "Nice," she observed as she studied the modern two-story brick structure sprawling before them.

"If you've got it, flaunt it," Dean appraised as he stepped out and led her to the massive double front doors. He pulled a small leather bag from his pocket and squatted down to study the lock.

Lisa looked over her shoulder cautiously. "Shouldn't you check to see if there's a maid or something before you pick the lock?"

"Good idea," he reasoned as he reached up and pressed the doorbell.

She edged back a step. "What if someone answers?"

"You try to sell them some brushes while I trot back to get our sample case," he advised as he rang the bell again, and then a third time. When the chimes inside receded, he inserted two slim metal picks into the lock, turned the handle, and swung the door open.

"This is illegal, you know," she advised.

"No kidding? Then you'd better wait out here in case I need bail money."

She edged in behind him. "What if there's an alarm, Sherlock?"

"I thought you were going to wait outside with the bail money, Watson."

"The door was open. *I'm* not doing anything wrong!"

They paused in the lavishly decorated marble foyer festooned with an expensive table featuring an artsy vase below a gilt-edged mirror hanging on the wall and peered tentatively into the first room on the right at built-in bookcases and a large executive desk with leather wing chairs poised on plush carpeting. Dean wandered over to the desk and checked the few papers scattered across the top, finding mostly household bills and stock reports, opened the neatly arranged desk drawers to find additional files of stock reports and pulled one labeled bank statements. He flipped through it and whistled at the six-figure balance as Lisa crowded against him inquisitively. He nudged her aside, replaced the file, and wandered back out into the foyer and into the main room, where he paused to study a gigantic modern painting with recessed lighting high on the wall behind two posh black leather sofas and easy chairs.

"I don't get it," he observed, mystified by the wild display of colors and warped shapes.

"It's expressionist," Lisa advised sagely. "It communicates what the artist feels."

"Well, he must have been feeling hung over then," Dean allowed sourly as he turned into an elaborate dining room, which in turn led into a modern kitchen. Lisa moved around him to inspect a well-stocked refrigerator and pantry before following him into a long sunroom overlooking a swimming pool surrounded by ornate pool furniture. She clutched at his arm and pointed to the floor in front of the double French doors, where shards of broken glass littered the tile.

Dean pulled back one of the thin white silk curtains to expose the empty glass panel next to the door handle. "Someone broke in here."

"Really, Sherlock?" Lisa quipped. "How can you be so sure?"

"Through my awesome powers of simple observation and deductive reasoning, my dear Watson—take note there's no lost baseball lying about."

"You never fail to amaze me," she swooned as she followed him back into the main room and up the stairs into the hall. They peeked into what appeared to be three guest bedrooms, each with a private bath, finding each undisturbed. The last door on the right proved to be the master bedroom, delineated by its size and the scraps of men's clothing strewn about the floor beside the unmade king size bed with black satin sheets. A built-in entertainment center located against the wall at the foot of the bed flashed black and white static from a muted screen. An open door on the left revealed two towels cluttering the floor next to a shower in a large bathroom. Lisa pointed to a blinking red light on an answering machine next to the bed. Dean wrapped his hand in the edge of the sheet and pressed the play button.

"*Kenny, buddy, Ray here. Give me a call.*"

"*Kenny, why won't you call me, you son of a bitch!*" Sharon's tearful voice screamed out in the next message. "*Why are you doing this to me? You won't get away with this!*"

"*Kenny? Please answer the phone. I know you're there,*" Sharon's voice pleaded in message three, calmer now, but still with a desperate edge to it. "*You can't do this to me. We need to talk this out. My whole life is at stake. Please, please call me.*"

"*Kenny, darling, your father and I are going to the Bahamas for the weekend. Just letting you know. We'll be back on Tuesday. Love you,*" a female voice in message four advised.

"*Kenny, you son of a bitch! I swear I'll kill you if you do this to me!*" Sharon's voice raged in message five. "*You better call me, goddamn you! You can't do this to me! Call me goddamn it, or you'll regret it! I mean it!*"

"*Kenny Felton, I'll kill ya if y're messing around with my wife again, ya bastard! I'll blow y're shit away, ya asshole!*" Al Robert's voice raged in message six. "*I done told ya that. Somebody seen my wife in y're car today. I'm looking for ya, buddy!*"

"*Kenny, this is Ray. Where the hell are you? It's after midnight and I've been waiting for over an hour. If you ain't coming, I need to know 'cause I got other things to be doing.*"

Dean rewound the messages and walked over to the entertainment center where the TV discharged its silent static and studied the VCR above the TV with the record button pressed. He picked up a shirt on the floor, pressed the rewind button, waited until it stopped, and then pressed play. When the TV screen sprang into full color, Becky Roberts stood beside the bed in her bra taking off her skirt. Kenny walked over and pressed her to her knees in front of him as she smiled and began tugging at his belt. As the scene played out, Dean looked at the picture, back to the bed, and back to the entertainment center. Cleverly hidden in the top shelf, he found a video camera pointed at the bed.

Lisa turned away in revulsion. "Turn that thing off!"

Dean chuckled as he watched the tape. "Old Kenny-boy was hung. No wonder all the girls were chasing after him."

"You're as *disgusting* as he is," Lisa spat as she fled the room.

Dean used his shirt-draped hand to open the long drawer under the TV. Cassette tapes filled the compartment, each numbered and with names written on them. Keeping the shirt wrapped around his palm, he picked one up and read *Linda, vol. 5*. He replaced it in its slot and picked up another. *Allison, Becky, Vol. 6*. He leaned down to scan the labels of the other tapes, but there was no Sharon listed, and volumes 8, 9, 10, and 12 were missing from their slots.

"Are you coming?" Lisa demanded from the doorway, her head averted from the TV.

"Come have a look."

"Turn that filth off first!"

He glanced up at the TV, punched stop and then fast-forward to put the tape back to the end where he found it. "Felton has quite a collection of his sexual escapades here, but none of him and Sharon. It also appears four tapes are missing."

Lisa glanced contemptuously at the array of cassettes. "This place gives me the creeps. Let's get out of here."

Dean left the TV on and followed her downstairs, where she waited outside while he wiped his prints off the desk before locking the door.

"That man was an animal!" she swore as she slid in behind the steering wheel of her Volkswagen and he got in on the passenger side. "No wonder someone wanted to kill him!"

"His playmates didn't seem to mind starring in his productions."

"They're animals too!"

"You really are a sweet, innocent, naïve little thing, aren't you?" he taunted.

Her cheeks flushed angrily. "I'm not in the mood, Dean—and *please* don't call me *naïve*!"

Chapter 11

"Give me your take on what we found back there," Dean challenged, intent on drawing Lisa out of her brooding mood as she drove grimly staring straight ahead.

"Kenny Felton was depraved," she swore bitterly.

"This profession requires dealing with and around the scum of the earth," he advised firmly. "If you want to be successful, learn to ignore your feelings and focus on the facts. Felton being a scumbag with a harem is significant only if it helps solve our case."

Her lips compressed into a thin line. "We already knew Kenny was rich. We knew he did drugs and provided them to women he had orgies with. We knew he spent the afternoon with Becky. We even knew Sharon called him three times begging him to call her. The only thing we learned new was that he was making dirty movies of himself and his companions."

"*Ah*, but consider the significance of the movies—specifically, that there were no movies of him and Sharon present and four of the cassettes were missing from his collection."

"So?"

"Consider that someone broke into his house after he was killed, and that as far as we could tell, nothing was missing or disturbed other than those four cassettes."

She softened her rigid posture and glanced at him. "I'm listening."

"The intruder must have been looking for something specific—such as the videos of Sharon. If you couple that with her phone messages, it all adds up to some form of a perceived threat to her. She said it would ruin her, remember?"

"Which only strengthens the case against her," she insisted.

He sighed. "True. We need to question the other female companions Kitty told us about, and add Little Joe, Bear, and Ray-whoever to our list. Do you know how we can get up with them?"

"Linda Thomson is a cashier at the carwash. I know Allison Neely and Janice Murray, but don't know where they live or work. I've never heard of Little Joe, Bear, or Ray-whoever."

"Okay, let's go get this foreign piece of crap washed then."

A gleam appeared in her eye, signaling the shock was wearing off. "Is this on the expense account?"

"You're getting awfully pushy!"

"Since we're on the subject, you owe me ten dollars for gas too, since I had to fill up yesterday," she added.

"I suppose I could arrange a modest advance," he agreed easily, pleased her mood was returning to normal.

"You're so kind," she replied sweetly. "A hundred dollars ought to do it."

"A *hundred*? Based on your demonstrated net worth, it'll take you *years* to work it off."

"If you'd quit adding people to our list of suspects maybe we could wrap this thing up and earn that bonus." She pulled into the carwash as he dug out his wallet and handed her the money. "That's

Linda Thompson behind the register." She indicated a young blonde behind the counter.

"She's hot," he observed. "Why don't you loiter around out here out of the way while I go in and lay my world famous, rascally charm on that little honey?"

"Jackass!" Lisa swore as she snatched the money from his hand and got out to place her wash order with the attendant. Pleased with her sulking, Dean high-stepped into the reception area and paused before the petite, blue-eyed, eighteen or nineteen year old with a curvaceous figure wrapped in a tight blouse and skirt, sporting a gaggle of bracelets on each wrist and a ring on every finger of her two hands. *Nice looking chick*, was his basic, predominate male-sexist thought as he graced her with his most engaging smile, clandestinely acknowledging that Felton seemed to have an eye for good-looking women.

"Hi, pretty lady," he crooned. "I don't suppose I could ask you a few questions, could I?"

She returned his smile with a brilliant flash of white teeth. "You're Dean Davis, that detective fellow Kitty told me about, ain't you? She said you'd probably be by to talk to me. Do I get a hundred dollars too?"

Dean blinked as his engaging smile drifted away. "Actually, I just need some basic background information, if you can spare the time?"

Her blue eyes dulled as her white teeth disappeared. "I get a break in fifteen minutes. You can wait for me in the restaurant across the street. My boss don't like strange dude's hanging around trying to talk to me while I'm working."

Dean limped back out to Lisa standing under the canopy watching her VW work its way down the line on the automated wash cycle.

"You look miffed," she observed, eyeing him cynically.

"She wanted to know if I was going to pay her to talk to me."

"You mean she didn't find your world famous rascally charm irresistible?"

"She agreed to have a cup of coffee with me on her break." He took her elbow and steered her across the street. "You can't blame her for trying since she's just a poor little struggling working girl."

"And you called *me* naïve?" she allowed as they slid into a booth. "I do seem to recall the name *Linda* listed on one or two of Kenny's home movies."

"Hi, Lisa," Linda greeted when she entered the restaurant. "Your detective boyfriend's real cute. *Hey, Carla! Bring me a Coke and a wedge of lemon pie!*" she yelled as she slid in beside Lisa and fixed her baby-blues on Dean expectantly. "I only got ten minutes, so what do you wanna know?"

"I appreciate your time," he opened.

She flashed her pearly whites. "I ain't ever talked to a real detective before."

"As Kitty told you, we're investigating the murder of Kenny Felton and hoped you could give us some information concerning his death."

"Why ain't I getting paid like Kitty did?"

"I'll be glad to pay you if you can tell us who killed Kenny Felton," he offered affably.

"Kenny and I were friends and all, but I don't know nothing about him getting killed." She dug into her pie as the waitress slid the saucer before her and placed her Coke on the table.

"Do you know of anyone who may have wanted to harm him?"

She shrugged. "The police say Sharon did it."

"Do you know of any reason Sharon would want to harm Kenny?" Lisa asked.

Linda licked her fork. "I guess because he got tired of her and dumped her. She called and yelled at him one time when I was there."

"What did she yell about?"

"I could just hear Kenny's side of it. He called her a slut and hung up on her."

"Do you know of any other reason, other than him being tired of her, involved in their breakup?" Dean asked.

"Kenny was a good time Charlie," she tossed back around a mouthful of pie. "He wasn't a one woman kind of guy."

"And he dispensed drugs freely to his friends, right?" Lisa prodded.

Linda smiled. "We called him the *Candyman*."

"We understand Little Joe and Bear were his source for the drugs," Dean inserted. "Do you know where we can find them?"

Her eyes narrowed. "If I see them around, I'll let them know you wanna talk to them."

"Who is Ray?"

"Ray Mize, Kenny's best friend?"

"Do you know where we can find him?"

"Over at the dry cleaners his daddy left him when he died, of course."

"Were Allison Neely and Janice Murray part of your group of friends?" Lisa asked.

"They hung around for a short time, but they weren't ever part of our inner circle."

"Do you know where they work?" Lisa pressed.

"Allison works at the bank. Janice is a checkout girl at the IGA."

"Other than Sharon, do you know of anyone else who may have been upset with Felton about anything?" Dean asked.

"Not enough to kill him over," Linda replied as she swallowed another bite of pie and licked her lips. "Lots of people were jealous of his money."

"Who were some of the other men or women who were part of your group?" Lisa asked.

"There were always people coming and going, 'cause we partied a lot." Linda scraped her saucer and shoveled the last of the crumbs into her mouth. "I didn't pay too much attention to the hangers on."

"How about married women?" Dean asked.

"Sometimes, if they were bored. I'm really going to miss him."

"Were you aware Felton liked to, uh, make home movies?"

She grinned. "Sure. He was kinky like that, always talking about being a big shot movie producer and making me a porn star. I knew he was full of shit, but it was fun and all. Look, I've gotta go. Is the pie and Coke on you?"

"I've got it covered," Dean replied, pulling out one of his cards and passing it over to her. "Please give me a call if you think of anything that might help us in this case."

"Ain't you going to ask me for my alibi?"

He smiled, thinking if she were a killer, he'd eat his hat if he owned one. "Where were you around midnight on the night Kenny Felton was murdered?"

"In the backseat of a friend's car. Wanna know what we were doing there?"

"Uh, no, that's not necessary."

"Okay, bye now." She hurried out of the door.

"I guess I *am* naïve," Lisa said. "Being in perverted movies doesn't seem to bother her."

Dean tossed a five on the table. "Birds of a feather. Let's go meet Allison at the bank to see what she has to offer since Linda was a bust."

"We did find out how to get up with the others," Lisa allowed as she followed him out. "And I got my car washed and waxed on the expense account in the process."

"Nothing was said about *waxing*!"

Lisa parked at a metered space in front of the bank. Dean deposited a nickel into the parking meter after dispatching her inside to ask Allison to join them for coffee and settled into the frigid interior of the drugstore next door, where the two soon joined him in a back booth.

Allison, a tall, well-endowed brunette with honey-almond eyes and a dark complexion, avoided looking directly at him as she clasped her hands together in her lap under the table. "I don't appreciate Kitty getting me involved in this."

"We'll try to keep our conversation as confidential as possible," Dean assured her.

"So what do you want to know?"

"We understand you were dating Felton?"

"I only went out with him a couple of times."

"Are you aware that he taped himself in intimate relationships with women?" Lisa asked.

Allison drew back. "I don't know anything about that!" Her face flushed and her eyes darted about, signaling she was not an adept liar.

"We've seen one of the tapes with your name on it," Dean accused.

She paled. "Oh my god! This could ruin me! Has anybody else seen it? I can only imagine what you must think of me. I wasn't thinking right when it happened!"

"Do you mean you were using drugs at the time?" Lisa asked.

"This is so *humiliating*! He gave me something and I didn't really understand what was going on at the time. I'm not like that, honest! Can you get the tape for me? I've got some money saved. I'll pay you!"

"I can't guarantee you we can do that," Dean advised. "This is a murder case. We don't know where it's leading yet, or what might be evidence, but trust me, if you'll help us, we'll do our best not to embarrass you in any way."

Her eyes lifted, pleading. "What do you want to know?"

"Do you know who may have wanted Felton dead?"

"You mean besides me?"

Lisa shot a startled glance at Dean. "Did you want him dead?"

She lowered her head. "Not enough to do it myself, if that's what you mean. I wanted to break things off with Kenny ... but he threatened me."

"How did he threaten you?" Dean asked.

Tears rimmed her eyes. "He said he would show the film to others. My mother would be scandalized. He even threatened to show it to his father and get me fired from the bank. He was an evil man. He told me I had to do favors for him or he would ruin me."

"He was blackmailing you?" Lisa demanded.

"He wanted me to do some awful things. If this gets out—"

"What did he want you to do?" Dean pressed.

She flushed. "I was supposed to meet him, but I didn't show up. He was furious."

"Exactly what were you supposed to do, Allison?" he asked.

"Please, this is so embarrassing ..."

Lisa took her hand. "We're sorry to have to put you through this, Allison. As Dean said, we will do our best to protect you. You have our word on that."

Tears slid down her cheeks as she bowed her head. "He wanted me to ... go to bed with him and Sharon ... to make another movie," she whispered.

"When did he want you to do this?"

"About a week ago. When I didn't show up, he began threatening me. He said he was going to make copies of the tape he already had of us and show them around. I begged him. He just laughed at me. I was so scared … I was relieved when I heard he was dead! *Please* get that tape back for me. Please, I don't want anyone else seeing it!"

"Who else knows about the tape?" Lisa pushed.

"Only you and Becky Roberts—the other girl in the tape with us, as far as I know," she whispered. "I swear I'm not like that, Mr. Davis. I didn't know what I was doing. What will it cost me for you to get it and destroy it? Please, I'm *begging*!"

"If it's determined it's not part of the evidence in Felton's murder, we'll do our best to ensure it disappears without anyone else seeing it," he hedged. "We won't charge you for that."

Lisa quickly handed her a napkin as she began sobbing and Dean waited patiently until she dried her eyes, blew her nose, and composed herself.

"Allison, you said Felton wanted you to make another tape with him and Sharon a week before he was killed. It's my understanding he and Sharon broke off their engagement some two weeks before that. Didn't you think that odd?"

"I didn't talk to Sharon about it. He just told me to be at his house at a certain time. At the last minute I couldn't bring myself to do it."

"Do you know why he and Sharon broke up?" Lisa asked.

"I started seeing Kenny right after they broke up, but he never said why they separated."

Dean leaned forward. "Allison, I have to ask—where were you around midnight on the night Felton was murdered?"

She recoiled in shock. "A-Are you implying *I* might have killed Kenny, Mr. Davis?"

Lisa squeezed her hand. "Allison, we just need a simple, basic alibi to help eliminate you as a potential suspect."

"I-I don't have an alibi. I was home in bed watching the Late Night Show."

"Were you alone?"

"My mother was in the house, but she was asleep. I did *not* kill Kenny, Mr. Davis. I don't have the courage to do something like that." She stood. "I've got to get back to work!"

"Thank you for talking to us," Dean said, rising. "Here's my card. If you think of anything that might help us, please give us a call."

"I'd be so grateful if you can find a way to help me, Mr. Davis." She wiped at her eyes and hurried out.

"Do you consider her a suspect?" Lisa asked.

Dean sank back down in the booth and sipped his coffee. "She doesn't seem the type, but Felton *was* blackmailing her. Desperate people do desperate things. She and Sharon were both desperate at the time and as such are viable suspects, but I don't think either one of them murdered Felton."

"Are we really going to try and help her?"

He frowned. "Breaking back into Felton's house to remove potential evidence is not an appealing prospect. Going to the sheriff with what we have is the smartest thing we can do under the circumstances."

"But that could blow the lid off of this sex thing and hurt a lot of people unnecessarily if the videos aren't part of the murder scheme," Lisa argued. "Isn't there any other alternative?"

"Allison admits Felton was using the tape to blackmail her. I suspect he was doing the same with Sharon. Technically a crime has been committed, even if the suspect is dead and the victims don't want to involve the police. If he was blackmailing Sharon, that's a possible motive for her to kill him. The phone messages further implicate her. I think we *have* to go to the sheriff with this. I'm surprised he hasn't already searched Felton's house and found the tapes and the phone messages. Searching his home should have been standard operating procedure in a murder case. Let's go see Janice Murray while I mull this over."

The manager at the IGA informed them Miss Murray had called in sick that morning. Lisa got her address by posing as a concerned friend. Her mother answered the doorbell and informed them Janice had a virus and was asleep. Dean left their business card with a request that she call them, stressing it was urgent that they talk to her concerning the murder of Kenny Felton. Her mother's demeanor made it clear she was not thrilled with the prospect of her daughter talking to two private detectives concerning the issue.

"We've got Ray Mize left on our list since we don't know how to get up with Little Joe and Bear," Dean said as they got back in the car.

"Let's go," Lisa agreed.

Ray Mize, a short, stocky, unattractive man of thirty, with short blond hair, deep brown eyes, bushy eyebrows and a bad complexion, led them back through the musky interior of the dry cleaners to his cluttered office at the rear. Lisa and Dean sat in straight-backed chairs before his desk as he settled in behind it in a squeaky, worn leather chair beside a small oscillating fan circulating tepid air around their heads as the aroma of dry cleaning fluids stifled their sinuses.

"I appreciate your talking to us, Mr. Mize," Dean began.

"So what do you wanna know about Kenny?"

"I understand you two were best friends?"

"Yeah, so?"

"Do you know anyone who may have wanted to harm him?"

Mize arched his bushy eyebrows. "Are you on a witch hunt or something? They already got the bitch that done him in, ain't they?"

"Currently, Sharon Lucas is only a suspect. We've been hired to attempt to clear her."

"How you gonna clear her when she did it?"

"By finding the real murderer. Do you know anyone that may have had a reason to—"

Mize stood abruptly, his face reddening. "You and sweet-cheeks here need to get on out of here and quit wasting my time."

"Why are you so certain Sharon Lucas killed him?" Lisa asked.

"You don't hear so good, do you, cupcake?" He leaned across his desk. "I said *get out*! I ain't got nothin' to say to either of you!"

"Let's go, Lisa, the sheriff can handle this one," Dean bluffed, rising.

"*Up yours*, stud! The sheriff don't worry me none."

"Are you aware Kenny provided drugs to women and made sex tapes with them which he then used to blackmail them for additional sexual favors?" Lisa demanded.

Mize plunked back down in his chair in disbelief. "Do *what*? Where do you get that shit from? Kenny ain't blackmailed any of those little sluts. You hear me? They were all more than willing to hop in the sack with him."

"Where were you around midnight on the night Kenny was murdered?" she pressed.

"None of your damned business," he retorted, again rising from his chair. "I've got nothin' else to say to you. Get on out of here or I'll have you arrested for trespassing!"

"If I could just ask you a couple more questions—" Dean pushed.

"*Get the hell outta here!*" He glared after them as they walked back through the maze of rumbling machines and piles of waiting laundry.

"Pleasant little asshole, wasn't he?" Dean observed.

"Is he a suspect?" Lisa asked.

"He didn't appear to be intimidated by the sheriff questioning him, and I didn't detect any motive for him to kill his good buddy Felton, not to mention his call to Felton's residence was made *after* he was killed."

"I guess that means no, but he did seem to know something about the tapes."

"I'm sure Felton showed them to him since they were friends, but I can't say he knew Felton was using them for blackmail. How about lunch while we regroup, *cupcake?*"

"I'm with you, *stud!* Your treat?"

"You're the one who just got an advance, *sweet-cheeks!*"

Chapter 12

They settled into a booth in the crowded diner and gave their lunch orders to a harried waitress. When she rushed off, Lisa focused on Dean plaintively.

"Okay, Sherlock, we've got four and a half days left to earn that bonus and we don't even have a viable suspect yet beyond Sharon. Any suggestions?"

"Al Roberts and Allison Neely are distant possibilities."

"What are you going to do about the tapes?"

"Telling the sheriff what we've discovered makes the most sense since they could have a strong bearing on the Felton murder."

"How are you going to explain breaking into Kenny's house?"

"Touchy point," he agreed.

She leaned forward and lowered her voice. "Why don't we meet with Mr. Felton at the bank first?"

"For what purpose?"

"To see if he would agree to allow us to safeguard the tapes until this thing is resolved. If the tapes turn out not to be evidence we could destroy them and prevent a scandal."

"Do you actually think he'd go for something like that?" Dean scoffed.

"Why wouldn't he? This thing certainly has the potential to expose his son for the scumbag he was. I'm sure he'd want to prevent that if possible, and we'd be in a position to help Allison like you promised. I know I'd sure hate to be in her shoes right now."

He grinned. "Now *that's* a tape I'd love to get my hands on!"

She wadded up her napkin and threw it at him. "You're such a low-life schmuck!"

"Lisa, even if Mr. Felton did agree to allow us to secure the tapes, it's still risky business where Sheriff Parsons is concerned. If it turns out the tapes are evidence, he'd most likely charge us with impeding his investigation."

She slumped back in the booth. "This investigating stuff isn't what it's cracked up to be."

"Are you kidding? We've got everything going for us in this case: sex, drugs, blackmail, damsels in distress, potential scandal, murder and mayhem. What else could you want?"

"A clue as to who did it."

"It's all a matter of deductive reasoning while weeding through the obvious suspects."

"Whatever happened to 'the butler did it'?"

"Maybe he did," Dean suggested as the server slid their plates before them. "Speaking of which, I wonder why the break-in at Felton's house hasn't been reported? Surely someone has been there since the murder."

"Not necessarily," she argued, shaking salt on her fries. "His parents were in the Bahamas and maybe the butler only comes in once or twice a week since the bed hadn't been made or the bathroom cleaned since the afternoon of his death."

"Eat up then and let's go see Mr. Felton to check on this butler thing," Dean replied airily. "That's as good a lead as anything else we've got at the moment."

"We'll *never* earn that bonus!" she swore as she stuffed hot fries in her mouth and fanned her lips.

✲ ✲ ✲

Mr. Felton, a meticulously groomed middle-aged gentleman in an expensive gray suit, viewed Dean's Levis, loafers, and golf shirt with moderate disdain as he and Lisa settled into the expensive leather chairs in front of his desk before leaning forward to peer at their business cards which lay on the blotter before him.

"You insisted on meeting with me on a personal matter, Mr. Davis?"

"Miss Bryant and I have been hired to investigate your son's death," Dean answered.

Mr. Felton surveyed him evenly. "By whom were you hired, if I may ask?"

"By Mrs. Peters, Sharon Lucas' grandmother."

"For what purpose?"

"To clear Miss Lucas of the murder of your son."

His countenance chilled. "I see. I view the tragic incident as entirely a police matter. They have my full support."

"Are you aware all the evidence against Miss Lucas is circumstantial?"

"And you presume her to be innocent, Mr. Davis?"

"That is my premise."

He scowled. "I'm led to believe they have an eyewitness to the crime."

"The witness they have can only give a partial identification as to Miss Lucas being the culprit," Dean advised, leaning forward in his chair. "Mr. Felton, the real purpose of our visit is to inform you we have uncovered some unsettling things in our investigation concerning your son's murder which could be very detrimental to your son's character if they become public, and could hurt other people unnecessarily. We need your assistance to prevent that from happening."

Mr. Felton's eyes hardened. "And you want to sell me this information to protect my son's reputation, Mr. Davis?"

Dean sat back in his chair. "Our primary purpose in meeting with you is to protect the other people involved."

"Please continue, Mr. Davis."

"The problem is, the material is in your son's house and may be evidence in his murder."

"Then it is a police matter, is it not?"

"Technically it may be, but since we're not certain it *is* evidence we haven't brought it to the attention of the sheriff yet."

Mr. Felton's eyebrows lifted. "And why not, if I may ask?"

"Have you been to your son's house since the murder?"

"No. We were out of the country when it happened and haven't had the opportunity since we've returned. Why do you ask?"

"Your son's house has been broken into and it appears someone has already removed some of this potential evidence. Our desire is that ,in the eventuality the remaining portion turns out not to be evidence, to, well … *destroy* it. We were hoping you would help us do that."

"And how do you know this potential evidence is in my son's house, or even that his home was broken into?"

"Because we broke in there ourselves."

Mr. Felton's eyes narrowed. "And what is the nature of this potential evidence you say you discovered there, Mr. Davis?"

"It's a collection of video tapes. Home movies if you will, made by your son in some rather compromising positions with various females in the community."

"That's preposterous!"

"We are further led to believe drugs were used to induce some of the women to participate."

"*Ridiculous*! I've heard all the nonsense I care to—"

"There are even indications your son was attempting to blackmail some of the women to induce them to provide additional sexual favors."

Mr. Felton's pallor changed to a heated red as he stood abruptly. "That's just not feasible! What you are insinuating is *impossible*. My son would *never* do such a thing. How *dare* you come into my office the day before his funeral and—and *suggest* such a thing! *Get out!*"

Dean stood as well. "We can do that, sir, but our first stop will be the sheriff's office. This material should be protected until we know if it's relevant to your son's murder. If we involve the sheriff, we can't guarantee this information will not become public. If it does, it will be very damaging to your son's reputation, and also to several young ladies in this community."

"Are you threatening me, Mr. Davis?"

"No, sir, I'm not, and frankly I'm getting tired of trying to explain it all to you. I'm probably already on shaky ground by not going to the sheriff with this information to begin with. The fact is it appears your son was providing drugs to young women and then filming himself having sex with them. It also appears he may have been blackmailing them, and that may have been a motivation for his murder."

"Was Miss Lucas one of these young women you refer to?"

"She hasn't admitted it, but it appears so. There's a message on your son's answering machine from Miss Lucas made the day he was killed that would indicate such."

He sank back down in his chair and covered his face with his palms. "Who else knows about this?"

"We know of several people who were willing and unwilling participants in the filming."

He dropped his palms from his face in disbelief. "Some of these women *willingly* participated in this … this … *venture*? I thought you said they were drugged?"

"Not all of them were drugged as an inducement, although drugs do seem to be involved in each case. Some of the women who willingly participated were also married."

"*Married*?" Mr. Felton's face flushed as his eyes grew fearful. "How much do you want, Mr. Davis?"

"Pardon me?"

"To keep this-this *scandal* quiet? How much do you want?"

"Sir, our only goal is to clear Miss Lucas of the murder, if in fact she is innocent of the crime, and to protect the unfortunate victims in the tapes. We don't expect to profit from this."

His eyes again narrowed as the color returned to his features. "You want nothing from me to keep this quiet, yet you want control of the material? Would that not put you in a position to use this *filth* for your own means?"

Dean sank back down in his chair. "If I had wanted control I would have simply taken the tapes when I was there. I suggest we conduct a joint inventory of the material and secure it in a safe place until we determine its relevance to your son's murder. If it is determined to be evidence, we can turn it over to the sheriff. If it turns out it's not, I propose we destroy it and let that be the end of it."

"Since this is potential evidence, what are the repercussions if we remove this material jointly and store it in a safe place?"

Dean took a deep breath and chose his words carefully. "I admit I'm on shaky ground here, but in my opinion, currently none since the sheriff is convinced Miss Lucas is the guilty party in your son's murder, and as such, has shown no interest in widening his investigation to consider other potential suspects. He bases this on her having the motive because of the fight they had in her apartment before his death, the witness who saw Miss Lucas, or someone who looks like her, running from the murder scene back to her apartment, and the actual murder weapon itself found beside her door. At some point, you'll be free to dispose of his estate. The only significant issue is that nothing is destroyed until the investigation has run its course."

"What mutually agreed upon place would you have us store this material?"

"We could fit it into one of your safety deposit boxes here at the bank. I suggest we set it up where it takes both of us jointly to enter into or remove the items."

"And you expect no compensation for this?"

"None."

"Remarkable."

"There's nothing remarkable in having no desire to profit off other people's misery."

"And Miss Bryant here?"

"She's my partner, bound by my agreement the same as I am. Beyond that, she probably has more basic integrity than I do."

"How do we go about securing this material?"

"We go to your son's house, box it up, and bring it back here where we sign the joint entry and removal forms."

"When do you want to do this?"

"The sooner the better since it appears someone has already broken into your son's home and, I fear, removed some of the material."

Mr. Felton stood. "In view of that, I propose we go there immediately."

� ✕ ✕

When they arrived at Kenny Felton's house, Mr. Felton paused before the door with the key in his hand. "How did you break into my son's home, Mr. Davis?"

"I picked the lock."

"And the other person who broke in?"

"They knocked a small window pane out of the French door on the back patio."

He nodded, inserted the key, and swung the door open. Lisa and Dean followed him in, where they paused at the door to the study to stare at the books pulled out of the racks, papers littering the floor, and the drawers emptied onto the carpet.

"Someone has been here since we were," Dean advised. "It's best if we don't touch anything."

Dean led the way though the house as Lisa and Mr. Felton followed, stepping carefully around the sofa cushions thrown about and the litter from the drawers of the end tables dumped on the floor in the living room. The kitchen showed little sign of disturbance, but both French doors stood open in the sunroom. Upstairs, they found the master bedroom ravaged, with the mattresses dumped on the floor and the contents of the drawers and closet sacked. All of the tapes were missing from the drawer under the TV, which was still silently playing. On an impulse, Dean punched the reject button on the VCR and a tape slid out. He pushed it back in, punched rewind, let it spin, and then punched play. Felton and Becky sprang into view locked in the throes of passion. Lisa turned away from the screen as Mr. Felton paled.

Dean punched stop. "This appears to be the only tape left. That was Mrs. Becky Roberts with your son. This tape was made on the afternoon of your son's death." Dean picked up the answering machine from the rubble on the floor and punched the play button. The messages from Ray, Sharon, Al Roberts, and Mrs. Felton played through. He rewound the tape and placed the recorder back on the floor. "At this stage, I suggest we call the sheriff. There were tapes of several other women, so whoever has those tapes is a potential murderer, or at the very least, as you suggested, has some powerful material to blackmail a number of women in this community. I think the opportunity to contain this thing has evaporated."

Mr. Felton pointed at the VCR. "What about that tape?"

"It, along with the cassette from his answering machine, should be turned over to the sheriff," Dean replied. "The woman in the VCR tape was a willing participant, and that was her husband threatening your son's life on the answering machine, so it is definitely evidence. The other tapes were the ones that concerned me."

Mr. Felton nodded cautiously. "But three of those messages could also implicate your client, Mr. Davis."

"True, but if my client is guilty of murdering your son, there's nothing I can do to help her anyway. I suggest you make the call to the sheriff." He scooped up the phone from the floor and handed it to him.

Mr. Felton hesitated. "Should I mention you were here earlier today?"

Dean nodded. "I recommend full disclosure at this point."

"And the missing tapes you say were here?"

"I'd say those tapes are definitely evidence now that they've been removed and need to become part of the official investigation into your son's murder."

"But … you admitted you broke in here yourself."

"Unless you file a complaint there's nothing the sheriff can do other than berate me for not coming to him in the first place. I guess I've got that coming."

"What of the other young women in the tapes?"

"All I saw were some arbitrary names."

"You don't think it would be better to—"

"Before, sir, we had a plausible excuse, now we would be suppressing evidence. Neither of us can afford that. Besides, it may lead to your son's actual killer."

"But what of his reputation?"

"Let's hope the sheriff uses discretion. I'm sorry, Mr. Felton, I had hoped this would turn out differently. Please make the call."

He begin dialing.

Lisa and Dean sat stiffly in front of Sheriff Parsons' desk.

"If you didn't violate the *letter* of our agreement, you sure as hell violated the *spirit* of it!" he bellowed.

"Technically, I guess you could say that, Sheriff, but I assure you it was never my intent," Dean answered meekly. "You see, I thought—"

"You *didn't think*, Davis! I ought to pull your license! And your associate's license as well, damn it!"

"Partner," Lisa corrected.

Sheriff Parsons slammed his hand down on his desk as she cowered. "Stay out of this, Miss Bryant, or I'll call your father down here! You know better than to pull a stunt like this, Davis! You were a police officer once. You know the goddamn rules of evidence!"

"At the time I wasn't sure it was evidence, Sheriff. I was mainly concerned with protecting—"

"Shut *up*, Davis! If you had come to me in the *first* place when you *broke into* Kenny Felton's goddamned house, I might have another suspect to deal with and *your client* might be *free* now! But *noooooo*, you have to play the Lone Ranger! I ought to lock you up for this!"

"Sheriff, I honestly thought—"

"I done *told* you that you *didn't think*, so don't *contradict* me again!" Sheriff Parsons bellowed. "You're just damned lucky Mr. Felton refuses to file a complaint against you. I'd put you in the deepest, darkest hole of my jail I could find and throw away the key!"

"Sheriff, I'm really—"

"*Save* it, Davis! Give me *one* good reason why I shouldn't suspend your license?"

"On what grounds?"

"Those damn telephone messages your client left lend even more credence to her being the murderer, yet you failed to notify my department, as you agreed you would do."

"Why didn't you get a warrant and search Felton's house as part of your *own* investigation, Sheriff?" Dean argued. "If you had done so, you would have found this potential evidence yourself."

He blanched. "There was no reason to search his home, goddamn it! We have the murderer and the motive!"

"You have what you *think* is the murderer and a *conceivable* motive."

"Get the hell out of my office!" He waved his hand at the door. "I'm sick of looking at you, Davis!"

Dean and Lisa scurried out and didn't slow down until they were in Lisa's VW headed out of the parking lot.

"For goodness sakes, don't speed or run a stop sign anytime soon," Dean counseled as she gunned the engine and swerved out into the street.

"*Gee*, that was *fun*, Dean!"

"*You're* the one who talked me into going to Mr. Felton instead of the sheriff!" he accused.

"He wasn't yelling at *me*!" she countered. "He knew *I* didn't know any better. *You're* the former policeman who *should* have known better!"

"Oh, right, I see where this is heading. When the going gets tough—*you* get *going*! Now I see how things are in *this* partnership!"

"He was *threatening* to call my *father*!"

"*He was threatening to lock my ass up and throw away the key*!"

After a strained silence, she glanced at him sulking in the passenger seat. "So okay, what do we do now?"

"Leave town on the next train."

"It's your turn to cook."

"*What*! How can you think about food at a time like this?"

"I'm hungry."

"Well I ain't by-god cooking tonight."

"Okay, then you've got to treat. How does steak sound?"

"On my dime?"

"I bought lunch! If I've got to listen to you rant and rave, I'm going to do it on a full stomach at *your* expense."

Dean crossed his arms. "Then make it some place that serves adult beverages. I'm in serious need of a double shot of something hard, and make it quick!"

Chapter 13

Dean chugged his second Jim Beam and Coke and motioned for another at the crowded bar in Big Jim's Steak House.

"You're going to get drunk," Lisa fussed as she sipped her white wine.

"So?"

"You need to keep a clear head so we can put a game plan together."

He clutched the fresh glass the bartender slid in front of him. "I'd rather get drunk instead."

"You're just feeling sorry for yourself because Sheriff Parsons chewed you out. I thought you were tougher than that."

"He was right. I knew better. I should have gone to him in the first place. Sharon might be out of jail now if I'd been thinking straight. Those tapes put a whole new slant on this case. *Dumb, dumb, dumb!*"

"So let's find out who took the tapes."

"*Before* we find Felton's murderer or *after?*"

"I'll put my money on Ray Mize," she mused.

"Okay, I'll take everyone else at even money," he countered, sulking as a heavy hand clasped his shoulder.

"You'n that detective guy askin' 'round 'bout us'uns?" a low, guttural voice growled in his ear.

He half turned to find a massive, thickset man in his late twenties sporting a bushy black beard and cold black eyes staring at him. A slim, light complexioned man with sandy hair, roughly the same age as the big man squeezing his shoulder, lurked behind the semi-giant.

Dean smiled solicitously. "Bear and Little Joe, I presume?"

Bear's grip tightened on his shoulder. "We 'uns need you 'uns to step outside."

"I just ordered a fresh drink. Care to join us?"

Bear's black eyes didn't blink. "You'uns need to step outside *now*."

Dean shrugged irritably in an effort to loosen the big man's claw on his shoulder. "We 'uns are having cocktails and waiting on a table for dinner, but we 'uns would love to converse with you 'uns if you'd care to join us."

Little Joe smirked. "You and your girlfriend don't wanna go getting Bear all riled up now."

"I'm his *partner*," Lisa corrected.

The grip on Dean's shoulder intensified. "You 'uns come on outside *now*."

Dean lifted his glass and took a sip as the annoyance built. "I prefer we 'uns talk in *here!*" The near giant's grip released his shoulder and wrapped around his hand, freezing his glass in midair and sending pain lacing up his arm as he winced. "You're *really-really* beginning to annoy me, big guy—" he began as the giant tilted his hand and poured the drink in his lap, his calm, beady-black eyes never leaving Dean's.

Several things occurred in rapid sequence: cold liquid soaked Dean's crotch, his wrist and knuckles stung when his fist connected with Bear's bushy jaw, Little Joe's eyes widened in astonishment, and Lisa yelped in surprise as he flew backwards across the room. He landed on his back on a table covered with glasses, skidded through a group of people as they scrambled out of the way overturning chairs in a mêlée of curses and breaking glass, hit the floor on his left shoulder, and slammed face first into the leg of a second table upsetting it and sending additional drinks flying. Bear jerked his body up from the rubble and propelled it toward the double doors, where he crashed through headfirst as they parted wildly before him, landed on his chest and skidded across the entrance into the grass. As he scrambled groggily up onto his hands and knees, a size sixteen boot caught him in the ribcage and curled him into a fetal position, where he lay desperately trying to find air in an oxygen-depleted world.

Little Joe lurched over to him jerking Lisa along behind him as she struggled to free her wrist from his grasp. "You shouldn't oughta hit ol' Bear like that."

Numbing darkness clutched at him. "*Ack!*"

"Bear don't like to be hit none," Little Joe explained as Bear drew his big boot back and kicked Dean in the other side of his ribcage.

"*Ack!*" Dean choked in a surge of searing pain.

Little Joe's sneering face faded in and out of focus above him. "It makes ol Bear mad as hell."

"*Ack!*" Dean gasped.

"*Don't you dare hurt him!*" Lisa shrieked, struggling to free herself from Little Joe's grasp as he drew his leg back and kicked Dean in the stomach.

"Sweetie, me and Bear's just playing with him, ain't we now, Bear?"

Lisa slammed her purse into Little Joe's face. "*Leave him alone!*"

Little Joe's lips curled in rage as blood trickled from his nose. "You little bitch!"

Lisa kneed him in the groin, doubling him over as he released her arm and clutched at his privates. She then swung her purse at Bear as he scooped her up in one arm and pinned her against his massive chest, where she continued to flail away at him with her clenched fist and purse. "*Put me down, you bastard!*"

Little Joe, eyes glazed and still clutching his crotch with one hand as he panted in pain, limped over and knelt beside Dean, grabbed a fistful of his hair, and lifted his head. "Me and Bear don't like people nosing around in our business."

"*Ugh, ack, ugh,*" Dean wheezed.

"You asking questions and all makes me and Bear mad. You understand that, Mister Big Shot Detective?"

Dean fought for oxygen as spots swam before his eyes. "*I—ack, ugh!*"

Little Joe punched him in the mouth. "Good, then we understand each other." He pulled his fist back again and the world went black.

When Dean regained his bearings, Lisa held his head in her lap. Somebody handed her a white towel from the crowd of hovering strangers, which she used to wipe at his sticky face.

"Are you alright, Dean?"

"I th-think so …"

"You probably need to get him on out of here, lady, 'fore 'em hombres come back to finish him off," a male voice cautioned from the crowd.

Lisa glared up at the circle of faces. "He needs an ambulance!"

"N-No ambulance … j-just get me to the … c-car," Dean gasped.

"Shouldn't have swung on old Bear like that," another voice advised as others chuckled.

"Old Bear don't like that," the first man snickered as a derisive chorus of agreement rippled through the crowd. "Seen him take on five men one night and whooped 'em all."

"Will somebody please help get him to my car?" Lisa pleaded.

"Why'd the durn fool go and hit Bear anyway?" another mocking voice asked.

"He's new around here, I expect." Several hands tugged at Dean and pulled him to his feet. "Now don't go bleeding on my shirt, Mister," one complained.

Dean sagged forward, unable to stand upright as pain tore at his midsection, and collapsed back onto his knees to heave up the puny contents of his stomach, which consisted mostly of the two bourbons he had drank.

"*Pew wee, now he's puking!*" someone warned as those around him scattered.

Lisa knelt beside him and swabbed at his face with the towel as he gagged and spit out the blood and bile clogging his mouth. He staggered up with her help, draped his arm across her shoulder, and stumbled to her car as the crowd straggled along behind them. Lisa opened the passenger door to her VW, helped him inside, pressed the towel into his hands, and hurried around to the driver's side.

"You might want to get him looked at, lady," a voice called as she started the engine and lurched away. "I think he's got some busted ribs!"

Dean sagged against the door, gasping. "Tough place ... to get any sympathy ..."

The doctor assured them none of his ribs were busted, but Dean wasn't entirely convinced of this himself as they departed the emergency room with him shuffling along in a half crouch with sharp, shooting pains stabbing at his midsection. His image in the glass door showed lips swollen from Little Joe's administrations, his right eye half closed from the contact with the leg of the second table, and several large knots and small cuts on top of his head from Bear's expulsion of his body headfirst through the doors of Big Jim's Steak House. Unseen in his pitiful reflection, but definitely present in ample abundance, was a roaring drumbeat in his head and bleary double vision to polish off the list.

Lisa helped him out of the VW, half carried him into the apartment, and propped him against the wall in the bathroom. He undressed and eased into the shower, stooped and hurting, as the hot water cascaded down over him. He gingerly dried off, struggled into his pajama bottoms, and limped out shirtless to sit on the side of the bed, still half-dazed.

Lisa pulled the sheet down and gently helped him lay back. "You shouldn't have hit that big guy, Dean," she scolded as she hurried back into the bathroom to get ready for bed.

"No … shit?" he gasped.

"He was way bigger than you," she admonished as she returned to the bedroom and switched off the light. "What were you thinking anyway?"

He swallowed painfully. "You're … weird …"

"You should meet the guy I live with."

He grimaced as a stab of pain worked through him. "You could have … got hurt jumping on … Little Joe and Bear … like that."

"I had to do *something*!" She slid into bed next to him. "*You* weren't doing much to defend yourself!"

"Very … funny. Are you … wearing that … slinky black thing?"

"You're not very observant for a PI, and certainly in no shape to criticize."

"I … appreciate you … trying to help me."

She snuggled up close to him. "I confess it's becoming something of a burden."

"But don't … do anything stupid … like that again … okay?"

"Goodnight, Dean."

Even doped up from all the painkillers the doctor gave him, in addition to the physical and emotional trauma he was suffering, he was still acutely aware of the warm softness of her body curled next to his in the slinky black thing kindling a faint smidgen of desire within him.

Thankfully, he slept amidst his aches and waning lust, his last conscious thought a promise to himself that a big bear and a little weasel were going to pay a huge price for this injustice.

Dean awoke the next morning in an empty bed and tentatively stretched, grimacing from the pain that permeated every fiber of his body, before swinging his legs over the edge and sitting up in a half stoop. He stumbled to the bathroom cursing Bear and Little Joe to peer through his one good left eye at the swollen right one above his battered lips. He then examined the huge bruises on both sides of his ribcage, finding the pit of his stomach tender to the touch and requiring him to stoop as he stumbled down the hall to the kitchen, where he found Lisa sitting at the table.

She appraised him with a cold stare. "You look like hell."

He whimpered as he eased into a chair across from her. "It hurts to even breathe."

She poured him a cup of coffee and placed a bottle of pills on the table. "I went out and got your prescription filled. Take two of those and quit whining."

He popped four pills and tried to glare at her through his one good eye. "Why are you in such a foul mood?"

"Due to your stupid antics last night, I didn't get anything to eat. I picked up some eggs and sausage while I was out."

He worked his mouth tentatively and decided his teeth were too suspect for solid foods. "Coffee will do for me."

She pulled a skillet from the cabinet. "Suit yourself, macho man."

"What's your problem?"

She whirled to face him. "You're such a damned fool!" She shook her fist at him. "I'm tempted to black your other eye. I don't know why I fool with you, I swear I don't!" She whirled back to the counter to hide her tears.

He limped over and put his hand on her shoulder. "Hey, why are you so upset?"

She turned and buried her face in his sore chest and hugged his aching ribs. "You could have got killed, Dean!"

"Yeah, well I feel pretty stupid right now, if that's of any consolation to you."

She stepped back. "Sit down and I'll fix us some breakfast. You need to eat something."

As she busied herself with the eggs and sausage, he limped over to the table and eased into the chair, focusing on a plan of action. "I thought you might go talk with Janice Murray today, assuming she's feeling up to it." *I, on the other hand, will take my brother's old car and nose around to find out where Bear and Little Joe hang out—if I can get the damned thing cranked.*

She turned to him. "Oh really?"

"Maybe she can provide us with some fresh leads while I'm recovering."

"You're trying to get rid of me."

"Have I mentioned you seem to be developing a cynical deportment lately?"

She slammed his plate down in front of him. "Imagine that! We'll go see Janice together, so just forget about whatever you're trying to pull on me."

"*Geez*, Lisa, you're becoming paranoid!"

After breakfast, he limped to the bedroom, dressed, retrieved a box from the top of his closet, took out a long barreled .44

magnum revolver, slipped it into the waist at the small of his back, and shrugged into his one and only sports jacket to conceal it.

"Nice," Lisa praised when he shuffled out of the bedroom. "At least you're beginning to dress like a real detective now, even if you do look like a dumb pugilist."

Janice Murray, a tall, slim brunette with dark brown eyes set in an attractive, heart-shaped face, but not as overly endowed or curvaceous as the other women in Felton's life tended to be, opened the door to her mother's house and focused on Dean's battered face.

"Gracious! What happened to you?"

Women can be so damned direct and insensitive at times, he fumed. "Uh, could we have a word with you?"

"Let's talk somewhere else." Without preamble, she closed the door after her to mask her mother hovering anxiously in the background, and Lisa and he fell in on each side of her as she turned onto the sidewalk. "So who beat your face in?"

"A couple of your friends, Bear and Little Joe," he replied as Lisa smirked at him.

"They're not friends of mine. Look, I know Kitty told you about me seeing Kenny. I really don't have anything to say to you. I just want to put all of that behind me now."

"Was Kenny blackmailing you?" Lisa asked.

She turned to Lisa. "Why would you ask me something like that?"

"We know about the tapes," Dean replied.

She turned to him. "What tapes?"

"Was he blackmailing you?" Lisa repeated from the other side.

"I don't know what you're talking about," she insisted, turning back to her.

Lisa placed her hand on her arm reassuringly. "Janice, we're here to help you."

"Help me what?"

"Are you aware that Kenny was taping himself having sex with different women?"

"*What?*" Her face paled. "How do you know that?"

"Did you use drugs when you were together?" Dean asked.

She stumbled over to a bench in a neighbor's yard and sank down. "I-It's not something I normally do. In fact, I'd never done drugs before. I took them as a lark ... to experiment ... and because I was nervous. I've ... lived a sheltered life. I thought he cared for me. He ... he *taped* us together? Are you sure?" Lisa sat down and hugged her as she lowered her face to her hands and convulsed into sobs.

"Is there a problem here?" a frail old woman with white hair dressed in gardening clothes and a broad brimmed straw hat asked as she stared at them from a few feet away.

"Our friend is just upset," Dean explained. "Just give us a moment, please."

The old woman took a tentative step forward. "Janice, do I need to call your mother, child?"

Janice wiped her eyes and composed herself. "No, Mrs. Calloway, I'm fine." She led Lisa and Dean back onto the sidewalk. "There's a place we can talk just ahead." They followed her to a clump of trees in a vacant lot, where she sank down on a fallen tree.

"I have some money ... not much—"

"We don't want your money," Lisa reassured her.

Janice wiped at her eyes and drew a shuttering breath. "What do you want then?"

"We don't know for sure if a tape of you and Felton exists," Dean informed her. "But if one does exist, we're trying to find out who has it. So try to calm down and help us. That's the only way we can help you."

Her eyes filled with hope. "Why do you want to help me?"

Lisa sat down on the log beside her. "Because other women have been victimized by Kenny and we need your help to help them. You could possibly be helping yourself as well."

"I … don't know who killed Kenny. I know you're here to try to clear Sharon, but I don't know if I can help you. I assume she killed him."

"How many times were you and Felton together?" Dean asked.

"Just … just the one time like that," she whispered. "I can't imagine what you must think of me. I swear I didn't know he was doing anything like that."

"Was there anyone else with you at the time other than him?"

Her eyes widened. "Why would you ask something like that?"

"Sometimes more than one woman was involved in the taping," Lisa soothed. "Some of the women were drugged and didn't know what was happening."

Her eyes flashed up and then away. "Please, this is so hard for me."

"I understand," Dean assured her. "Whatever you tell us will be kept in the strictest confidence, if possible. Did he ever ask you to have sex with him and other women?"

"*No*! Of course not! What kind of a person do you think I am? I would never agree to anything like that! I was only intimate with him that one time. I'm so embarrassed! This can't be happening to me."

"Do you know of anyone who may have wanted to kill him?"

"Bear and Little Joe were mad at him, but I can't imagine them actually killing him!"

Dean glanced at Lisa. "Why were they mad at him?"

"They came by Kenny's house and argued over money. Kenny said they had to be patient. I thought there was going to be a fight."

"Do you know where we can find Little Joe and Bear?"

"M-Maybe at the Bloody Bucket, off the North Highway, about five miles out. I-I went there with Kenny once. He said they hang out there. It's not a very nice place."

"Is there anything else you can tell us that might help our investigation?" Dean pressed.

She shook her head. "I only saw Kenny a few times. I wish I had never met him now. If this gets out my whole life will be ruined."

Dean handed her his card. "Please call us if anything comes to mind, no matter how trivial. We'll do our best to keep you out of this."

"If there is a tape will you really help me?"

"You have our word on it."

Chapter 14

L isa shifted into reverse and backed out of the drive. "I feel sorry for the women in Kenny's life. He was such a creep."

Dean nodded absently. "That he was."

"I certainly don't view Janice as a suspect. Do you?"

"Nope, but we've got two more suspects in Little Joe and Bear now."

"So where do we go from here?"

"To the Bloody Bucket."

"Are you crazy?"

He reached behind his back and pulled the .44 magnum from his waistband. "No, just better prepared this time."

Her eyes widened. "Put that away, Dean! Get rid of it!"

He slipped it back into his waistband. "*You're* the one who's crazy."

"What are you even *thinking?*"

"I'm thinking I have this aversion to getting my ass kicked."

"That thing will only get you in serious trouble!"

"Or keep me out of serious trouble. Chill out, I'm licensed to carry. Now drop me off at the apartment so I can get my brother's car."

"You're not going anywhere without me."

"You'll only be in the way."

"Do you want some lunch?"

"Lunch? Would you quit changing the subject?"

"Let's get a cheeseburger." She wheeled into the Dairy Queen. "We need to think this thing through."

He glowered at her. "Lisa, it's been fun and all, but you leave me no alternative—you're fired."

She smiled at the carhop as she approached her window. "Two cheeseburgers, one large and one small order of fries, and two medium Cokes."

The carhop scribbled on her pad. "Do you want those all the way?"

"Hold the onions on one, please."

"Are you listening to me, damn it?" Dean demanded.

She turned back to him. "You can't fire me."

"And why the hell not?"

"Because I'm not your employee, I'm your partner."

"That's bullshit!"

"You signed the papers."

They sat in strained silence until the carhop returned with their orders. Lisa handed his burger and fries over. "Do you want ketchup?"

"Yes."

She passed the tubes of ketchup. "You're not really serious about confronting Bear and Little Joe, are you?"

"Without you hanging around my neck, my Smith and Wesson and I'll be just fine."

"What if you screw up again?"

"I'll bet you fifty dollars against your slinky black thing I don't screw up again."

She feigned astonishment. "*You* want to sleep in my slinky black thing? I thought you hated it?"

"*Cute*! Now drop me off at my brother's car, damn it."

She drove up the north highway for five miles and parked in an unpaved parking lot before what appeared to be little more than a shack with a warped roof and rough board sides.

Dean opened his door. "Wait here. If I start getting the raw end of the deal, attract some attention."

She got out and hurried around to him. "I'd look silly standing out here in the parking lot waving my arms and screaming while they beat you to death."

A battered truck with several coarse looking construction type men parked near them and they ambled to the door casting appraising glances in Lisa's direction as Dean attempted to stare them down with his one good eye.

"Let me be clear about this, Lisa, I'm going in alone."

"So go. I'm going in alone too."

"You can't go in that place without an escort."

She nodded in the direction of the construction crew. "I'll bet one of them would be delighted to escort me."

"Great idea—frizz your hair, smear your lipstick, show some cleavage, pop some bubblegum in your mouth, and make goo-goo eyes at that big dumb one on the end there. Maybe he'll even let you sit on his lap."

"As a general rule I'm not attracted to big dumb men, you being the peculiar exception of course."

"If things go wrong, maybe you can even encourage him to hustle on over and help me."

"And if he's not inclined to hustle on over and help you?"

"Then start screaming and waving your arms around."

She turned to the door. "I'll be at the bar."

"You'll stand out like a Barbie doll in a whorehouse in there."

"I suppose that's meant to be, like, a compliment or something?"

"It means those rednecks will be all over you like ticks on a hound dog."

She preened. "I'd prefer to think of them as *swarming like bees to honey*. I'll flirt with the bartender. He'll protect me."

"I've got a better plan—act baffled and ask for directions to the nearest mental institution. That shouldn't require too much imagination on your part and provide a degree of protection."

She glared at him. "When they start pounding on your head again, I'll rescue you just like I did the last time."

"You can't *imagine* the immense comfort that gives me!" He jerked the door open, entered, and released it, forcing her to lurch forward to keep it from whacking her backside.

"*Jackass*!"

One of the rednecks slouched at a table with his buddies rose. "Are you okay, lady? I could put a couple more dents on that gent's noggin for you, if you'd like?"

Lisa flashed him a brilliant smile. "I'm fine, but thanks for the offer."

The obviously disappointed redneck sank back down in his chair as they paused to get their bearings amidst the low intensity, dust covered neon lighting advertising a myriad of miscellaneous ales while inhaling the pungent odor of stale alcohol permeating the heavily smoke filled air.

Dean focused on Little Joe standing at the jukebox studying the song selections and crossed the irregular plank flooring as Little Joe turned to stare at Lisa in opened mouth wonder as she slid onto a barstool. "I'd like a word with you."

Little Joe's incredulous eyes shifted to Dean. "Huh? Are you fuckin' crazy, man? Get the fuck outta here! And take that fuckin' fanatical little hoity-toity, nut-kickin' wench with you!"

"Don't call my partner *hoity-toity*," Dean warned cheerfully as he popped him in the mouth, staggering him back against the jukebox. He easily slipped Little Joe's roundhouse right as he lurched back at him, sank his fist into the pit of his stomach, linked his arm under Little Joe's as his lips formed a perfect oval spewing air out beneath his bulging eyes, helped him over to a table, and plunked him down into a chair. "Now, where is your big dumb partner?" he inquired, ignoring the sharp pains emitting from his ribcage.

"You 'uns lookin' fer me?" a deep voice demanded.

Dean turned to the giant striding out of the men's room with eyes hostile and fists clenched, thinking him even bigger than he remembered. He pulled the huge Smith and Wesson cannon out of the back of his pants and pointed the long barrel between Bear's bewildered eyes, stopping him cold as everyone in the room ducked to get out of the line of fire.

"As a matter of fact I am, shit-face." He kept the barrel of the pistol in Bear's face, whose eyes were nearly crossing as they focused on the business end of the revolver.

"Now hold on there, mister," the bartender cautioned from his half crouch behind the bar as the rednecks near the door cowered behind their table in an apprehensive group. "Don't do nothing crazy now, you hear?"

"Barkeep, put your palms on the bar where I can see them," Dean called over his shoulder. "The rest of you keep your hands visible. If everybody keeps their head, there's a better than even chance no one will get killed."

The scattering of men brought their hands up into view, shoulder height, palms out.

"Can I leave, Mister?" a thin, nervous man at the bar begged. "I just came in for a quick brew. I ain't got no dog in this fight. I got kids back home and a sickly wife."

"Nobody leaves!" Dean ordered. "If I have to kill one of these assholes, I'll need witnesses." He fixed Little Joe and Bear with a hard stare. "*Do* I need to kill one of you assholes?"

They shook their heads in unison, eyes fixed on the ominous barrel of the Smith and Wesson.

"Good. Now get down on your hands and knees and crawl out into the parking lot where we can talk in private."

They exchanged bewildered glances.

"On your hands and knees, damn it! *Crawl*!"

They scrambled down on all fours and lurched towards the door as Dean stalked after them.

"What—what do you want us to do, Mister?" the bartender asked as Dean herded them to the door.

"Just go about your business. My only interest is in these two—"

"*Watch out!*" Lisa yelled.

Dean swung the barrel of the pistol against Bear's head as he half turned and lunged at his legs, collapsing him in a heap as Little Joe rose up. He slapped the side of Little Joe's head with a resounding whack of metal against skin and bone, peeling his scalp back in a long gash above his ear. As he collapsed onto the floor as well, Dean stepped forward and administered a series of swift kicks to the face and stomach of each of them as they twitched and moaned. Breathing hard, he turned to the other patrons in the bar as they sat frozen in their chairs. "Anyone else got a problem with doing things my way?"

They shook their heads fearfully.

"Now you two get your ass out into the parking lot," he panted. Bear and Little Joe rolled over and groped their way out the door as blood seeped from their head wounds. "Lisa, come stand by the

178

door. If any of these gentlemen moves, call out and run, because I'm going to start pumping holes the size of watermelons through these walls."

"*Dean, please*!" Lisa whispered tersely as she hurried over. "*This is crazy*! *Don't hurt them anymore*!"

"I tried to get you to stay out of this, maybe next time you'll listen!"

He herded Bear and Little Joe out into the middle of the parking lot. "Okay, sit on your hands, stretch your legs straight out in front of you, and listen close, because I don't like to repeat myself and you two have already pissed me off to the max. I'm going to ask you some questions. If I don't like the answers, I'm going to cap your knees first, and then work my way up to your balls. Do you understand?"

"P-Please, d-don't shoot us, okay?" Little Joe begged as blood trickled down his cheek. "We're sorry about last night. It was just business, you know?"

"So is this." Dean pointed the pistol in his face and cocked the hammer back with a solid click. "Question one: who killed Kenny Felton?"

Little Joe shrank back wide-eyed as Dean pressed the muzzle of the cannon to his forehead. "Hey! Wait now! I don't know. Honest, now. Sharon Lucas did it, I guess. Hell, I don't know. It wasn't us, is all I know. Please don't shoot me!"

Dean believed him, which he found disappointing. "What were you and Felton arguing about just before he was murdered?"

"Arguing? I-I don't know nothing about no argument with Kenny. Who said we were arguing about something?"

Dean aimed at Little Joe's right knee. "*I* ask the questions here, and *you* just gave me the wrong answer."

Little Joe recoiled away from him. "*No-wait-I don't understand what you're asking me*! We didn't even see Kenny the day he died!"

"You were arguing about money, shit head, and I said it was *just before* he was murdered. Now do you want to try answering the question again?"

"Yes, please! See, I remember now. We did argue about money just a few days before somebody done him in. Yeah, I remember now. See—he lost some of our money. Didn't he, Bear? He was investing it for us in that stock market thing. I swear. That was all it was to it. We was just mad about it, is all. We gave him twenty thousand cash 'cause he said he'd double it for us in a few weeks, only it'd been over two months and we ain't seen our money. He said the market was down and we needed to be patient. We worked things out between us. It was just a misunderstanding is all it was, honest."

"Where are the tapes?"

Little Joe blinked. "Tapes? What tapes?"

"The ones of Felton and various women."

"Oh, you mean his slut tapes? Yeah, I know about them. He'd show us them sometimes. He liked to brag a lot. But I don't know where he kept them. Honest. He kept them somewhere in his house. I don't know where. He'd just put one on sometimes for us to watch. He liked to show us what a big stud he was."

"Who were the women in the tapes?"

Little Joe's forehead furrowed in concentration. "Well—there was Kitty. And Sharon, of course. She was the hottest bitch by far. And, uh, there was some married chick, but I can't remember her name. There was a skinny girl, and a girl that worked at the bank, but I don't know them that well. Hell, we didn't ask their names. We just watched the chick-flicks with him."

"And helped Felton drug them."

"Hey, now wait a minute! We did business with Kenny, but what he did with his stuff was none of our concern. You know? It was just business, is all."

"Where are those tapes now?"

"Hell, I don't know, I swear! We just watched them. I don't know nothing else about them."

Dean swung the muzzle to Bear as he shrank back. "So what was last night all about?"

"Y-You mean with you?" Little Joe answered. "Hell, you was asking questions about us and our business. We intended to warn you off is all, but then you had to go and hit Bear there. Things got out of hand after that. Honest. We got no quarrel with you other than that. We're sure sorry about that, ain't we, Bear?"

Bear nodded, his eyes still fixed on the muzzle of the Smith and Wesson.

"Why do you think Sharon killed Felton?"

"Hell, the police arrested her, didn't they?" Little Joe wailed. "What else was we supposed to think? They even got an eyewitness, or so I heard. Look, Mister, can't we just let bygones be bygones here? We don't want no trouble with you, and we promise we won't cause you no more trouble. It was all just a misunderstanding between us and things got out of hand."

Dean un-cocked the pistol. "Here's the real deal, friend, I'm going to take my partner and leave. From here on out you make it a point to stay out of my way and we'll let the matter stand settled between us. But if you give me cause, I'll be back to deal with you, and I won't be in such a mellow mood the next time around. Understand?"

"Thanks, Mister," Little Joe whimpered. "You won't have no problem with us!"

"Lisa, let's go!" Dean called over his shoulder.

She hurried out and scrambled into the VW as he turned and got in on the passenger side.

"I thought you were going to kill them, Dean!" she gasped as she drove off.

"They're going to need stitches and have terrific headaches for a few days, but they'll be alright."

"How could you do something like that? You scared me half to death!"

"I was just playing by their rules. And by the way, I won the bet."

"What bet?"

"That I wouldn't screw up."

"So you want my gown now?"

"I'd prefer to take it off while you're wearing it."

"You're sadistic *and* depraved!"

"That's a given."

"So do you still think Little Joe and Bear are suspects?"

"I'm convinced Little Joe and Bear didn't kill Felton. That narrows our viable suspect list back down to Sharon, the mystery woman, Al Roberts, and Allison Neely again."

She took a deep, steadying breath. "Maybe Sharon really did do it. All of Kenny's friends seem to think so and she seems to have the strongest motive so far."

"I think the video tapes fit into this somewhere. Whoever broke into Felton's house and took those tapes is a strong suspect in my book. Hell, it could have been any of the women he was trying to blackmail into his orgies."

"But why kill him?" she argued. "They could have broken into his house and stolen the tapes without killing him. Do any of them strike you as killers?"

"We don't know all of the women in the tapes."

"So how do we find out who the others are?"

"We talk to Kitty again. Hell, she probably helped recruit them for Felton's little parties."

She frowned as she peered in her rearview mirror. "I've got a police car on my bumper."

"Are you speeding?"

"No."

"Then ignore him."

"I don't think I should."

"Why not?"

"He's got his little blue light on."

Dean sighed in exasperation. "*Then pull over, damn it!*"

Chapter 15

Lisa lurched over to the side of the road and watched the cruiser drift in behind them in her rearview mirror. "Someone must have called the police for what you did back there!"

"For what *I* did?"

"*I* didn't bash anyone over the head with the barrel of a gun!"

Dean glanced over his shoulder. "We're in luck—it's your cute little deputy. If you bat your eyelashes maybe you can get us off."

"Officer Miller? *Really?*" She tugged the mirror down to study her makeup and pressed her lips together to even out her lipstick.

"You're a little hussy with no shame!" he scolded derisively.

She used the end of her finger to smooth out her eyeliner. "A girl likes to look her best!"

"You want to look your best for someone who's going to *arrest* us?"

"*You're* the one who suggested I bat my lashes and try to get us off!"

Deputy Miller stooped to peer into the window and tipped the brim of his trooper's hat with his finger tips. "Howdy, Miss Bryant."

Lisa flashed him a dazzling smile. "Why, Officer Miller, what a pleasant surprise!"

He nodded at Dean in the passenger seat. "Mr. Davis."

"Is there a problem, Deputy?"

He took in Dean's raw, discolored face. "Not at all, Mr. Davis. Chief Parsons would like to see you down at the jail at your earliest convenience. I didn't mean to alarm you, I'm just delivering the message."

"Did Chief Parsons say what he wanted to see me about?"

"The dispatcher just asked us to keep an eye out for you and deliver his request." He stepped back and tipped his hat to Lisa. "Ma'am, you have a nice day now and drive safely."

Lisa flashed him her dimples again as he backed off to allow her to pull out onto the highway. "Well, thank you, Officer, that's so nice of you, and you have a nice day yourself!"

"Don't forget to re-adjust your damned mirror," Dean lamented as she pulled away. "And for the record, it's damned embarrassing to have such a pathetic little flirt as an associate!"

She smirked as she adjusted her mirror. "*Partner*!"

✵ ✵ ✵

Sheriff Parsons' cold brown eyes searched Dean's misshapen visage with amusement as they settled into the chairs in front of his desk. "I heard you got on Big Paul McKinley's wrong side last night."

Dean fixed his good eye on him. "Would that be the grizzled cretin they call 'Bear'?"

"You're lucky Jim's Steak House doesn't want to press charges against you."

"Sorry to disappoint you, Sheriff. Is that why I've been summoned to your high office?"

The sheriff shifted his gaze discretely to Lisa's bosom. "I understand there was a bit of a ruckus up at The Bloody Bucket this afternoon as well."

"I wasn't aware that nefarious establishment was in your jurisdiction."

Sheriff Parson's eyes moved back to him. "Allison Neely attempted suicide this morning. What do you know about it?"

Dean's sore stomach did flip-flops as Lisa lurched forward in her chair. "You said *attempted?*" she gasped. "Is she alright?"

Sheriff Parsons glanced at her breasts. "She swallowed a large bottle of aspirin, but her mother got her to the emergency room in time to get her stomach pumped out." He cut his cold eyes back to Dean. "You didn't answer my question, Davis. What do you know about this?"

"It's news to me, Sheriff."

"You met her yesterday at the drug store. Several people who saw you there said she was upset. When she returned to the bank, she claimed she was ill and asked to go home early. What happened between the two of you that would cause her to make an attempt on her own life?"

Dean held his stare. "Sheriff, my conversation with her is confidential in nature."

"Is she a client of yours, Davis?"

Dean shifted uneasily. "Well, no, she's not a formal client, per se."

"Then answer my question, damn it, or I'll charge you with withholding information in an ongoing criminal investigation."

Dean slouched in his chair. "Sheriff, I'll respond to your question only under duress—"

"*Quit* wasting my time, Davis!"

"Allison Neely was one of the women in Felton's home videos."

Sheriff Parsons leaned forward. "Why didn't you tell me this before? In my book this comes close to suppressing evidence, Davis!"

"She was distraught and offered to hire me. I turned her down, but I did promise I'd do what I could to recover the tape for her at no charge. I don't see her as a suspect or the tape as potential evidence in the Felton murder case."

The sheriff slammed his palm down on his desk. "*You* don't make the decisions as to what is evidence in this case! I've warned you about interfering in this investigation and tampering with potential witnesses!"

Dean stood. "You know, Sheriff, I'm getting damned tired of your insults and threats. Charge me with something or I'm walking."

"*Sit down*, Davis!"

"Do you intend to read me my rights?"

The sheriff's bushy brows drew together in a menacing fashion. "I can hold you for up to seventy-two hours without charging you—"

"I don't think you want the hassle of dealing with the aftermath, Sheriff."

"Get out of my office, Davis—and take your associate with you!"

"*Partner*," Lisa corrected as she scooted out ahead of Dean.

"You two don't seem to like each other very much," she observed sourly as Dean climbed into the passenger seat. "Why don't you try to get along with him? You're unnecessarily abrupt and defensive when you talk to him."

"Every time I *talk* to him he's threatening to lock me up and throw away the key!"

She backed out. "I never realized you were so thin-skinned. So what should we do now?"

"Go to the hospital and check on Allison."

✡ ✡ ✡

The head nurse escorted a thin, gray haired woman with tear-swollen eyes into the small sitting room where Lisa and Dean waited and introduced her as Allison's mother.

"Mrs. Neely, I'm Dean Davis and this is Lisa Bryant. We're friends of Allison. We're obviously very distraught about what has transpired. We hoped we might have a word with her, if possible?"

She hesitated, taking in his swollen features with a modem of misgiving. "Allison has never mentioned either of you as a friend."

"Actually, we're private investigators working on a case she was assisting us with," Lisa injected, handing her one of their cards.

"Private investigators?" She sank down in a chair. "Does this have anything to do with Allison's ... accident?"

"We're not sure, Ma'am," Dean replied. "We've been retained to look into the Kenny Felton murder. Allison was very helpful to us in the course of our background investigation."

She lifted her hand to her throat. "I'm aware Allison became acquainted with Mr. Felton just before his ... *demise*, but it's my understanding they were only friends. Are you inferring there was more to their brief relationship, Mr. Davis? Does his death have anything to do with Allison's current situation?"

Dean glanced at Lisa. "I certainly hope not, but we can't be sure until we speak with her."

Her eyes clouded. "What do you know that you're not sharing with me? This is my *daughter*." She lowered her face into her palms and began weeping.

Lisa sat on the arm of the chair and placed an arm around her to comfort her. "Mrs. Neely, it may be that we can help Allison if you will allow us to meet with her in private."

She lifted her tear-streaked face. "She's very weak. She doesn't want to see anyone."

"Please ask her if she is willing to meet with us," Lisa implored gently. "This is very important to us and possibly to her."

Mrs. Neely wiped at her eyes with a damp tissue and heaved a shuddering sigh. "Give me a moment to see if she will receive you. I'd be grateful for any assistance you could give her." She hurried from the room.

"Being a private investigator is becoming less and less fun," Lisa observed in the silence.

"The hours and pay suck too," Dean added.

They rose together when Mrs. Neely returned. "She has agreed to meet with you. Please don't do anything to upset her. She's all I have in this world."

Lisa placed her hand on her arm. "We'll do our best, Mrs. Neely."

Allison lay on an inclined bed covered with white sheets dressed in a blue gown with a hospital identification bracelet attached to her left wrist. She focused sunken, dark circled eyes on Dean's distorted face as they entered. "Did I have anything to do with that?"

Dean pushed his battered lips into a semblance of a smile. "Not at all. I had a slight misunderstanding with one of Felton's friends. It's no big deal."

"D-Did you find the tape? Please tell me you have the tape!"

Lisa took her hand. "We're still working on it, Allison."

Allison sank back in despair. "No one can help me now."

"Allison, the chances are good we can find the tape and destroy it before any of this becomes public knowledge," Dean reassured her. "There's no reason to go to such extremes as this. Give us some time to help you."

She stared dully up at the ceiling. "I got a call from a man last night. He said he had the tape and that if I didn't want anyone else to see it I would have to ... *be* with him." She closed her eyes. "I can't bear the thought of becoming someone's *whore*, or the consequences if I don't. I'd rather die first!"

"Did the man identify himself?"

She shook her head.

"Did you recognize his voice?"

Tears trickled down her cheeks "No, he disguised it with a handkerchief or something."

Lisa handed her a tissue from the box beside the bed. "Is there anything he said that would give you any indication as to who he was?"

"No."

"Did he ask you to meet him somewhere?" Dean pressed.

She shuddered. "I hung up on him!"

"Allison, you're not in this alone," he soothed. "Sheriff Parsons knows about the tape. You need to inform him about the attempted blackmail as well."

"Sheriff Parsons knows!"

"I was forced to tell him or face obstruction charges for withholding evidence in an ongoing murder investigation. I'm sorry, but I had no other alternative. If you'll work with us we'll find this bastard and destroy the tape. Harming yourself serves no purpose, and unfortunately there may be other victims out there who also need your help."

She swallowed. "W-What do you want me to do?"

"You have my card. Call me when they release you. We're going to hunt this thug down. In the interim, you've got your mother scared to death, so do what you can to comfort her."

She nodded miserably as she fought to suppress her tears.

Lisa hugged her and then stopped by the waiting room to reassure Mrs. Neely before hurrying out to Dean waiting at the hospital entrance.

"We've got to find the creep who has those tapes before he hurts any of the others," she allowed grimly as she opened the door to her VW. "I'd like to pistol whip that jerk myself!"

"*Now* you're talking!" he praised as she started the engine. "This also explains the second break-in at Felton's house. I never considered that some jackass might try to corral Felton's harem for his own pleasure. Let's go talk to Janice Murray next to see if she's received a phone call from this double-dealing asshole."

"Do you think this man could also be the one who murdered Kenny?" she asked.

"Possibly, but he could also just be an opportunist attempting to exploit the situation. Felton seems to have been pretty free about showing his art collection around."

Lisa leaned over and kissed his cheek. "Thanks, Dean."

"What're you getting so mushy about?"

"Because deep down under that carefully contrived gruff exterior you're really a pretty decent guy overall."

"Oh, for heaven's sake—can we go now?"

✲ ✲ ✲

Janice Murray stared at Dean's face in bewilderment when she opened the door. "What happened to you?"

"It's a long story. Could we have a word with you in private?" he asked as her mother appeared anxiously behind her.

She stepped out and closed the door. "From the looks of you, I assume you're not bringing good news?"

The curtain lifted beside the door as her mother peeped out at them. Dean took Janice's elbow and guided her down the walkway. "Has anyone contacted you?"

"No. Why do you ask?"

"Someone tried to blackmail one of the other victims."

She drew back. "What? Who? What did they want?"

"We don't know who," Lisa replied. "They wanted her to 'party' with them in exchange for not showing the tape to others. We need your help if he should contact you."

Her face paled. "If there really is a tape of me, I'll be scandalized!"

"Calm down," Dean soothed. "The other victim tried to take her life over this—we don't need you doing anything as foolish."

"*What*? Oh, no, I-I don't think I could … oh my god!"

"Easy now, we just want you to know we're here to help if he should contact you, and to reassure you that you're not in this alone. I suspect you might hear from him soon if such a tape exists and he'll probably make the same demands on you."

"What should I do?"

He took her shoulders and turned her to face him. "You should go to the sheriff and—"

She pulled away. "*No*! I don't want anyone else involved in this!"

He tugged her back around to him. "Listen to me, Janice, there could be an element of personal danger to you if you don't. This may not be a simple matter of blackmail. We could be dealing with Felton's murderer here. The sheriff can protect you far better than we can."

Defiance rose in her eyes. "What have I got to lose? This thing will ruin me if it gets out. Tell me exactly what you want me to do."

"If you won't go to the sheriff, then think rationally if this slime ball should contact you. Agree to meet with him and then contact us immediately. We'll devise a plan from there."

"What if he doesn't call?"

"Then I'd assume he doesn't have a tape of you, which can only be a good thing, right?"

"Who is the other girl?"

"I'm not at liberty to say."

She nodded. "I appreciate your discretion, Mr. Davis. Thank you for offering to help me."

"It's our pleasure."

Janice's mother came out onto the porch. "Darling, don't you want to invite your friends inside? I've got fresh tea made."

Dean waved her off. "Thank you, Ma'am, but we've got another appointment."

She wrung her hands, covertly studying his swollen features. "Yes, well …"

Lisa hugged Janice. "We'll stay in touch. Call us the minute you hear anything."

"I will!" she called after them as they turned to the car.

"I'm feeling better about this detective thing," Lisa mused as they drove away.

"Yeah, but the hours and pay still suck," he reminded her.

"So do we notify Kitty, Becky, and Linda next?"

"I think we should, even if they were willing participants in Felton's videos and seem to have less to lose reputation wise. Until we know who we're dealing with in this scheme, we have to assume he's a potential murderer."

"What about Sheriff Parsons? Are we doing anything illegal by not notifying him? I mean, blackmail is a crime, isn't it?"

"We're definitely in the wrong by not bringing him into the picture, but on the other hand, we've sworn to protect the victims. Let's hope Allison confides in him as I've advised."

"What do you think he'll do if he finds out we knew and didn't tell him?"

"Lock us up and throw away the key."

"This detective stuff sucks."

"Don't forget the lousy hours and pay."

Chapter 16

L isa dropped Dean off at the restaurant across the street from the carwash and hurried over to arrange for Linda Thompson to meet with them on her break. When the two slid into the booth across from him, Linda stared at his banged up image with sarcastic amusement.

"Lordy mercy, Mr. Detective, what in the world happened to your handsome face?"

Dean winced. "I walked into a door." He waited while she ordered a slice of lemon pie and a Coke before briefing her on the missing tapes and the attempted blackmail of one of the women involved.

She licked her fork. "So why are you telling me all this for?"

"We were hoping you would help identify him if he should call you."

"What makes you think he'll call me?"

"It's just a guess since he contacted the other woman and tried to blackmail her. I think that's probably his motive for stealing the tapes in the first place, but I can't rule out he's also the man who murdered Felton."

She pursed her lips. "Ray Mize is weird enough to do something like that."

"Murder Felton?"

"No, silly, steal the tapes."

"Will you help us identify the man if he should contact you?" Dean pressed.

"What do you want me to do?"

"If you can't identify him on the phone, agree to meet with him and contact the sheriff immediately."

"Why do you need to involve the sheriff in this?"

"Blackmail is a crime, and like I said, we could be dealing with a murderer here."

"So I could be putting myself in danger, right?"

"I'm certain the sheriff will do everything in his power to protect you."

"So what do I get out of helping you find this bozo? I mean, I'd be putting my personal safety on the line so you can earn a big fat fee, right?" She worked on her pie with her fork. "Detectives make gobs of money for helping people, so I'm thinking you should be willing to spread some of it around to the people who help you."

Dean stifled his rising irritation. "We're not charging the other woman involved or you."

"I haven't asked for your help, have I?"

"Well no, but—"

"Look, I don't give a damn about this jerk-off trying to blackmail me over some stupid tapes. Do you want my help or not?"

"We'll pay you a hundred dollars if you help us identify him," Lisa cut in.

"Two hundred," Linda countered.

Lisa slid from the booth and picked up her purse. "The pie's on us."

Linda grimaced. "Now hold on, girlfriend, I was just trying to see where the ceiling was. A hundred it is. I'll talk to the pervert if he calls, and I'll set up an appointment to be his little blow-up dolly for you. But I don't want the sheriff involved. Understood?"

"I appreciate your help," Dean said, rising. "You have our number."

"See ya," she chirped as she forked a lump of pie into her mouth.

Becky Roberts, dressed in a crisp white short skirt that enhanced her tanned legs, and a tight blue silk blouse that left little to the imagination, opened the door to her apartment, her flawless makeup and hair only heightening her sassy charisma as she eyed Dean speculatively.

"Did Al do that to your face?"

"Uh, no—"

"It *looks* like something he'd do."

Dean drew himself up with as much decorum as he could muster as Lisa turned her head to stifle a snicker. "We need a moment of your time to discuss a new wrinkle in the Felton murder."

"You two have already got me in a world of shit with my hubby, so get lost." She slammed the door in their face.

Dean knocked on the door again. "Mrs. Roberts, we need to talk with you!"

"*Go away!*" she ordered through the door.

"There have been some developments in the Felton case you need to be made aware of," he called through the door.

"Such as?" her muffled voice demanded.

"Such as certain video tapes are missing from Felton's house."

"*So?*"

"Whoever has them is attempting to blackmail one of the other women."

The door opened a few inches for her to peer through the crack. "What's that got to do with me?"

"Has anyone contacted you in an attempt to coerce you into anything?"

"Who says I'm involved with those tapes?"

"The other woman involved said you were in the tape with her."

She scowled. "Al's on the warpath and doesn't want me having anything to do with you."

"If those tapes are made public, I'm sure Al would be very disturbed by them," Dean threatened. "Could we come inside and discuss this matter in private?"

"Go away or I'll call the cops!"

"Becky, have you been contacted by this man?" Lisa asked.

"You might be in some danger," Dean cautioned when she stared at them sullenly. "Maybe we can help."

"You can help by leaving me alone!" She slammed the door again.

"She's heard from him," Lisa whispered.

"I'm warning you, I'm calling the cops right now!" Becky yelled from inside. "You better get on outta here now!"

"Mrs. Roberts, you're making a mistake in not talking to us," Dean pleaded. "This individual might be dangerous. Please talk to us or the sheriff before you do anything rash."

"I'm dialing the police right now! I mean it! Get on off my doorstep!"

Dean stuck one of his cards in the door. "I'm leaving my phone number. Please call me before you do something you might regret."

Lisa pulled him away from the door and back out to her car. "Let's tail her."

"Tail her where?"

She backed out into the street and pulled away from the apartment. "If we knew that we wouldn't have to tail her, would we?"

"Would you mind giving me just a tiny clue as to what the hell you're talking about?"

"She's on her way to meet the blackmailer. This is our chance to identify him."

"Are you crazy? We don't know he's contacted her, and even if he did, when or if she's agreed to meet with him."

"If this guy is the killer, it's our best lead since we've started this case," she argued as she turned into a side street and did a u-turn to park next to the curb in view of Becky's front door but partially hidden by the intervening buildings.

"This is ridiculous," Dean insisted. "Let's go talk to Kitty and see if she'll help us. We're wasting our time sitting around here like dummies."

"I've got a hunch—I'm betting she leaves to meet the blackmailer in the next half hour. If she doesn't, we'll go see Kitty."

"Hunches are for amateurs. We need to stick to the facts, not bet on long shots which rarely pay off."

"This is not a long shot!"

"Want to bet?"

"You name it."

"Okay, if she leaves in the next half hour I'll eat my shorts, and if she doesn't, you—"

"*Bon appetite!*" she chided as Becky rushed out to a battered Chevrolet parked on the street in front of her house.

"Damn! How'd you know she was going to do that?"

"Easy, Sherlock. Using my awesome powers of deductive reasoning, I noticed she was all made-up from head to toe and decked out in her finest in the middle of the day, which is something housewives don't normally do unless they're going somewhere. Furthermore, if you had any people skills at all, you would have noticed she was desperate to get us off her doorstep. She's probably running late for the appointment. Brilliant, huh?"

"Baloney! That doesn't prove she's going to meet the black-mailer, Miss Einstein. She could be going grocery shopping or to get her hair done for all you know."

"Her hair is already done, and women don't dress like that to go to the grocery store," she chided as she slipped out of the side street behind Becky Roberts' car. "Do I have to teach you *everything* about women?"

"Do women normally get all dolled up in the middle of the day to meet blackmailers and potential murderers for sexual trysts?"

"You really are clueless where women are concerned."

"You're missing my *point*!"

"*You're* missing mine!"

"Stay at least two blocks back," he cautioned. "This damned red Volkswagen stands out like a flashing neon light."

"I heard somewhere that one tends to over-look the obvious."

"So now you're suddenly the expert on tailing suspects too?"

"I got us this far, didn't I?"

Becky's car cut hard across the left lane from the far right lane and swerved in front of a dump truck onto a side street.

"Look out! She's turning left!"

A tractor-trailer rig in the left lane beside them forced Lisa to drive through the intersection before she could work her way over into the left lane and turn back to the junction. When they turned onto the side street, there was no sign of Becky's car.

"You've lost her!" Dean groaned.

"What did you want me to do, drive through the eighteen-wheeler?"

"You should have dropped back like I told you to, damn it! If you'd quit being such a know it all I could teach you something about being an investigator."

"*Oh, please!*"

"Just cruise around the area and see if we can spot her, okay?"

After a half hour of criss-crossing the side streets they gave up and drove to Kitty's run down apartment complex on the south side of town. After knocking and receiving no answer, Dean wrote a brief message on the back of his card requesting she call him and stuck it in her door.

"Let's drive by Ray Mize's dry cleaners," Lisa suggested as they drove off.

"Why, pray tell?"

"If he's not there, it's a good indication he's meeting with Becky. If he's in, it's a good indication he's not our man."

"That's assuming Becky was rushing out to meet the blackmailer in the first place, Dr. Watson, and that's certainly not a proven fact yet."

"If you can afford the loss of underwear, I'll make you another wager Ray Mize is not there. Double or nothing?"

"Don't be such a smartass. Besides, we never actually sealed the bet."

"We did so!"

"Did not! We were still negotiating when she came out."

"*You're such a cheat!*"

The clerk behind the counter informed them Mr. Mize had taken the afternoon off and that she did not have a means of contacting him.

"Told you so," Lisa quipped as they climbed back in the car.

"You're beginning to grate on my nerves."

"I can only imagine how rough it is on your ego for me to always be right."

"My ego is certainly not threatened by a couple of wild-assed guesses on your part."

"It's getting late."

"Your point?"

"I was hoping you would offer to feed me since I've proven myself invaluable to the team today."

"How do you eat so much and stay so skinny?"

"I need to keep my energy level up. There's a fish place out near the lake."

"I like fish."

✵ ✵ ✵

They ordered a large platter of catfish and hush puppies, which they devoured before a magnificent view of the setting sun across the tranquil lake. When they reentered the city limits, a police cruiser pulled up on their rear bumper and flashed its blue lights.

"I wasn't speeding!" Lisa objected as she pulled over to the side of the road.

"It's probably your cute little deputy wanting to discuss your driving record."

The patrol car pulled up beside them and the officer rolled down his window on the passenger side. "Mr. Davis?"

Dean leaned across Lisa. "Yeah?"

"Would you follow me to the jail, Sir? Sheriff Parsons wants to see you."

"Again?" Dean called back. "Are you guys his personal messenger service?"

"Sir?"

"We'll follow you there," Lisa advised as she jabbed her elbow into Dean's sore ribs. "Now what?" she asked as she pulled out behind the patrol car.

"Beats me, to the best of my knowledge we haven't done anything illegal since noon."

"*Fun-ny*. Try being professional this time, will you?"

"*Me?* He sets the tone!"

They followed the deputy at the front desk to Sheriff Parsons' office, where he knocked on the door and ushered them in.

"Hi, Sheriff, long time-no see," Dean greeted. "I assume you're in dire need of my sage counsel yet again. Have you considered setting me up a desk down here for convenience?"

"I've got a private room reserved just for you, Davis. Ray Mize is dead. What do you know about it?"

Dean eased into the chair in front of his desk to mask his shock as Lisa settled into the one beside him. "Well, let's see, I know you haven't read me my rights yet, so I assume I'm not a prime suspect. Why do you think I'd know anything about it?"

"Why do you always answer my question with a question, Davis?"

"Sorry, allow me to be a little more specific, Sheriff—I don't know a damn thing about Ray Mize's death. How was he killed?"

"How do you know he was killed?"

"Did you perchance want to discuss his fatal accident or suicide with me?"

"You're going to push me too far one of these days, Davis. I understand you had an argument with him at his place of business yesterday and that he threw you out. I also understand you went back earlier today asking for him. I want any information you have that might reflect on this case." His eyes narrowed as Dean sat pondering his answer. "Davis, if I find out you're withholding information—"

"I know, I know, you'll lock me up in your dungeon and throw away the key." He leaned forward. "Look, Sheriff, I might have a lead or two for you, and I'm more than willing to cooperate, as long as you appreciate a lot of what I know is confidential in nature unless it pertains to evidence in a crime. Help me out here, Sheriff. Tell me what's going on so I can help you with a clear conscience."

"Ray Mize checked into room 204 of The Traveler's Rest Motel at approximately 3:15 p.m. this afternoon. His body was found at 4:20 p.m. with three slugs in his chest from a large caliber weapon, possibly a .357 magnum."

"Who found him?"

"A guest in the room next door reported a loud argument involving a male and a female, followed by what she thought were muffled shots, around 4 p.m. The manager called the room and got no answer. He then proceeded to the room and knocked on the door. When he again received no answer, he used his master key to open the door and found the body."

"That doesn't explain why you think I have any information on this crime."

"Your business card was found on the floor beside the body. Now quit stalling and tell me what you know about this case."

Dean collected his thoughts. "To begin with, Mize was my chief suspect in the disappearance of Felton's video tapes. An unidentified male attempted to blackmail one of the women in those tapes for sexual favors. I suspect he may have arranged to meet a second woman at the motel for that same purpose and she subsequently killed him."

The sheriff picked up a pen and poised it over a pad on his desk. "Who were these two women being blackmailed?"

Dean sat back in his chair. "Keep in mind I can't confirm one of them was actually being blackmailed."

"Don't play games with me, Davis! If you withhold—"

"*Please*, Sheriff, you don't have to threaten me, I'm more than willing to give you the name of a potential murderer, especially if it helps clear my client. The thing is, I can only tell you what I know to be a fact, and then only as it directly pertains to the case at hand. I'm trying real hard to be cooperative."

Sheriff Parsons relaxed a fraction. "Who is the woman you know was being blackmailed?"

"Allison Neely—that's why she attempted suicide. I hope you can appreciate how sensitive that information is under the circumstances."

"Are you implying I'm *insensitive*?"

Dean suppressed a grin. "Not at all, Sheriff, I'm just emphasizing the obvious."

Sheriff Parsons glowered. "And the woman you *suspect* was being blackmailed?"

"Becky Roberts."

"The woman in the tape in Felton's VCR?"

"The same."

"Why do you suspect her as a blackmail victim?"

Dean briefed him on the sequence of events of that afternoon. "She gave us the slip between three and three-thirty," he concluded. "The Traveler's Rest Motel is less than a mile from where we lost her."

"That's pretty flimsy evidence."

"I don't know that I'd even call it evidence at this point, Sheriff, just an odd coincidence that might need looking into."

"And your business card being in the room?"

"I left one of my cards in Mrs. Roberts' door just before she left. I also gave Mize a card when I questioned him yesterday. It could be either one of those cards, or an entirely different one. If you need an alibi as to where I was at 4 p.m. this afternoon, I was driving around in circles with Miss Bryant here looking for

Mrs. Roberts' car after she cut across four lanes of traffic to shake us off her tail. Afterwards we drove to the catfish place out near the lake for dinner. Please feel free to check it out."

"You arrived there shortly after 5 p.m. and left just before 7 p.m. You had the all you can eat fried catfish special for two. In my opinion it wouldn't be a stretch to get from The Traveler's Rest Motel to the fish house in that period of time."

"I take it you've never ridden in a rickety Volkswagen with a very studious driver like Miss Bryant behind the wheel."

The sheriff almost smiled as Lisa glared at Dean. "Who are the other women in those missing tapes, Davis?"

"To my knowledge, they're not suspects in either the Felton murder or the Mize murder, Sheriff, and none of them have been contacted by the person who was trying to blackmail Miss Neely. I've promised them confidentiality until such time as circumstances dictate otherwise."

"You're walking a thin line, Davis."

"I understand that, Sheriff. Regardless of what you think, I have no desire to see a murderer go free. I'll help you anyway I can, as I promised you in the beginning."

"I could lock you up and haul you before the judge."

"Can you show cause as to how they may be involved in your investigation?"

He grimaced. "Get out!"

Dean crawled into the passenger seat as Lisa fired up the VW. "How about a cocktail? It's been a long day."

"Okay, I'm game," she agreed. "Where?"

"The Traveler's Rest Lounge."

"Good idea, we can get the inside scoop on the Ray Mize murder, right?"

"Nope, that's a police matter now."

"Okay, we can go over the Sharon Lucas case and put together a new game plan then."

"Negative, I'm too tired to do that either. Besides, it's bad to overanalyze a case. Sometimes you've got to put it out of your mind and let your subconscious work on it."

"So why are we going to the Traveler's Rest Lounge then?"

"To relax and have a few drinks, if that suits you. If you get lucky, I might even allow you to ply me with liquor and take advantage of me."

"*You wish!*"

Chapter 17

Dean lifted his glass after a semi-attractive bleached blonde with tired eyes set their drinks before them in the dimly lit lounge. "Here's to everything and nothing."

Lisa touched her glass of white wine to his glass of bourbon. "Why so gloomy?"

"Everything we do turns into a dead end. We don't have a single viable suspect in this case outside of Al Roberts and our own client."

"Maybe we're fooling ourselves and Sharon really did kill him."

He suppressed his own waning self-doubts. "I don't believe that."

"You can't ignore the fact a witness saw someone who looks like her running towards her apartment after the shot was fired, and you've got to admit that so far she seems to have the best motive."

"I still can't picture Sharon pulling a trigger."

"Don't let your personal feelings shade the facts, Dean. If Kenny was blackmailing her, she may have been desperate enough to do anything. You heard how distraught she was on the phone when she called him on the day he was killed."

"It still doesn't jell with the way I remember her."

"I assume she wasn't into drugs and group sex back then either."

He glared at her. "We weren't going to talk about this case, remember? We were going to relax. Let's talk about something different."

"Like what?"

He shrugged. "Pick a subject."

She dug in her purse, pulled out a coin, went to the jukebox, studied it a moment, and made a selection. As the slow, dreamy music filled the lounge, she walked back to him with extended hands.

"Want to dance, sailor?"

"I'm not much of a dancer," he protested as she pulled him out of the booth and folded into his arms.

"Just fake it then."

"You're not making a move on me, are you?"

She rested her cheek on his chest wistfully. "Unfortunately, you're nowhere near deserving of such yet."

Later, watching her make up the couch was distressing, even though he was in no physical shape to press the issue. The lingering thought of not being deserving was somewhat disturbing to him as well …

☆ ☆ ☆

Dean awoke alone in his bed and lay listening to Lisa rattling around in the kitchen. She appeared a few minutes later with two cups of coffee.

"I thought you were going to sleep all day."

He stretched his sore body gingerly. "I feel like I've been hit by a Mack truck."

"Actually, it more closely resembled a grizzly bear."

He propped up against the headboard as she handed him one of the cups and settled down on the side of the bed staring at him in amusement.

"What?" he demanded irritably.

"You look a little less freaky this morning with the swelling going down. I've been thinking—we need to focus on the mystery woman."

"So focus."

"How do we find out who she is?"

"You're the one doing the thinking, you tell me."

"She could be the key to this," she insisted as she hurried out to answer the telephone. "That was Mr. Jenkins, from apartment 330," she informed him when she returned. "He's back in town and seems anxious to talk to us. I told him we would be by within the hour."

Dean rolled his sore body out of bed. "Guess I'd better get dressed."

Lisa hurried back to the living room as the phone rang again.

"It's Charlene Peters," she advised sourly when she returned.

"What the hell does she want?"

"To talk to you, of course."

"Tell her I'm not here."

"I already told her you were."

"Damn!" He limped into the living room and picked up the phone. "Hello?"

"*Dean*! I've called your office every day, but never get an answer!"

"That's probably because I'm not here," he mumbled peevishly.

"Doesn't Lisa maintain office hours for you?"

"She's my partner, not my secretary," he advised impatiently. "And we spend most of our time in the field."

"You might consider getting an answering machine then so people can get up with you."

"What can I do for you, Charlene?"

"I thought we might do lunch."

"Uh, I'm really tied up at the moment."

"Surely you can take time to eat. I'll meet you somewhere."

"I usually grab a bite on the run when I'm working a case."

"Do I need to hire you so you can fit me into your schedule?" she teased.

"Right now Sharon's case has my full attention," he replied smoothly. "In fact, I'm late for my next appointment."

"I'm sure Sharon appreciates all your hard work," she replied graciously. "Keep me in mind when you get a spare moment."

"I'll do that, Charlene. Bye now!" He hung up the phone.

"What did she want?" Lisa asked.

"To do lunch and to advise me to get an answering machine because you're a lousy secretary," he replied. "Your next lesson will be on how to screen my calls."

"Is that in our partnership bylaws?" she asked as she turned to the kitchen. "Hit the shower while I make us a quick breakfast, but don't expect it every morning."

"Mr. Davis, I presume?" Jenkins, a short, slender man in his early fifties with wisps of thin, graying hair surrounding his bald head in a well-groomed semi-circle, demanded when he opened the door to his apartment. His somewhat dated, prim, un-rimmed thick spectacles, crisp white shirt, yellow and blue polka dot tie, and gray dress-slacked attire gave his countenance an air of contrived self-importance. "What happened to your face, if I may inquire?"

"I was involved in an unfortunate accident." Dean handed him his card. "I appreciate you calling. This is my partner, Lisa Bryant."

"I expected to talk to the police, not private investigators. I understand you are working on behalf of Miss Lucas. Is that correct?"

"We were hired by her grandmother. I'd have thought the police would have questioned you by now as well."

"It's inexcusable of them not to come by and talk to me. It has been almost a week since the unfortunate event occurred. I have been out of town, but I certainly was not out of town the night it happened. It is an intolerable waste of taxpayer's money to conduct such a shoddy investigation. Now I understand they have arrested the wrong girl for the murder while I was away. I can't wait to see how they explain that unpardonable blunder!"

Dean suppressed a surge of excitement. "Wrong girl? Sir, may we come inside to discuss this in more detail?"

"That's what you're here for, isn't it?" He stepped aside for them to enter. "The first officer on the scene that night ordered us to stay in our homes. He said someone would come around to take our statements. They never came by to see *me*, that's for sure. If they had, they wouldn't be making fools of themselves. Serves them right." He motioned for them to sit on the sofa as he settled into a well-worn easy chair facing them in the living room, which appeared as synthetic as he, with the same dated style of everything being too perfectly in its place.

Dean leaned forward eagerly. "Sir, if you could tell us what you saw that night?"

"Aren't you going to take notes, young man?"

Dean dug out his pad. "Of course, if you could just start from the beginning?"

"Will my name be in the paper?"

"The paper?"

"For helping you clear the Lucas girl. Everybody calls me 'Carl' but I prefer my full name. *Carlson*. That's spelled C-A-R-L-S-O-N. Everybody wants to shorten a man's proper name to slang these days. 'Carl' does not tell you anything about a man. *Carlson* speaks of ancestry and proper breeding."

"Indeed it does, Sir." Dean wrote *Carl Jenkins* on his pad. "Now, on the night of the murder?"

"I was standing at my window looking through my telescope at the stars, as is my custom. You see, I'm something of an amateur astronomer and have a very fine telescope. It helps soothe my nerves after a trying day. The vastness of our universe brings one's relative importance into focus in the overall scope of things. Have you spent time reflecting upon the proper place we each fit into God's scheme of things, Mr. Davis?"

"Uh . . ."

He nodded with a gleam of satisfaction. "I recommend it, Mr. Davis, recommend it highly. When you view God's creation up close, it tends to humble you and elevate you to the highest essence of awareness. It brings out the creative impulse to craft something as marvelous on such a grand scale as our Lord Savior did. His universe surrounds us, and sets the chaos of our insignificant little world into a semblance of order. He has shaped the planets and stars and galaxies of His glorious heaven in all of its splendor right above our very heads to remind us of His majesty." He sat back with a blissful look on his smug mug and Dean jumped at the pause.

"Sir, exactly what did you see from your window that night?"

"Call me Carlson, *please*."

"Right, Carlson, so that night while you were standing at the window viewing God's magnificent universe?"

"I saw the young man drive up in his fancy red car and go into Miss Lucas' apartment. She is such an exquisite young woman, albeit one of God's unfortunate fallen angels, I am sorry to say. I often marvel at her physical perfection as I watch her . . . uh, what I mean to say is, she is indeed deserving of a proper man of unshakable faith to lead her back to the righteous path."

"Err, and what else did you see that night, Sir?"

"*Carlson*. Call me Carlson. Well, shortly after this young fellow entered Miss Lucas' apartment, a second vehicle pulled in and parked beside his car. The occupant in this vehicle was a woman. She got out just as the young man came out of Miss Lucas' home and met him as he started to get into his car. He seemed to push her aside. She followed after him pulling at his arm. They struggled and he pushed her back. Then without warning: *Bam!* The young man fell to the pavement and out of my view. The woman then ran to Miss Lucas' apartment. I lost sight of her temporarily because the door to Miss Lucas' apartment is recessed and beyond my vision, but shortly afterwards, she ran back into view, jumped into her vehicle, and drove away."

Lisa and Dean exchanged startled glances as Mr. Jenkins looked from the one of them to the other. Dean finally found his vocal cords. "Mr. Jenkins——"

"*Carlson*."

"*Carlson*, can you identify this woman you saw?"

He shook his head. "No, sorry, I do not recall having seen her before. The light was dim and everything happened so fast. My vision has always been something less than normal, unfortunately." He indicated his thick spectacles for emphasis.

"How was she dressed?" Lisa asked.

He hesitated. "I think she was wearing a light colored skirt or something with a dark top. However, I am not absolutely certain of that. As I said, it was dark and my eyesight is not what it should be."

"What kind of vehicle was she driving?" Dean pressed.

"A white Ford Bronco. I'd guess it was several years old since it had rust spots on the rear quarter panel and hood."

"Can you give us a description of the woman?" Lisa asked.

"She was just beyond the street lamp, but I'd say she was light of hair, slim of build, and short in stature."

"Could you identify this woman if you saw her again?"

He shook his head. "Unfortunately, I never got a good look at her face."

"Carlson, may I borrow your phone?" Dean asked. "I think it's imperative we get Sheriff Parsons out here to take your statement."

He arched his eyebrows indignantly. "I would certainly hope so. That poor child has spent enough time in his despicable jail under false charges. This would never have happened if the police had bothered to conduct a proper investigation. I was appalled when I returned this morning to find her unjustly arrested for a crime she did not commit. I called Sheriff Parsons first thing, but he has yet to return my call. You *will* mention my role in helping free her when you talk to the press, will you not?"

Dean mustered as much sincerity as he could as he reached for the telephone. "I'll ensure every detail of your noble role in getting Miss Lucas cleared of this ridiculous murder charge is made known, Sir."

"Carlson!"

"Uh, sorry—*Carlson*!"

☆ ☆ ☆

"This is Sheriff Parsons," a gruff voice answered after several minutes of holding.

"Sheriff, Dean Davis. Miss Bryant and I are currently at Mr. Carl Jenkins' home."

"Please, *Carlson*," Mr. Jenkins corrected in annoyance from behind him.

"Uh, I mean at Mr. *Carlson* Jenkins' home, apartment 330, at the Belmont Apartment complex—"

"I got a message he called this morning. I can't imagine what that pious little hymn-singing, Bible-thumping, water-wading, head-dunking, holy-rolling hypocrite has to say to me."

"Uh, be that as it may, Sheriff, I think you need to hear what he has to say."

"And just what does that jackass claim to know about anything?"

"He witnessed the murder."

"Bullshit!"

"I've just heard his version of things, and there's no doubt Sharon Lucas is innocent."

"Then why in tar-nation hasn't he come forward before now!"

"He says he was told to stay in his apartment and that someone would come by to take his statement. He had to go out of town on business the next morning and just found out when he returned that Sharon Lucas was arrested for the murder."

"The damned fool!"

"He's actually quite upset that no one bothered to question him that night before he left."

"Damn it, Davis! If you're leading me on a wild goose chase ..."

Sheriff Parsons barged through the door fifteen minutes later with one of his deputies. After ten minutes with Carlson Jenkins, he bundled him up in his patrol car and drove him off to meet with the district attorney as Lisa and Dean hurried to Mrs. Peters' house.

"Oh, my goodness!" Charlene exclaimed when she opened the door. "What happened to you?"

"Just a little accident," Dean replied. "Is your grandmother in?"

"Have you seen a doctor?"

"Yes, I'm fine. I've got some great news for your grandmother."

"Mr. Davis, you've been injured!" Mrs. Peters observed as she appeared behind Charlene. "I sincerely hope I'm not responsible in some way?"

"It's nothing, Ma'am, part of the job. But I've got some excellent news."

She opened the screen door. "Come into the parlor. Would you like some tea or coffee?"

"No thank you, Ma'am." Lisa and Dean took the sofa as she and Charlene sat down in the easy chairs, and Dean quickly briefed her on Carlson Jenkins. "So, Ma'am, if his story holds up, Sharon should be released very soon."

She clasped her hands together in her lap. "And you say this Mr. Jenkins was doubtful he could identify the other woman he saw?"

"He never got a good look at her face due to the poor visibility and his bad eyesight."

"You've done an excellent job, Mr. Davis, as I expected you would. I'm very pleased."

"Thank you, Ma'am, but it was really more blind luck than—"

"*Coupled* with a lot of hard digging fraught with personal peril!" Lisa piped in, indicating Dean's tattered self with a nod of her head.

"Please excuse me," Mrs. Peters apologized as she hurried out to answer the phone. Some moments later, she returned. "That was Sharon, Mr. Davis. The authorities are releasing her from that horrid place within the hour. I've prepared your bonus check for you." She handed him an envelope. "Please forgive me, but I must leave now to pick her up and bring her home."

"Of course, Ma'am," he replied, standing. "But it's not really necessary to pay us a—"

"We're delaying her from picking up Sharon, Dean!" Lisa injected, rising.

"Perhaps Sharon could have you out to dinner soon to properly thank you herself?" Mrs. Peters suggested.

Dean swallowed the rising croak in his throat. "Thank you, Ma'am, but my schedule is very tight at the moment."

Charlene hooked her arm through his. "I'll walk you out, Dean. I'm *so* disappointed you haven't called! Now that you seem to have saved Sharon, I assume you're free tonight?"

"Unfortunately, we have to meet with another client," Lisa injected smoothly as she opened her door. "In fact we really must be going, Dean, or we'll be late."

"We certainly can't afford to be late," Dean agreed as he slid into the passenger seat.

"Call me!" Charlene insisted as Lisa fired up the VW and backed out.

Chapter 18

"What a *transparent* little twit!" Lisa raved as they drove off. "She has no shame! You owe me big time!"

"For what?" Dean demanded.

"For rescuing you!"

"Bull-crap! I had the situation under control, thank you very much!"

"Sure you did, Romeo," she purred. "She had you squirming like an eel!"

"I can't help it if women find my charisma overwhelming," he offered philosophically.

"*Beguiling* is more like it!"

"Whatever. I feel guilty as hell for taking this bonus money."

"Don't be silly! She offered it of her own free will, and we *did* break the case, which is what she hired us to do."

"Apparently with a lot of hard digging fraught with personal peril?" he scoffed. "You're shameless! We were lucky as hell and you damn well know it."

"And you haven't got one ounce of business sense!" she complained. "You nearly blew it back there!"

He ripped off the end of the envelope and pulled out the check. "There wouldn't have been a case if Sheriff Parsons had done a thorough investigation to begin with."

"What are you going to do with your half?" she asked.

"Umm, buy a car, for sure."

"I'm going to rent an apartment now that I can finally afford one," she mused. "They've got some really nice ones out at Lake Shore."

His stomach churned at the mention of the moving-out thing again. "Aren't they a little on the expensive side?"

"They're worth it with a pool, tennis courts, and such a marvelous view of the lake. I've always wanted to live there."

"They're unfurnished. Are you planning to sleep on the floor?"

"I can get my bedroom set from home and buy some inexpensive furniture for the living and dining rooms with my half of the bonus."

"It could be weeks, even months, before another case comes along," Dean argued. "It's not like this profession offers a steady income, you know."

Her heart skipped a beat. "Is that a firm offer to keep me on as your partner?"

"I'm just suggesting it would be wise to be conservative until you know for sure where your next paycheck is coming from," he hedged.

"Okay, I'll save half to live on and use the other half to upgrade my lifestyle."

"Whatever furls your sails," he replied despondently.

"Why so gloomy?" she taunted. "I thought you couldn't wait to get rid of me. Once I'm gone, you'll have your precious privacy back and won't have to sleep on that lumpy old sofa every other night."

"I *told* you, I've gotten attached to that fuzzy picture of the naked chick you hung on my wall. I'm sure going to miss that broad."

"*Ohooo, poooor baby!*"

☆ ☆ ☆

Dean cashed the check at the bank and split the money with Lisa. Afterwards she dropped him off at the apartment and rushed off to check on a unit at Lake Shore. Dean called his brother over to jump-start his old jalopy and chugged his way over to drop it off at his house before hitching a ride back with him to visit the used car lots. After a great deal of arguing and tire kicking, they agreed on a two-year-old silver-blue Mustang with low mileage. With several hundred dollars left over from his allotted budget, Dean splurged on dinner fixings and had the grill fired up when Lisa returned.

She opened the wine while he put on the steaks. "I found the most beautiful apartment! They'll connect the utilities tomorrow. Mother and I spent the rest of the afternoon furniture shopping. I'm so excited! She even bought me a gorgeous sofa set as a house-warming gift."

Dean turned the steaks glumly. "I take it you two have made up from your little tiff?"

"She's still skeptical about me getting involved with you again, and more than a little concerned about this private detective business, but basically proud of the fact we proved Sharon Lucas innocent. I like the car you bought."

"I practically stole it."

They ate and then cleaned the kitchen together. Dean showered and slid into bed as Lisa took her turn in the bathroom. She came out wearing her slinky black thing and slipped into bed beside him.

He stiffened as she curled into his arms. "What gives?"

"Would you prefer I sleep on the sofa?"

"I thought you were in an all-fired hurry to get away from me?"

"Are you sure it's just my art you're going to miss?"

"Is that a trick question?"

Her lips brushed his "You're *such* a coward. Why can't you admit you want me to stay?"

Lust surged through him as her hungry, sensuous lips devoured his, sending tingling currents of desire sweeping through him in delicious ripples. She moaned as he parted her nightgown, taking first one and then the other of her taut breasts in his lips. "Okay, damn it, I admit I want you to stay."

"Um, that's better," she whispered. "I've got a new proposal for you."

"Save it for later," he urged as he peeled her top off. "Are you sure about this?"

She arched into him, shivering with pleasure. "If you stop now I'll kill you!"

A heavy banging shook the front door. "Mr. Davis? This is the police! Open up, please!"

"What the hell!" Dean cursed as he untangled himself from Lisa and pulled on his trousers. "What now, damn it?"

"Get rid of them quick!" she urged.

He pulled a t-shirt over his head and hurried to the front door, where he found a deputy standing on the porch.

"Sorry to disturb you, Mr. Davis, but Sheriff Parsons dispatched me over here because your phone seems to be out of order. He would like to see you at Miss Lucas' place on the double."

"What the hell for?"

"She's dead, Sir."

✫ ✫ ✫

Lisa and Dean dressed in a state of shock and drove to the Belmont Apartments in the Mustang, where two police cruisers and an ambulance sat in front of apartment 220 with their lights flashing. Deputy Miller greeted them and escorted them to the apartment door, where Sheriff Parsons waited.

"What happened?" Dean asked.

"Your client got herself killed about an hour ago," Sheriff Parsons replied gruffly. "What do you know about it?"

Dean fought the swelling nausea. "I don't know a damned thing about it!"

Sheriff Parsons led them inside to the blanket-covered figure lying on the floor and pulled back the edge to reveal Sharon's wide-set open eyes staring upward above a flimsy blue nightgown covering her immobile form. The frozen expression on her face indicated surprise, even in her semi-glazed, unseeing state. A single thin line of congealed blood drifted down the left side of her scalp from a small hole left of center in her forehead.

"Shot at close range," Sheriff Parsons stated as Lisa gasped and turned away. "I need the coroner's confirmation, but it looks like a small caliber pistol, maybe a 9 millimeter. It appears she opened her door, someone popped her between the eyes, and she collapsed back into her apartment. A neighbor noticed her front door open, saw her lying on the floor, and called an ambulance and us. What do you make of it?"

Dean's insides turned to jelly as he stared down at what had once been the love of his life. He turned to look out into the parking lot with all the vehicles and flashing lights, unable to look at Sharon's corpse, as he forced his constricted throat to work.

"Damned if I know."

Sheriff Parsons stared hard at him for a moment and then seemed satisfied. "Give it some thought, Davis, and get back to me if you come up with anything useful." He nodded at Deputy Miller, who ushered them out of the apartment.

Dean stood in the center of the parking lot looking around at all of the people standing on their porches in their nightgowns and robes, noting that Carlson Jenkins' window was black and all of the lights were out in his apartment. His heart beat a slow, heavy pace as his mind flashed alternate images of the living, vivacious Sharon he had known against the strange, comatose mannequin lying under the blanket behind him.

Lisa held out her hand, her heart aching for the grief etched across his grim face. "Give me the keys, Dean."

Wordlessly, he fished the keys from his pocket and handed them to her.

✠ ✠ ✠

Lisa opened the door to the apartment and led him inside. "Are you okay, Dean?"

He sank down in the easy chair in disbelief. "Who would want to kill Sharon?"

"Do you want me to take the sofa tonight?" she asked hesitantly, sensing his desire to be alone in his current state of distress.

"Go on to bed. I'll be fine in here."

She slipped away and returned with sheets and a pillow, paused for a lingering moment wanting to comfort him before deciding that would be the wrong gesture in his present frame of mind, and then turned to the bedroom shamefully aware that she was still jealous of his feelings for Sharon, even in death.

When she disappeared down the hall, Dean turned off the lights and settled into the obscurity of the protective darkness welcoming the flood of memories he and Sharon had shared as the pain of her loss cut through him like a knife. In the tinges of early morning light he crept over to the couch and collapsed, physically and mentally exhausted.

☆ ☆ ☆

Dean awoke to a banging on the door, sat up in befuddled confusion still out of sorts from heavy sleep, and stumbled to the door to find a deputy there.

"Mr. Davis? I'm Officer Kelly. I need you to accompany me to meet Sheriff Parsons."

"What time is it?"

The deputy looked at his wristwatch. "It's a little after three in the afternoon, Sir. I tried to call before I came by, but your phone isn't working."

"What does the sheriff want to see me about?"

"There's been another murder."

Dean's pulse raced as he looked beyond him to Lisa's Volkswagen missing from the drive. "Who?"

"Mr. Carl Jenkins, Sir. A woodsman discovered his body around noon today on the outskirts of town. The sheriff would like me to bring you to the crime scene pronto."

"Give me a minute to get dressed!" He stumbled into the bedroom, pulled a shirt from the closet, slipped on some socks and shoes, and rushed back to the living room without bothering to shower or shave, where he saw a note on the kitchen table.

"*Dean,*

Mother and I are getting my new home sorted out. See you later this afternoon.

Lisa"

He scribbled his own note on the bottom of hers informing her he was going to see the sheriff and slid into the front seat with the deputy, who sped away with his lights flashing. On the outskirts of town, the deputy turned off the main highway onto a paved secondary road and traveled a short distance before turning onto a gravel road. A hundred yards along, he parked behind several police cars with a group of deputies and medical personnel clustered near a blue Chevrolet surrounded by yellow crime tape, where Sheriff Parsons stood talking to someone in a white lab coat. Dean hurried over to him as the deputy dogged his heels.

"What's going on, Sheriff?"

Sheriff Parsons turned to him. "You tell me, Davis! I haven't had a real murder in this town in the last twenty years. In the last week I've got more damned dead bodies lying around than I can deal with and all of them seem to be connected to *you* in some fashion or another."

"Can I have a look at the crime scene?"

"You know the procedure—don't touch anything."

"What have you got so far?" Dean eased forward to look into the back of the Chevrolet, where the left rear door stood open. Carlson Jenkins' body lay sprawled in the back face down in the far corner of the floorboard, wedged between the front seat and the bottom of the right rear door, dressed in a pair of white boxer drawers and a white undershirt smeared with congealed blood. His feet were clad in a pair of blue nylon stretch socks. The side window in the right door was shattered and a tuft of upholstery punched out from the side panel below the window. "Was this door open when he was found?"

"Nothing has been disturbed, Davis. A logger saw the car and got close enough to see the body. Coroner estimates the time of death at between midnight and two this morning."

"That's about three hours after Sharon was killed," Dean mused. "Do you know what kind of weapon was used?"

"We won't know for sure until after the autopsy, but it appears to be a small caliber much like the one that killed the Lucas girl earlier last night. That turned out to be a nine millimeter. We've recovered one of the slugs from the panel on the door after it went through the body and lodged there. The body has three holes in it, one in the left arm, two in the chest. One of the chest wounds exited his back and possibly went through the side window. We've searched the area without turning up anything other than one footprint near the rear door here." He indicated an area marked off with white tape and a red flag. "It appears to be a woman's. Lab's confirming the size for us now."

"Any fingerprints?"

"Plenty, but mostly smeared."

"Was he robbed?"

"His wallet contained seventy dollars and his wedding band and watch are still on him."

Dean stepped back. "It looks like our fine Christian man here met someone for a secret sexual tryst and got blasted in the midst of their passionate embrace."

"That's the way I read it, but who did he meet, and is this tied in to the Felton, Mize, and Lucas murders?"

"You get paid the big bucks to figure that one out, Sheriff."

"Is there anything you're not telling me, Davis?"

Dean looked him in the eye. "Sheriff, I don't have a clue. None of this makes any more sense to me than it does to you."

"Do you think the sex tapes fit into this somehow?"

"Possibly. I assume you searched Mize's place for them after he was killed?"

"Not a trace of them anywhere."

"Four murders in seven days," Dean speculated. "Whatever you're dealing with here is getting stranger by the day, Sheriff."

"No shit. And you've been no goddamned help at all."

"If I had anything to help, I'd gladly pass it along."

"Kelly, take this jackass on back home. All he's doing is cluttering up my mind."

Dean turned to the patrol car. "Glad to be of service, Sheriff."

Chapter 19

When the deputy pulled into the drive behind Lisa's Volkswagen, Dean climbed out and made his way up onto the porch as she rushed to open the door.

"Your note said the sheriff wanted to see you?"

He made his way past her to the refrigerator and opened a beer. "Somebody killed Carlson Jenkins last night."

"*What?*"

"Shot him in the backseat of his car on the outskirts of town. It looks like he was in the middle of a secret sexual rendezvous with an unknown female."

"Why do you say that?"

"His pants were pulled down."

"Are you serious?"

"As serious as the itch on a flea-bitten dog with a bad case of mange."

"What's going on around here? This is getting scary!"

"Sheriff Parsons says there hasn't been a real murder in this town in over twenty years and the four he's dealing with now all revolve around me somehow."

"That's absurd!"

"He's grasping at straws, but I can't say I blame him. So how did things go with you today?"

She suppressed her excitement, relieved he seemed to be his old self and not still grieving over Sharon. "I'm exhausted after spending the whole day with mother and a team of movers getting the furniture in and everything set up. If you'll help me load my things in the car, I'll show you around."

Dean looked around his shabby apartment. "Are you sure you want to give all this up?"

"Take these boxes out before I get all melancholy," she advised dryly.

They loaded her car and he followed her out to the Lake Shore apartments in his Mustang to unit 20, a corner high-rise with a broad view of the vast lake shimmering in a blue reflective haze in the background. She opened the door and led him into a foyer covered in dark gray slate decorated with a yellow wall table holding a vase of fresh cut yellow roses under a yellow-framed mirror. He followed her into the living room covered with light blue carpeting and paused before a dark oak entertainment center standing against the wall holding a television and a stereo, complete with albums stacked neatly on the bottom ledge and various knickknacks scattered about on the remaining shelves. He turned to appraise the blue couch and matching blue and white striped easy chair facing the entertainment center with matching end tables and a small reading lamp beside the easy chair. One end table held the telephone and a new message recorder. The other held a vase with fresh cut flowers.

"Nice," he allowed.

"I haven't had a chance to hang anything yet," she apologized for the bare walls as she pushed him into the neatly organized kitchen, complete with a new set of stainless steel pots and other various hanging utensils, with attractive dinnerware decorating the shelves. A petite stained glass dinette table occupied the tiny breakfast nook overlooking a small cement patio with a view of the lake. He followed her upstairs to a small, empty front bedroom with a large window overlooking the lake.

"A two bedroom," he observed. "Aren't they more expensive?"

"This one had the view," she explained, watching him fretfully as she gathered her courage to make her pitch. "It's only a few dollars a month more and I thought we might make it into our office if we're, you know, still going to work together."

"We don't have anything to work together on," he replied as she led him down the short hall into the master bedroom, "and this line of business calls for field work, not sitting behind a desk." He paused to survey her bedroom, vaguely recalling her king-sized bed with the white headboard from their high school days, now covered with a new gold and brown spread with matching throw pillows in place of the former pink and white ruffles with the ménage of stuffed animals. The painting of the fuzzy nude hung on the wall above it. An ornate telephone sat on one of the matching white end tables and a clock radio perched on the other. Her large white dresser with the huge mirror stood at the foot of the bed. He edged out onto the small balcony decorated with two wrought iron chairs and a small table absorbing the unrestricted view of the lake.

Lisa lingered behind him. "You don't like it, do you? Is it the colors?"

"The colors are fine."

"What then?"

"I'm not accustomed to things being so … *nice*. It sort of unnerves me."

"Mother helped pick everything out. It all feels strange to me, too."

"I'm sure it'll feel like home to you in no time."

"I really wanted you to feel comfortable here," she said glumly. "I was hoping if you liked it you might consider—"

"I know something that might help break this place in," he suggested, throwing caution to the wind and taking her in his arms, fearing he was losing her now that she had elected to move out of his apartment. "Let's pick up where we left off last night," he whispered, kissing her ardently as he edged her back into the bedroom.

She shivered as he nibbled her ear and pressed against him, her pulse racing wildly with anticipation and the heady realization that his actions were signaling his willingness to keep her in his life now that they had solved their case.

"They've finally got the phone hooked up," she mouthed against his lips as the phone on the nightstand rang. "I'll get it."

"That's what you've got a recorder for," he argued as he drew the zipper down at the back of her dress and allowed it to peel from her shoulders and slip to the floor.

She pulled his shirt up over his head as he kicked off his shoes. He unbuckled his pants, stepped out of them, pushed her back onto the bed, and buried his lips in her throat as the recorder downstairs kicked on and her distant voice reached them.

> "*This is the D and B Detective agency. We are unable to take your call at present. Please leave your name, number, and a detailed message at the tone and we will get back to you as soon as possible. Thank you for calling.*"

"Neat," he whispered as he unsnapped her bra and tossed it aside, freeing her firm breasts in explosive eagerness. "Now you won't miss any important calls while you're doing more important things."

She sought his lips, squirming in anticipation as he hooked her panties with a thumb and drew them down.

"Lisa, honey, thank goodness you're not there yet. I'm at the pay-phone at the entrance and wanted to warn you Daddy and I'll be dropping by in a few minutes."

Lisa stiffened and shoved him back so hard he rolled off the bed and hit the floor with a resounding thud.

"Daddy insists on seeing your new home, so I thought it best to show him around before you get Dean moved in. I don't think it would be a good idea for him to know about that part just yet since he'll definitely need some time to adjust to the thought of you two sharing an apartment together. I'll just zip him in and out to avoid any nasty little scenes. Love you, darling!"

Dean stared up at her dumbfounded from where he sat on the floor. "Before you get me moved in?"

Lisa jumped up and grabbed for her dress beside him. "Quick, get your clothes on! Daddy will go ape if he finds you here!"

"Where the hell does he think you've been for the last week?"

"Staying with one of my girlfriends! He still thinks I'm his innocent little girl!"

Dean drew his pants on and buckled them. "Well, he's sure as hell not that far off the mark the way things have been going with us lately!"

"Was that a car pulling up out front? Quick, hide in the closet!"

"The *closet?*" he demanded, reaching for his shirt. "If he opens the door we'll *both* have a heart attack!"

"Hide in—no, wait—let me think—this is silly! Of course you have every right to be here if this is going to be your home too!"

"When were you going to spring *that* on me?"

"Mother and I discussed it yesterday, but we don't have time to get into all that now."

"It would've been nice if you had included *me* in the discussion!"

"I was going to talk to you about it last night, Dean, but after Sharon's murder it seemed inappropriate to bring it up. I thought we could cut down on expenses by still being roommates."

"And your mother agreed to that?"

"Let's just calm down and act natural."

He pulled on his shirt. "What's natural? There hasn't been anything *natural* about us since high school!"

"Well *fake* it then, Dean!" She spun around with her back to him. "Zip my dress! Hurry!"

"Don't you want to put your bra back on first?"

"Oh, god, where is it?"

"On the other side of the bed, I think."

She dove across the bed, snatched her bra, bounded back up, dropped the front of her dress, slipped on her bra, and fastened it. "How do I look?"

He snickered. "Like you just got caught in the act."

"Where's my hair brush? Is my mascara smeared? They're at the front door!"

"Calm down," he soothed as he kissed the back of her neck and zipped up her dress. "I'll jump off the balcony."

"No! You might break a leg or something!"

"I'd prefer that to hiding in a closet."

"Daddy's just going to have to accept that I'm a woman now. You go down and stall them while I put myself back together."

"Stall them *how?*"

"Offer them a glass of wine or something, just buy me some time!"

"I need something a lot stronger than wine—do you even *have* any?"

"In the cabinet to the right of the stove!" She pushed him to the door. "I only need a minute!"

"Lisa, dear? Are you home? I saw you car outside——" Mrs. Bryant froze in horror as Dean came bounding down the stairs.

Belatedly, it occurred to Dean he was barefoot with his shirttail hanging out when Mr. Bryant, standing just behind Mrs. Bryant, scowled and turned red while deliberately sizing him up in his disheveled state.

"Why, Dean! I didn't expect you to be here!" Mrs. Bryant gasped.

I didn't expect you to be here either, Dean thought dolefully. "Mr. and Mrs. Bryant! It's good to see you again. Lisa will be down in a minute. Um, err, would you like a glass of wine?" He hurried to the kitchen, opened the cabinet, grabbed the first bottle of wine he saw, and searched the drawers for a corkscrew.

"It's in the drawer to the left of the sink, dear," Mrs. Bryant trilled from behind him as she wrung her hands.

"Do you know where the glasses are?" he asked. "I'm still a little disoriented around here."

Mr. Bryant drew himself up indignantly. "*Clearly* we *both* are!"

Mrs. Bryant grabbed the bottle from Dean's hands. "Here, dear, let me do that! Just get the glasses, if you will. They're in the cabinet to the left of the stove."

Mr. Bryant locked eyes with Dean in a significant manner before stepping aside in order for him to reach the cabinet.

"I called earlier ... we didn't expect anyone to be home," Mrs. Bryant explained in a nervous twitter as she jabbed at the jug with the corkscrew. "James wanted to see where Lisa was going to be living so I thought we'd just pop in and—oh, dear, it seems I've pushed the cork into the bottle!"

"What the hell's going on here, Mildred?" Mr. Bryant demanded as his wife squinted anxiously down the neck of the bottle.

Her hands shook as she poured the wine, splattering droplets onto the counter around the glasses Dean set out. "I hope James and I aren't intruding, Mr. Davis?"

"Uh, no, uh, not at all, I'm just helping Lisa, um, get settled in."

Mr. Bryant's complexion changed to a dark purple as his eyes dropped deliberately to Dean's bare feet. "*Evidently!*"

Mrs. Bryant thrust glasses at them. "Well! Here's to uh—to uh ..."

They stood frozen in suspense with their glasses half extended towards each other for an awkward moment before Lisa swept into the kitchen to rescue them.

"Mother! Daddy! What a pleasant surprise! Welcome to our home!" she gushed as she kissed her father on the cheek and hugged her mother.

Mr. Bryant set his glass firmly on the counter. "*Our* home? Will somebody please tell me what the *hell* is going on here?"

Me too, Dean echoed mutely.

Mrs. Bryant thrust a glass at Lisa. "We're making a little toast, dear! Let me pour you a glass so you can join us!"

Lisa lifted her glass to them. "To our new home!"

The three of them took a sip as Mr. Bryant glared at Dean. "I'm not much of a wine drinker," he allowed, his tone something less than cordial. "Young man, let's you and I go somewhere private and have a *man's* drink!"

Mrs. Bryant paled. "But, James, we're expected at the Masterson's for—"

"They can wait! Dean and I need to talk! In fact, cancel the damned dinner engagement altogether, this might take awhile!"

Lisa clanked her glass down next to his on the counter. "*Daddy!*"

Dean turned to the door. "Give me a minute to get my shoes, Sir."

Lisa jerked at Dean's arm. "You two *will not* leave this house together!"

"You stay out of this," Mr. Bryant thundered. "This is *man's* business!"

"Man's business, my foot!" Lisa wailed. "For your information, I'm a grown woman now and I *will* be included in any discussions that concern me, and Mother will be included as well. Now everybody sit down so we can talk about this like adults!"

Lisa and her father glared at each other as Mrs. Bryant and Dean edged over to the table. Mr. Bryant stormed over and sat down across from Dean, who didn't have to make eye contact with him to read the hostility simmering there. Lisa sat down facing her mother, her own expression fierce. Her mother settled into her chair flushed with consternation. Dean sank down with butterflies swirling in his stomach and took a nervous sip of his wine.

Mr. Bryant eyed Dean's wine glass with disdain. "Do you have anything stronger than *that* around here?"

Lisa hurried to the refrigerator, grabbed a beer, and sat the can in front of him. "That's the best I can do on short notice."

Mr. Bryant scowled, popped the top on the can, took a long draw, and wiped his lips with the back of his hand as he glared at Dean. "Now tell me what this is all about, young man!"

Lisa sank down in her chair. "He doesn't have to answer to you, Daddy."

He turned to her. "Then *you* tell me what the hell this means, young lady! I'll *not* have my only daughter—"

"It's not *your* decision to make, James," Mrs. Bryant scolded. "She's been living on her own since she went off to college and is quite capable of making her own decisions now."

Dean sipped his wine and settled back to enjoy the show, thinking the poor man didn't have a snowball's chance in hell against these two tyrants, but was instantly dismayed when Mr. Bryant displayed some semblance of common sense by dodging their crossfire to refocus on him again.

"You hurt my daughter once before back in high school, young man! What makes you think you have the right to waltz back into her life again after all these years?"

Dean set his glass on the table carefully. "I probably don't have the right—"

Lisa leaned forward angrily. "Dean and I are partners now, Daddy!"

"*Partners*? In what way?"

"The D and B Detective Agency."

"The *wh*—are you *insane*? That has no viable, realistic future! I didn't send you to college to squander your life away looking through other people's bedroom windows or to live with a deadbeat out of wedlock!"

"You sent me to college to get an education so I could make informed decisions in my life! I've made the decision to become partners with Dean! I demand you apologize for calling him a deadbeat!"

"What the hell are you going to do if this foolishness doesn't work out?"

"If it doesn't work out, then I'll be the wiser for it!"

Mr. Bryant turned to his wife. "How long have you known about this, Mildred?"

Mrs. Bryant sank back, flustered. "Lisa and I have had several discussions about her and Dean's relationship—"

"Why didn't you discuss this with me before it got out of hand?"

She drew herself up. "Mother and daughter discussions are private and I'll not break her confidences unnecessarily."

"Are you saying you *agree* with what she's doing with her life now?"

"I don't necessarily agree with what she's doing, and I've made my reservations clear to her, but I do support her right to make her own decisions in this matter."

Mr. Bryant turned back to Lisa. "So you're willing to shame yourself by living out of wedlock with this man? I thought you had more pride in yourself than this."

"This is a different generation, Daddy. People today don't live by the same code of ethics and values you and mother grew up with!"

"This is a small town! People still notice these things. They talk and gossip!"

"Most people honestly don't care, and the ones that do are going to talk and gossip anyway. I'm sorry, Daddy, I wish I could be your perfect little girl, but I can't pretend to be something I'm not. I can only pray for your understanding and forgiveness for being who I am."

Mr. Bryant reached for her hand. "Do you love this man?"

"Yes, I do, Daddy," she whispered tearfully. "I've always loved him."

His eyes narrowed. "Do you love him enough to go against my wishes in this matter?"

She drew a deep, shuddering breath. "The only two men I've ever loved in my whole life are at this table with me right now. I won't be forced to choose one over the other, or have my love for one conflict with my love for the other."

Mr. Bryant held her stare for a long minute before turning to Dean. "Do you love my daughter?"

Dean's heart hammered. "I—"

"Do you *truly* love her?"

His throat tightened. "I—"

"Because if you *do*, you won't allow her to demean herself this way! Look me in the eye and tell me you're willing to allow her to destroy her life and her reputation!"

Spots swam before Dean's eyes—the old coot was going for the jugular. "I—"

Lisa stood, trembling with fury. "That's enough, Daddy! Our feelings for each other are a matter between the two of us! I will not have him discussing such with you!"

Mr. Bryant sank back in his chair. "Can I have another beer?"

Dean went to the refrigerator and got them both one. They popped the tops on their cans as they met each other's eyes across the table and tilted their heads back to drink.

Mr. Bryant lowered his can. "I knew your father before he passed away, Dean. He was a fine man, a fine, hard working, honest man. I hope he raised you with those same traits. Now, you listen to me closely—you take good care of my little girl or you'll have me to contend with, and I promise you it'll be a lot worse than those bruises on your face if it comes to such! Is that clear?"

Dean nodded. "Err, yes sir, very clear."

Mr. Bryant finished his beer in a long draw, slammed the can down on the table, and stood abruptly. "Let's go, Mildred. We'll be late for dinner with the Masterson's." He leaned down to kiss Lisa on the forehead. "If things don't turn out like you expect, darling, you know where home is." He walked out of the kitchen as Mrs. Bryant hugged Lisa and hurried after him.

When the front door closed, Dean expelled his pent-up breath. "*Now* do you want to clue *me* in on what the hell's going on around here?"

"Do you want to share an apartment with me or not?"

"It's got its merits, but I think we need to establish a few guidelines and reach an understanding about things before—"

She jumped up. "Don't you *dare* start trying to negotiate terms! You can just go on back to that dank cave you live in and rot there for all I care!" She ran up the stairs and slammed the bedroom door, her nerves ragged as the tears flowed in torrents.

Dean broke in her new couch that night, but only after he knocked on the locked bedroom door and received no reply from within other than racking sobs before eventually slipping back downstairs and into a troubled sleep thinking his old lumpy couch was a lot more comfortable than her new-fangled one and that women were a strange breed indeed.

Chapter 20

Dean awoke with a sore neck and stiff back, limped into the kitchen where Lisa was clattering around, glanced at her as he poured a cup of coffee, and eased into a chair at the dinette table.

"Good morning," she greeted without looking at him as she worked at the counter.

"Is it?" he challenged.

"You must be starved since we didn't get around to eating last night." She turned to face him. "Okay, no games, you're angry, right?"

"It's more along the lines of highly aggravated," he affirmed.

She turned back to place bacon in a pan.

"Lisa, I'm not one to spar around. In the future, I propose we agree to never storm off during a disagreement."

Her shoulders slumped. "I'm sorry ... I just needed to collect my thoughts after that awkward scene with my father."

"That was definitely a challenging event."

"I'll make it up to you somehow."

"Three eggs and about half a pound of bacon will be a good start."

"I'll even throw in some biscuits." She bit her bottom lip. "Dean, I know you haven't asked for any of this." She sat down across from him. "I did some serious thinking last night. I admit I came back here a week ago because I thought I was still in love with you."

"Lisa, please—"

"No, Dean, please hear me out. It's important I say this. Yesterday, before my parents showed up, I was dizzy with desire for you, and then after they arrived, shamefully grateful to you for enduring that scene and not exposing me for a fool in front of them. I see things in an entirely different light this morning. I've always known I couldn't love another because I loved you, and I felt inadequate because you didn't love me back. Being around you for the last week, I came to realize you couldn't love me, or anyone else, because you were still in love with Sharon. That insight makes me happier than I've been in years. It gives me back my confidence in myself and restores my pride. Because of that, I've come to genuinely like you now when I've never really liked you before, even when I thought I was in love with you. I've come to appreciate you for the rogue you are. I enjoy being a detective and partners with you. I'm terrified of putting our professional relationship at risk by entering into a physical relationship with you again. I'm so confused!" She wiped at a stray tear trickling down her cheek with the back of her hand and lowered her head.

Dean tipped her chin up as a surge of humility worked through him. "Lisa, I'm not sure how I feel about things either. I'm not as good at expressing myself as you are, but I do know in the last few days I've come to, well, to *enjoy* having you around. I'm not sure what that means, or where it's leading, but I see you in a different light now than I did before as well."

She smiled. "So where do we go from here?"

He pulled her up, turned her to the stove, and shoved. "Damned if I know, but I *do* know you're burning my bacon."

"Jackass!" She forked strips of bacon from the frying pan. "What do the last two nights mean to you, Dean?"

"You mean us almost making love? They mean I want you. Hell, I'm practically panting with lust. But I also know you deserve more than that and I don't want to take advantage of you."

"So *now* you don't want to advantage of me?"

"That's part of it. Another is this investigative business doesn't offer much of a realistic future, as your father pointed out. I've only had one lousy case, which we solved by accident, and I'm practically broke again already. I honestly don't know what my future holds."

"Don't you think that's all the more reason to pool our resources?"

"I haven't ruled that out, I'd just like for us to be a little cautious and make sure we understand each other's expectations. You're more important to me now than you were back then, and I don't want to hurt you again."

She turned to him. "I think you're afraid you'll end up in a creek again."

He grinned. "With you, that's always a distinct possibility, but realistically, if this detective thing doesn't work out, I'll probably go after that undercover job in Houston."

She set their plates on the table and sat down across from him. "So you think it would be a mistake for us to move in together?"

"I think it's something we should think through very carefully," he replied.

She nodded, hiding her disappointment. "Okay, let's take things one day at a time, but I want you to acknowledge something, Dean. Getting to know you as you really are, instead of harboring some silly little girl notion of who I thought you were has made me stronger than I was a week ago. I don't want you to be afraid of hurting me or being overly concerned about taking advantage of me. I'm a big girl now who can take care of herself and I want you to trust that."

"Done deal," he agreed. "Now, moving on to less troubling waters, I'd like to go to Sharon's viewing today and her funeral tomorrow."

"Then you need something decent to wear. It wouldn't hurt you to get a whole new wardrobe. I'll send a funeral wreath in our company name and we can go shopping."

He picked up his fork. "Works for me."

She hesitated. "There's one other thing. I had your telephone number transferred here. I'll have it changed back to your place today."

He grinned. "Hell, just leave it as it is until we figure out what we're going to do—at least you've got a damned recorder!"

"Thanks for not yelling at me."

"Would it do any good?"

She grinned slyly. "Not really."

He was less than enthused with the results of their shopping spree, and felt something akin to a used car salesman when all was said and done, but Lisa was delighted with the outcome. Of the three outfits she selected, she dressed him in a navy blue jacket, a light blue shirt, tan pants, black loafers, and a blue and tan striped tie to wear to the funeral home.

When they wheeled into the parking lot a black limousine pulled up to the entrance ahead of them and deposited Mrs. Peters and Charlene, both dressed in black.

"Mrs. Peters and the wicked little sister have arrived," Dean observed as the funeral director escorted them inside.

"Please, Dean, show a little respect!" Lisa chastised. "We're here for Sharon."

"Okay, let's go get this over with," he allowed. "But for the record, I hate funerals, especially for people who've been murdered."

"Have you given any thought as to who may have killed Sharon?"

"Nothing makes sense. From the crime statistics, over ninety percent of homicides are committed by perpetrators who know their victims." He opened the door for her. "So I'm thinking along the lines of who knew all four of the victims rather than just focusing on Sharon."

Inside they joined a slow moving, subdued group of people in the viewing room surrounded by flowers and funeral wreaths. Mrs. Peters sat in a high-backed velvet chair and Charlene stood beside her near the pearl gray casket where Sharon reposed. Lisa and he fell into the line of people waiting to offer their condolences as low organ music piped out of hidden speakers in the background and shuffled forward until they stood before them.

Mrs. Peters clutched his hand. "Dean! I can't believe my baby is gone."

"Mrs. Peters, you have my deepest sympathy."

Mrs. Peters patted his hand. "She always loved you, Dean. She meant to thank you personally for clearing her name before——" She dropped his hand and snatched a lace handkerchief up to dab at her eyes.

Charlene smiled and held out her hand. "Dean, thank you for coming."

He took her outstretched hand and was surprised to feel a scrap of paper pressed into his palm. "You have my deepest sympathy for your loss."

Her hand clung to his for a tenuous moment as he attempted to extract it, and then he palmed the piece of paper as she turned to Lisa with an icy stare.

"Lisa, thank you for coming."

"I'm sure you know how special Sharon was to us all," Lisa replied graciously.

"Yes, wasn't she?" Charlene replied before deliberately looking beyond her. "Mrs. Powell, so nice of you to come!"

Lisa and Dean reluctantly made their way to the casket to view Sharon, still radiant in an artificial way as she lay against the pure white silk lining of her coffin, her expression calm compared to the surprised, vacant look she had worn on the floor of her apartment. Dean was grateful no blemish marked her forehead where the bullet had penetrated her skull as a rush of deep sadness worked through him, making him think again of what could have been.

Lisa steered him to the far side of the room out of the main flow of traffic and leaned in close. "What did the Ice Queen pass to you?"

He inclined his head to her and lowered his voice. "You're pretty observant. I'm impressed."

"She's just blatantly obvious. Did you see how she brushed me off? What have I ever done to her?"

"She's always been weird," he allowed.

"Read her note. I'm just *full* of curiosity."

"It's *my* note."

"Do you want me to punch your sore ribs right here in front of all of these people?"

"Okay, I'll share." He opened the note and peered down at it as Lisa crowded against him.

"*Dean, please call me after the funeral.*"

She stiffened. "She just won't give up!"

"Well, frankly, since I can't seem to get to first base with *you* and she's all grown up and filled out now—"

Her eyes narrowed. "This is *not* the time or place to play your *sick* little *mind-games* with me, Dean!"

"*Ouch!*" he whined as she clasped his elbow and steered him to the door.

☆ ☆ ☆

They elected to dine at the fish house after the viewing and sat before the large window overlooking the lake enjoying the magnificent scene as the sun set in a golden hue.

"So who knows Kenny, Sharon, Ray Mize, and Carlson Jenkins?" Lisa asked as the dying rays of the evening light lit her face in a warm glow, sparking her eyes into deep, enticing pools of cobalt blue.

Dean stared at her fretfully, conscious that at this precise moment he wanted her more than he'd ever wanted any woman—including Sharon. "Carlson Jenkins seems to be the odd man out in the equation. The other three pretty much ran in the same circles."

She tilted her head. "Why are you looking at me like that?"

"Like what?"

"Weird."

"Did I ever mention you've got the bluest eyes in the whole-wide world?"

"Is that a come on?"

"You're kind of slow on the uptake, aren't you? Of course it's a come on."

She glared at him. "Quit playing games with me."

"I'm not playing games. I'm seriously coming on to you."

"Are we going to talk about this case or not?"

"We don't have a case, remember? We've already done our job and been well paid for it. The rest is up to our pal the sheriff."

"It's our civic duty to provide any evidence we come up with to his department," she insisted.

"We don't have any evidence, just speculation. It's sort of like me speculating on whether you're wearing panties or just pantyhose."

"You're making me mad."

"Why am I making you mad?'

"I don't appreciate being teased about my undergarments over dinner."

"Can I tease you about them over dessert?"

"Stop it!"

"You're no fun."

"You're crude."

He sighed. "Okay, if you insist, I'm betting Becky Roberts killed Ray Mize because he was blackmailing her for sexual favors with Kenny-boy's home movies."

"So how do we prove it?"

"We don't."

"Why not?"

"No one has hired us to prove it. We don't wear badges, and in case you've forgotten, the High Sheriff doesn't like us mucking around in his business."

"I don't like you very much sometimes."

"You admitted just this morning you *genuinely* like me now."

"I take it back."

"Would you like a bottle of white wine?"

"Are you attempting to ply me with alcohol?"

He leered. "Whatever it takes."

"Dean, Lisa, what a pleasant surprise," Mrs. Bryant interrupted as she and Mr. Bryant paused at their table.

Dean stood and offered his hand. "Mr. Bryant, Ma'am."

"Perhaps we could join you?" Mr. Bryant proposed as Lisa and Mrs. Bryant exchanged panicked glances.

"Please do," Dean responded smoothly. "We were just ordering a bottle of wine. Not being a connoisseur myself, perhaps you could make a suitable suggestion?"

Mr. Bryant smiled as he seated Mrs. Bryant. "Whatever you and the women prefer. As I said last night, I'm not much of a wine drinker. I'll just stick to my Scotch, if you don't mind."

"In that case, I'll have beer myself and the ladies can pick the wine," Dean said as he and Mr. Bryant seated themselves across from each other.

Mr. Bryant looked him in the eye. "I hope there's no lingering animosity over our, err, little talk last night, Dean? I was hasty in my choice of words when I called you a deadbeat."

"None at all, Sir. I have the same concerns you do, and I've been called a lot worse."

"And *that's* all we're going to say on *that* matter," Lisa injected.

"I most *certainly* agree," Mrs. Bryant added.

Mr. Bryant grinned in wry amusement. "I believe the women are laying out our parameters for dinner conversation, Dean. So, are you a sportsman, by chance?"

"I don't hunt or fish, Sir."

"Me either, so at least we have that much in common. Do you golf?"

"Poorly, but with passion."

"Maybe we can get together at the club one weekend."

The waitress appeared to fill their dinner orders. When she hustled back with the drinks, Mr. Bryant lifted his Scotch to them.

"To you and Lisa's, uh, successful venture in your, uh, new undertaking!"

They touched glasses and drank.

Mrs. Bryant leaned over and placed her hand on his arm. "Dean, doesn't this investigation thing often carry an element of danger to it?"

He hesitated as Lisa flashed him a warning look. "If you're referring to my facial features, Ma'am, it can carry a bit of risk at times, but for the most part, it's fairly boring work."

Lisa sizzled him with a penetrating glare. "He got his *face rear-ranged* because he engaged his *mouth* before engaging his *brain*, Mother. Dean often has a problem with that."

Mrs. Bryant paled. "I trust you will watch over Lisa as best you can, Dean?"

"You can count on that, Ma'am."

With all of the individual concerns laid to rest, they settled back to enjoy the meal and talked only about intrinsic things to insure they did not poach on hallowed ground. After a pleasant evening, they parted on amicable terms.

Lisa sank back in her seat as he pulled away from the restaurant. "Thanks, Dean."

"For what?"

"For the most part, you were very gracious and well-behaved tonight."

"You can't blame your parents for having your best interest in mind. But there's one thing that still puzzles me."

"What's that?"

"*Are* you wearing panties or just pantyhose?"

Chapter 21

Dean parked in front of Lisa's apartment, cut the engine, and followed her to the door, where she fished her key from her purse. "Did you get an extra key made for me?"

"Under our current arrangement, I think you should call first before coming by."

"I can't. You had my telephone disconnected and stole my number, remember?"

"Goodnight, Dean. Thank you for a lovely evening."

He leaned forward and brushed her lips. "What? No nightcap after I splurged on dinner and even picked up the tab for your parents?"

She stepped back from him. "Is this leading somewhere?"

"It might."

She studied him insipidly. "Where?"

"Hell, I don't know. We could give it another night together and see where it leads. I'm already sort-of kind-of getting attached to this place."

"Please don't play with my emotions, Dean."

He sighed. "Okay, then you can have the couch tonight. But I warn you, you'll find mine was a lot more comfortable."

"Then I suggest you go sleep on it."

"I was thinking more along the lines of sharing your bed."

"What would that mean in the morning?"

"That we had a wild night of joyous sex?"

She turned to the door. "Goodnight, Dean."

"Okay, you win—you can put a pillow between us. That damn bed is so big we'll never know the other is there anyway."

She turned back to him. "You want to sleep in my bed without making love to me?"

"Actually, I want to sleep in your bed *and* make love to you—I just don't want to buy an expensive diamond for the privilege."

"You're impossible."

"You should meet my partner."

She turned to the door. "The sofa is my best offer. Take it or leave it."

"*Oh, joy!*" he grumbled as she led him in.

☆ ☆ ☆

When he came out of the shower, he paused to study the lump under the sheets on the far side of the bed. "Are you asleep?"

She tossed about irritably. "How could I be with all that commotion going on in there?"

He eased over and sat on the side of the bed. "Have you changed your mind about sharing the bed?"

"Have you changed your mind about what it would mean afterwards?"

"I meant that figuratively, not literally."

She rolled over and propped up on her elbow to face him. "What are you suggesting?"

"I'm suggesting we could at least snuggle to see if we're compatible sleeping together, you know, to see if you snore or pull the covers?"

"I don't do either, thank you."

"How can I be sure?"

"Take my word for it. Besides, I don't trust you being close to me right now."

"I'll make you behave. I promise."

"Do you know how strange that sounds, Dean? I mean here we are, two adults sexually attracted to each other all alone in the same bed with the lights out, and you want to snuggle up to me but not make love to me. That's really bizarre, don't you think?"

"Just think of it as an experiment."

She flounced over with her back to him. "Go to bed, Dean."

"Here?"

"On the sofa. I left you a blanket and a pillow while you were in the shower."

"Are you saying I have to agree to move in before you're willing to sleep with me?"

"*Good night, Dean!*"

✫ ✫ ✫

He awoke early the next morning consumed with stirrings of desire, slipped out of his lumpy bed on the couch, and by the time she joined him a half hour later dressed in a white cotton robe, had the coffee going, waffles cooking, and the bacon draining. She stretched and rumpled her hair as he slid coffee in front of her.

"You look like death warmed over—didn't sleep well?"

She glared at him over the rim of her cup. "A romantic you are not—and no I did *not* sleep well, thanks to you!"

The phone rang as he forked up a waffle on a plate. "I'll get it. You eat up. Maybe you can improve on your horrid early morning disposition." He set the plate and a jug of syrup on the table and hurried into the living room to pick up the phone on the third ring.

"Hello?"

"Is this Dean Davis of the D and B Detective Agency?" a male voice inquired.

"Yes it is. How can I help you?"

"Do you want to know who killed Ray Mize?"

"Who is this?"

"Al Roberts did, that's who."

"Can we meet to——" He listened to the dial tone.

"Who was that?" Lisa mumbled when he returned to the kitchen.

"An unidentified caller who claims Al Roberts killed Ray Mize."

She sloshed her coffee in surprise. "*What?*"

"He asked me if I wanted to know who killed Ray Mize, and when I asked who he was, he said 'Al Roberts did, that's who,' and hung up on me." He slid a waffle on a plate and sat down across from her.

"Do you believe him?"

He shrugged as he poured syrup on his waffle and helped himself to the bacon. "Al could have followed Becky to the Traveler's Rest Motel when she met Mize there. He was already suspicious of her fooling around with Felton. It's feasible."

She nibbled on a strip of bacon. "But if Al was following her, why didn't we see him when we were following her? And since she gave us the slip, why not him as well?"

"Maybe he wasn't following her. Maybe he saw her car at the motel or something and put two and two together."

"How would he have known what room she was in? She didn't register, Ray Mize did."

He scowled. "Hell, you're always claiming to be the bright one, you figure it out. I'm trying to eat my breakfast here and this waffle is dry as a bone."

"What are you going to do about it?"

"Add more syrup."

"I *mean* about the anonymous caller?"

"Pass the information along to Sheriff Benny-the-Weenie, I guess. It's not my problem."

"You don't have much of a community conscience."

"I do if somebody is paying me."

☆ ☆ ☆

Sheriff Parsons drummed his fingers on his desk. "And you rushed all the way down here to tell me this, Davis?"

"I said I would keep you informed," Dean allowed expansively.

"And this anonymous fellow just up and called you out of the blue this morning?"

"That's right."

"Why did he call you instead of me?"

"I didn't get a chance to ask him."

"And that's all he said?"

"That's verbatim as he relayed it to me."

"And what time did he call again, exactly?"

"Around six-thirty—could have been six twenty-nine or six thirty-one."

"Don't be a wiseass, Davis, I tend to find it annoying."

"You said 'exactly' so I'm trying to be precise. I was a little distracted at the time."

"How so?"

"I was cooking waffles."

"Waffles?"

"And bacon. I like mine extra crispy so I really have to keep a close eye on things."

The sheriff's cold brown eyes reluctantly shifted from Lisa's treasure trove to him. "I'll look into the matter."

"I'm sure you will, Sheriff. Now if you'll excuse us, we'll be on our way."

Lisa led Dean out to the car in a huff. "I'm really beginning to dislike that guy, he doesn't appreciate anything we try to do to help him. What's his problem anyway?"

"If we do anything to help him, he figures it'll only make him look bad because he didn't think of it himself. I think I'll attend Carlson Jenkins' funeral after Sharon's this afternoon."

"Why?"

"Community conscience and all that civic duty stuff."

"Bull malarkey. What are you up to?"

"You see some strange people at funerals."

"Are you looking for suspects?"

"Damned if I know what I'm looking for, but you've about got me talked out of it with all your in-depth analyzing. Lighten up."

"Why didn't you want to go to Kenny Felton's and Ray Mize's funeral for the same reasons, whatever your reasons are to begin with?"

"I didn't figure it would do any good."

"Why not?"

"I'll tell you, but only if you'll admit I'm way out ahead of you here, as usual."

"Okay, I admit you're way ahead of me here as usual, so tell me."

"Felton's funeral was restricted to family only, and Mize is being buried somewhere up in Virginia."

"How do you know that?"

"I read it in the obituary section of the newspaper."

"Jackass."

✲ ✲ ✲

They sat in the back of the funeral home chapel behind approximately a hundred people who attended Sharon's funeral. Mrs. Peters cried throughout the moving ceremony as Charlene sat dry-eyed beside her. They then followed the hearse to the cemetery, stood by the gravesite for the final portion of the ritual, and paid their condolences again to Mrs. Peters and Charlene. Charlene took Dean's hand and squeezed it while trying to hold his eyes with her own as he deliberately focused on the second green canopy and freshly dug grave awaiting Carlson Jenkins a short distance beyond her. After completing the task, they hurried back to the funeral home for his service.

Carlson Jenkins' observance had less than ten people in attendance. Mrs. Jenkins sat alone on the front pew crying throughout as Lisa and Dean sat in the back of the nearly empty chapel.

Dean leaned near her. "I find it strange his services are being held here instead of at the church he was so devoted to."

Lisa leaned in to him. "And why are there so few people in attendance?"

Afterwards they trailed after the same hearse back to the same cemetery and gathered around the second gravesite of the day. As the minister droned on with his recital, two workers a short distance away shoveled dirt over Sharon's coffin, tugging Dean's thoughts to happier times.

Lisa nudged his arm. "So have you seen anyone who looks suspicious yet?"

He pulled his mind back to the present. "Nope, have you?"

"All I've gotten out of this whole mess is depressed. You were the one working the gut feelings." After the short prayer service, they paid their condolences to Mrs. Jenkins.

"Might I have a word with you, Mr. Davis?" Mrs. Jenkins requested as they passed.

"Certainly, Ma'am."

Lisa and he stood aside as the few mourners shuffled past, and then accompanied her back to the waiting limousine.

"Since you were successful proving Miss Lucas innocent of the Felton murder, I'd like to hire you to assist me in finding my husband's killer, Mr. Davis," she said without preamble. "Would you consider working for me in this endeavor?"

"I appreciate your confidence in me, Ma'am, but I'm sure Sheriff Parsons is conducting a thorough investigation."

"Sheriff Parsons and my husband were never on cordial terms, Mr. Davis. Beyond that, I have little confidence in his abilities to conduct a proper investigation, as demonstrated by his false arrest of the Lucas girl. It's important my husband's killer be brought to justice. It would give me a great deal of comfort knowing you were on the case."

"Our fees are one hundred dollars a day and expenses, Mrs. Jenkins," Lisa injected. "We'd be glad to assist you if we can."

"Do I need to sign a contract?" she asked.

"A small retainer is customary," Lisa replied. "Say, five hundred dollars?"

"Will you take a check?"

"That will be fine."

Mrs. Jenkins reached into her purse for her checkbook. "I assume you can start right away?"

"We can," Lisa replied. "We'll need to meet with you to establish some background information. When would that be suitable?"

"I need to pick up my car back at the chapel. Would it be convenient for you to stop by my home in half an hour?"

"We'll meet you there," Lisa acknowledged.

Dean waited for the limo to pull off before turning to Lisa. "Why the hell did you do that?"

"To heighten your community conscience," she chided smugly. "Now we're being paid to stay on the case. Wasn't that your stated criteria?"

"You should be ashamed of yourself for cheating a poor old widow woman out of her money like that."

She arched her eyebrows. "How am I cheating her?"

"This is a police matter, and they won't charge her a dime for finding Jenkins' killer."

"How much confidence do you have in that happening?"

"About as much as I have in *us* doing it!"

She rolled her eyes. "This is our *profession* now, Dean. We're *certified investigators* for hire, aren't we?"

"*Con artists* is more like it!"

☆ ☆ ☆

They spent an uncomfortable half hour drinking strong, bitter coffee at Mrs. Jenkins' dinette table, where they learned her life with her husband was modest and unassuming. They had few social friends outside of their church, where Mr. Jenkins was a deacon and taught Sunday school. When Dean tactlessly mentioned he found it odd for her to hold Mr. Jenkins' service in the funeral home chapel and that hardly any of his former flock had attended, she tearfully explained the congregation was in deep shock over the manner of his death. Dean assumed she meant with his pants down, so to speak, and that the parishioners therefore had distanced themselves from the scandal. When she wiped her nose and got herself back under control, they further learned Mr. Jenkins was a sales representative for a tractor company where he had worked for over twenty years. According to Mrs. Jenkins, he did not drink, smoke, chew tobacco, chase wild women, or use the Lord's name in vain. His sole hobby, outside of reading the Bible daily, was astronomy, and he spent practically every night when he was home locked away in his room upstairs stargazing through his telescope while she watched TV. There was no one she knew of that would want to harm him in any way, nor a man, woman, or child that he had a personal relationship with outside of their church group. They rarely dined out, never accepted invitations to parties or social gatherings outside of the church sponsored events, nor invited other couples into their home. Dean deemed they made watching goldfish in a bowl an exciting prospect as he watched her refill his coffee cup for the fourth time with some trepidation, his nerves already jangling from the excess caffeine.

"Mrs. Jenkins, could you please give us some insight into your husband's activities on the night he was murdered?" he asked.

She poured a spot of coffee into Lisa's mostly untouched cup and set the pot back on the stove. "It was a strange and confusing evening, Mr. Davis, quite out of the ordinary, actually. He came home early that afternoon and worked in his study upstairs alone. We had dinner at 5:30 sharp, as he prefers it. Afterwards he again retired to his study. At 8:30, he came down and told me he was going out for a walk to get some fresh air. He came back minutes later, which I thought odd because he normally takes longer walks. He seemed very agitated and rushed upstairs without a word. A short time later, I saw the police arrive at Miss Lucas' house. I went up and knocked on his door and he responded by telling me to stay in the house and to turn out the lights. I watched some of the activity from the front window and saw them bring her body out on a gurney covered in a sheet. I was confused and frightened by the events. I again went up to his study, where he very curtly told me to go to bed. Later, I'm positive I heard him on the phone. He came into the bedroom around 10:30, said he had to go out for a while, and for me not to wait up for him. He left and never returned."

"Is that something he regularly did?' Lisa asked. "Go out late at night?"

She shook her head. "No. I don't recall him ever doing that before."

"Did he often go for walks in the evening?"

"It was his custom to take a brisk one-hour walk several times a week."

"Did he mention why he was going out so late?" Dean asked.

"No, he just rushed out the door, but he did seem in better spirits than earlier."

"Did anyone call him here at home that evening?" Lisa asked.

"I don't recall the phone ringing at all that evening."

"Mrs. Jenkins, would you give us permission to have your phone records checked to trace any calls he may have made?" Dean asked.

She nodded. "Of course, Mr. Davis, whatever you need."

Dean waited while Lisa and Mrs. Jenkins called the telephone company, gave them the approximate time and date of calls they were interested in, and for Mrs. Jenkins to verify permission for them to receive the information on who he may have called. The phone company informed Lisa that they would contact her the following day.

When they finished, Dean stood. "Ma'am, would you mind if Miss Bryant and I looked around your husband's study?"

"It's the door at the top of the stairs. I'll put on another pot of coffee."

Mr. Jenkins' study contained a cheap desk with a clean top and a battered desk chair on rollers. A large, expensive looking telescope stood by the window on a metal tripod. A well-worn easy chair perched in the corner next to a reading lamp on a tarnished brass pole. A small bookcase filled with rows of well-thumbed books stood against the wall to the left of the desk.

Dean sat down and opened the middle drawer of the desk to find a row of neatly arranged sharpened pencils with the erasers to the right, lying front to rear in descending order of length. Beside the pencils lay four ballpoint pens, the tips facing the lead of the pencils. Three blank tablets were in the center. He took one of the pencils and lightly scrubbed the top sheet of each pad in hopes of finding indentations of names or numbers, but nothing appeared. He tore off the top sheets and tossed them in the trashcan after ensuring it was empty, and replaced the tablets in the center drawer. He opened the top drawer on the right and found a checkbook. The entries, dating back several months and showing a balance of three hundred dollars with change, appeared to consist of ordinary, mundane household bills. Envelopes and stationery were in the second drawer on the right. The top drawer on the left held a roll of stamps, a small handheld battery operated calculator, and a spare set of thick glasses. A telephone directory rested in the bottom drawer. Dean pulled each drawer out and felt underneath for anything taped to the bottom, finding nothing. He opened the phonebook and flipped through several of the pages, noting blue tick marks by some of the names in the columns.

"Go through this and make a listing of all the names and numbers with marks," he directed to Lisa as he stood up.

She sat at the desk and extracted one of the pens and a pad to make the list as he wandered over to the bookcase to look at the titles. He found at least eight Bibles of various colors and thickness, all well worn. He thumbed through each, finding many of the passages marked and cropped, but nothing suspicious caught his eye. He worked his way through thirty or forty books on astronomy. Again, many were marked and cropped with notations, but nothing held his attention. He examined a small collection of the classics, which he opened and leafed through, moved to the easy chair, pulled the cushion up, and searched the sides, finding a quarter and a dime, which he placed on the edge of the desk. He pulled the chair out of the corner, but found nothing under it.

"What are we looking for exactly?" Lisa asked as he stood at the window looking out.

"I think he saw Sharon's murderer that night. From the angle of the window here, he couldn't see her front door because it's recessed into the side of the building, but he could have seen the killer approach and then run back down the walkway. I suspect he sensed something was wrong and decided to have a look. The timing fits with him rushing out and then returning minutes later upset and running back upstairs. I believe he rushed over, saw Sharon's body, and hurried back here in shock. I also think he recognized the murderer this time. I looked up at this window that night and the lights were off, so he must have been standing in the dark watching. It could be he came back here, waited for all the activity to settle down, and then called the killer to arrange a meeting, which got him killed when they met. I know it's a long shot, but it's feasible."

"But why would he turn off the lights and hide in the dark without reporting what he saw to the police?"

"Damned if I know."

He examined the telescope as Lisa returned to her list, put his eye to the vertical eyepiece jutting out on top, and nearly blinded myself with the setting sun. He blinked the spots out of his eye, and when his vision returned, noticed the black hinges holding the scope in place on its tripod showed clear signs of wear in a half moon crescent near the knob. He tilted the telescope to the bottom edge of the hinge and pulled it to the far right of the worn arch, settled his eye over the eyepiece, and looked directly into Sharon's bedroom window, the image so sharp it transcended the silk curtains allowing him to read the label on a blouse on the foot of her bed.

"*Hello*! Come check this out," Lisa called from behind him.

He peered over her shoulder at Sharon Lucas' name, which had a blue tick mark beside it. She flipped the pages to the P's and pointed to a blue tick mark beside Mrs. Bernice Peters name as well.

Lisa looked up at him. "Both he and Mrs. Peters claimed they didn't know each other, yet he marked both Sharon and Mrs. Peters' number. Why?"

"Interesting, come check this out." He led her over to the telescope and swiveled it to show her the markings on the hinges and then set them to their limits. "Have a look."

She pressed her eye to the scope and stiffened. "He was a peeping tom!"

"It would seem so. Now look at this." He pointed to the end of the telescope, where faint markings showed wear. "That's a camera attachment. I suspect he's been taking pictures of heavenly bodies, but not all of the twinkling star variety, if you get my drift."

Lisa scowled. "What a pervert!"

"That camera and his photos have to be here somewhere." He checked the room again, but found no camera or pictures. He opened the closet and went through the boxes stacked there, but again found nothing but the ordinary, precisely stacked clutter of accumulated junk. He checked the top shelf and rifled through the boxes there as well, but found nothing. As he tapped on the walls and baseboards for a hollow spot, Mrs. Jenkins poked her head into the room.

"I heard you knocking, do you need something?"

"Mrs. Jenkins, did your husband own a camera?" he asked.

"I recall he bought one to use with his astronomical studies."

"Do you know where he kept it?"

"I assume it would be here in his study."

"I've not been able to locate it. Did he store things anywhere else in the house?"

"We have a storage unit on the backside of the apartment complex, but I haven't been there in some time."

"I'd like to have a look if you don't mind."

"I believe the key is in the envelope with his personal things the sheriff returned to me. I'll check." She returned as Lisa finished her list. "Here you go, Mr. Davis. It's the silver one here. Unit 11 is ours. Would you like me to accompany you?"

He took the keychain. "That won't be necessary, Ma'am. Would you please scan this list of names and see if you find any of them odd?"

Her forehead creased as she read. "They are all members of our church, with the exception of Mrs. Bernice Peters and Sharon Lucas, who I don't believe we've ever had the pleasure of meeting."

"I'd like to check the storage unit now, if you don't mind."

She led them downstairs.

Chapter 22

Lisa and Dean made their way to the backside of the apartment complex to a double row of metal storage units, each the size of a single garage with wide, roll up doors and a metal clip at the bottom to hold a lock clamped through a hasp attached to the cement floor. Dean knelt in front of number eleven, fit the key into the lock, pulled up on the handle to roll the door to the top, and walked into a tidy interior containing an orderly row of boxes stacked against one wall with a wooden table on the opposite side holding a Nikon camera and two 8x11 white stationary boxes. Lisa flipped on a light switch beside the overhead door and a low wattage bulb cast a weak yellow arc in the dim interior.

Dean picked up the camera. "It's still got film in it."

Lisa lifted the cover from one of the boxes and gasped. Dean set the camera down and moved over next to her to view the top photo, an 8x11 grainy black and white portraying a naked Kenny Felton standing beside Sharon's bed with a nude Sharon kneeling before him as he grasped her hair in his right hand to guide her.

Lisa moved away as he flipped through the stack of pictures. "How can you look at that sick pornographic rubbish?"

"You'll get used to this sort of stuff if you stay in this business. I've seen a lot worse. Some people even think it's erotica, but I call it evidence. Here are some pictures of Kitty with them and some others with Becky. Old Carlson was having himself a good time with his little telescope. Stay here and guard this crap while I go brief Mrs. Jenkins and get her permission to call in our pal, Sheriff Dudley Do-right."

Lisa glanced at the pictures on the table. "Dean?" He turned back to her. "How does it make you feel … you know, seeing Sharon like this?"

He turned and hurried away to find a place to throw up, but that was his own damned business.

Sheriff Parsons and one of his deputies leered down at the table of photographs as they worked their way through the stack with morbid glee. "So you've been retained by Mrs. Jenkins? With a stretch of your questionable imagination, this could be considered in the category of privileged information."

Dean stifled a grimace. "I had a hard time convincing Mrs. Jenkins to allow me to call you, but I'm certain this has something to do with Jenkins' murder, and possibly even some of the others, which makes it potential evidence."

Sheriff Parsons glanced at Lisa hovering by the door in a state of acute mortification and then back to Dean. "For the record, I picked up Al Roberts this afternoon for questioning in the murder of Ray Mize, although I'm still curious as to why your so-called anonymous caller would pass such information along to you instead of me."

"It's hard to say what his motive was," Dean allowed. "Did you come up with anything during your questioning of Roberts?"

"Not a thing at present. Have you got any other tidbits of information concerning this case you need to pass along to me?"

"A couple of long shots, maybe."

"Spit them out."

"Roberts has a friend who works with him at the saw mill named Clyde Hawkins."

"I know Hawkins. What does he have to do with anything?"

"Hawkins apparently informed Roberts when he saw Becky with Felton on at least two occasions, and sat outside Felton's house with Roberts on the night Felton was murdered."

"So?"

"He appears to keep pretty close tabs on Becky. I think if you look close, you'll find he's my anonymous caller with the tip that Roberts murdered Mize."

"Why would he do something like that?"

"Mrs. Roberts admits to having an affair with Hawkins. If he somehow knew she was meeting Mize at the motel, he could have got Roberts all worked up enough to kill him. With Mize dead and hubby in jail, he'd have clear sailing with Becky by eliminating two of his rivals at once. As I say, it's a long shot, but I believe it has merit and he might provide you with a few more leads if you press him. I also suggest you question Mrs. Roberts about going to the motel to meet Mize."

"Uh huh. Anything else?"

"Do you have any leads on the woman in the white Ford Bronco?"

"Lots of people drive white Ford Broncos."

"I'm convinced we're missing a thread somewhere that sews all of these murders together, but I'm getting nowhere in trying to find the missing link."

"When you find that thread and get it all sewed up, give me a call."

"Have you got a reading on the slugs in the Jenkins' murder yet?"

"The slugs from Jenkins' body matched the slug from the Lucas girl."

"That confirms we're looking for one killer for the both of them."

"Did you find anything else in Jenkins' study that might shed some light on this case?"

"Nothing that aroused my interest, other than the telescope, which led here, and the names of Sharon Lucas and Mrs. Peters tagged in his phonebook for whatever reason. Carlson Jenkins and Mrs. Peters both claimed they've never met, and Mrs. Jenkins agrees. Other than that, I think it's important to get the unexposed roll of film in his camera developed as soon as possible in hopes it might give us more clues to pursue."

"Let's get one thing straight here, Davis, there ain't no *us* in this investigation, and I've got better things to do than to run around doing your bidding."

"Sorry, Sheriff, I almost thought we were on the same team there for a minute."

"Take your associate and run along now—she's looking a bit thin around the gills."

"I'm his *partner*!" Lisa retorted from the doorway. "And I'm just fine, thank you!"

Dean grinned. "As always, it's been a pleasure, Sheriff."

"That despicable old goat," Lisa grated as they climbed into Dean's Mustang. "He's as perverted as Carlson Jenkins and Kenny Felton. What is it with this town? I've lived here all my life and suddenly it's turning into a regular little Peyton Place. Why didn't I see all of this slime and filth before?"

"You lived a sheltered life and looked out at the world through rose colored glasses before you got into this line of business."

"I'm not in the mood for one of your smug little lectures, Dean!"

"Well pardon the hell out of me! What's eating at you all of a sudden?"

"I've dealt with all of the degenerates and their foul wickedness I want to for one day. Four people have been killed, I've watched two of them get buried, discovered that practically everyone in this burg is sleeping with everyone else, and that the rest are sneaking around taking pictures of them. Along the way I've also discovered our sheriff, the very one I helped get reelected, is a lecherous old incompetent fool whose sole ambition in life is to protect his image. I'm tired and disillusioned and feel soiled by it all." She turned to the window to hide her tears.

"I've got just the cure for an overdose of reality," he offered.

"And what would that be?"

"A long hot bath and a cold stiff drink." He pulled into a liquor store. "Any preferences?"

"You decide."

When Dean got her home, he ran the tub full of hot water, sprinkled in a liberal amount of her foamy bubble bath, and left her to undress and slip into the tub while he went downstairs to mix up a jug of frozen margaritas. Using a recipe on the side of the tequila bottle that called for eight ounces of the fiery liquid, he figured double that couldn't be all bad in view of her mood, and carried the concoction upstairs to pour them each a glass as she lay immersed up to her chin in the thick suds.

"So do you want to talk about things?" he encouraged as he settled down on the edge of the sink with his concoction.

"No, I want to forget about things."

"Okay." He sat in silence as she soaked. When she emptied her glass, he refilled it along with his own, the frozen liquid building a warm glow in him. He could see it mellowing her out as well from the tranquil look in her eyes, and refilled their glasses a third time as she used her toes to add hot water.

She smiled up at him with a lopsided grin. "*Mm*, this is good, just what I needed."

"I'll make another batch." He topped off their glasses and hurried downstairs, pleased with himself, this time figuring if sixteen ounces was that good, the remainder of the jug could only be that much better.

He hurried back upstairs, replenished her glass and reassumed his seat on the edge of the sink as he watched her luxuriating in the warm suds, idly wondering why in the world he didn't pull her out of the tub and ravish her. For the life of him, he couldn't figure that one out, so opted to get drunk with her instead.

The shrill ringing of the telephone on the nightstand beside Dean's head jarred him into consciousness. He groped for the receiver as his head pounded behind aching eyeballs.

"Hello?"

"Mr. Davis, I've stopped payment on that check!" a chilled voice trilled in his ear. "I expect you'll be hearing from my attorney soon!"

"Mrs. Jenkins? What—" The phone slammed down in its cradle on the other end of the line, sending painful currents through his throbbing skull as he worked his tongue around in his mouth wondering where all the sludge had come from.

"*Ohooooo*, I'm going to be *sicccccckkkk*," a pitiful moan whimpered from the covers beside him. A feeble hand worked its way out from under the sheet and tugged it down to reveal bloodshot eyes embedded in a twisted face squinting up at him in the harsh light of day above bare shoulders. "I feel *awful*!"

The clock on her side of the bed showed nearly noon. He groped his way up into a sitting position and clasped his head as his senses stabilized somewhat. "I'll get us some coffee and aspirin."

"*Ohoooooo*," she moaned.

He tried to remember why they were nude as he stumbled to his pants, which lay in a crumpled heap near the bathroom door, with his shirt and underwear nowhere in sight. He slipped on his jeans and went downstairs bare-chested to put the coffee on to brew. As he waited he tried to piece together the events of the night before, but all was lost in the dull pounding of his head. He put the pot, cups, and a bottle of aspirin on a tray and took it upstairs.

"Wake up, Sleeping Beauty. Take these and wash them down with some coffee."

She pulled the cover down to her chin and reached a trembling hand for the three aspirin he held out to her. He poured their coffee, downed four aspirin himself, and sank down on the side of the bed to ease the trembling in his legs.

She cut her eyes at him nervously. "So?"

He glanced at her cautiously. "What?"

"You know ... last night?"

He searched his broken memory bank for any scrap of remembrance. "Um, what about last night?"

She blushed and looked away. "Was it ... you know?"

He swallowed back the swirling ebbs of nauseous bile in his stomach as his pounding heart intensified the pain in his swollen head, thinking *good grief*, w*hy do women ask dumb things like that?*

Her swollen eyes widened. "It was *awful*, wasn't it?"

"Huh? Why would you think that?"

"Because you're not saying anything!"

"It was great! Honest!"

"Liar!"

"Why would I lie about something like that?"

"*You still think I'm a terrible lover*!"

"*Hey*, I've *never* thought you were a terrible lover! Where do you get that stuff from anyway?" he soothed in an attempt to calm her, acutely aware of how unnerving bawling females were when they let loose with the waterworks. "Don't cry now, I'll get you a washcloth!"

"I'm not crying!" she shouted after him as he dashed for the bathroom. "I'm just disappointed because I don't even remember *doing it*!"

He found his shirt in a wad on the floor and his soggy underwear lying in a limp heap amidst a thin film of suds in the bathtub, grabbed them up, wrung them out, and tossed them in the clothes hamper along with his shirt, rinsed a washcloth in cold water, and rushed back into the bedroom.

"Here now, wash your face and blow you nose."

"I was terrible!" she wailed. "Admit it!"

"You weren't terrible, and besides that, if you don't remember, it doesn't count anyway."

"That doesn't make sense! If we did it, we did it, whether I remember it or not."

"Not so! If you don't remember, it doesn't count!"

"A-Are you sure?"

"Absolutely," he lied righteously.

She wiped her face with the cloth and blew her nose, wanting to believe him.

He took a nervous sip of coffee as another anxious flash swept through him. "Uh, Lisa, you *are* on the pill, aren't you?"

"*You liar*!" she screeched. "I *was* terrible and now you're afraid I'm pregnant and you'll be stuck with me for the rest of your life!"

He took her cup, set it on the nightstand, and hugged her to him. "Lisa, I swear, you were great! I wouldn't lie to you about something like that."

"Really?"

"I'd make love to you again right now if I didn't have such a pounding headache." He refilled her cup as she pulled the cover back up to her chin. "I'm going to hop in the shower while you finish your coffee and then make us some breakfast."

"By the way, who called?"

"Oh, that was just Mrs. Jenkins calling to say she cancelled the check she gave us."

"*What! Why?*"

He paused at the bathroom door. "She didn't say, but she did mention her lawyer would be contacting us soon."

Chapter 23

Lisa, still looking like she had a ways to go to normal, put her napkin to her lips and belched politely as only women can do. "No more. I'm ready to burst."

Dean poured more orange juice in her glass. "Protein and vitamin C, that's the cure for a hangover."

She pushed the remains of her eggs, bacon, and toast away with a trembling hand. "I can't believe we got fired."

He glanced at the blaring headline on the front page of the morning paper laying on the table with the article beneath it quoting an unnamed source and outlining the peeping tom scandal surrounding the Carlson Jenkins murder. Though not in-depth, it was accurate, naming Sharon Lucas and Kenny Felton in the sexually explicit photographs the sheriff's department had uncovered. From the tone of the article, it appeared Sheriff Parsons was doing a fine job of investigating the recent multiple murders and hinted the good officer was pursuing other promising leads and close to making an arrest in the unsolved homicides that had plagued their small community in the past week.

Dean shoved the paper aside dourly. "Let's focus on facts and probable motives."

Lisa batted her lashes. "Are we developing a civic conscience now? We're fired, remember—no *moola* for our valuable time?"

"That jackass knows better than to let something like this go public. I hope Mrs. Jenkins sues his pants off."

"It sounds like she intends to sue ours off as well."

"We didn't do anything but turn over evidence in an ongoing murder investigation to the sheriff's department, as was our *civic duty*. I'm not worried about her suing us, but I am mad as hell at our dippy little sheriff and his dumb-assed posse for letting this leak to the media. I want to solve these crimes now even if we have to do it on our own dime—and hopefully expose him for the fool he is in the process."

Lisa rubbed her hands together eagerly. "Where do we start?"

"Mostly in the dark," he allowed grimly. "Let's go back to the basics. Normally, you follow the money, but in this case, there doesn't seem to be any money involved, so let's focus on establishing a motive that ties all of these crimes together."

"The only thing I can see is the drugs and sex," Lisa offered.

"Okay, so we follow the drugs and sex. Let's go back to Kitty and Becky and start from the beginning."

"But they weren't victims," she protested. "They were willing participants."

"No, but they played the sex game for the drugs."

"Which means they had no incentive to kill Kenny," she argued. "Why would they want to cut off their source?"

"They're both still subject to blackmail, just as Sharon was, who was also a willing participant, so let's examine the drug and sex ring to try to develop a motive that fits all four of the murders.

"The first murder victim was a rich tyrant that ruled over a coven of captive nymphs who could join his club, but apparently couldn't resign their membership. Supporting this, we have some sexually explicit home videos he made and tried to use to blackmail at least two, if not more, of them into making additional tapes. Someone subsequently broke into his house and stole four of those tapes, which I think were most likely of Sharon, and the same or an entirely different person broke in on a second occasion and stole the remainder, with the exception of the one overlooked in the VCR.

"Next, we have the best friend of murder victim number one found nude and murdered in a motel room, who is also our most viable suspect for stealing the remaining tapes the second time around since he knew they existed and where Felton kept them.

"Then we have a murdered beauty queen who was involved in drug-induced group sex and desperate to keep something secret, most likely the videos she starred in.

"Finally, we have a quasi-religious fanatic found murdered in the backseat of his car with his pants down around his ankles who turns out to be a peeping tom.

"For suspects, we've got an unknown woman lurking around who drives a white Ford Bronco seen at the scene of the first murder by peeping tom murder victim number four, who resembles Sharon as reported by a second witness who claims to have seen her running away from victim number one's body in the parking lot. We also have a nymphomaniac housewife who willingly participated in Felton's home movies for drugs whose husband threatened to kill Felton on more than one occasion, the last on the very day he *was* killed. Lastly, we have the nymphomaniac housewife herself, who we suspect rushed out to meet murder victim number two after he stole Felton's tapes and attempted to blackmail her and at least one other woman for sex.

"We have no suspects at all in murder victims three and four.

"To complicate things, murder victim one was shot with his own .38 snub-nosed revolver, murder victim two with a .357

caliber howitzer, and numbers three and four with the same 9 millimeter automatic. We need a common denominator that ties all of this together."

Lisa pursed her lips. "What if there isn't a common denominator, only tragic interrelating circumstances? There were three different murder weapons, why can't there be three different killers?"

Dean stood and paced around the kitchen. "That's a distinct possibility, but if there is a common denominator it has to be the drugs and sex thing. Let's take the murders in the order they occurred. The facts are Jenkins swore he saw a female in a white Bronco outside of Sharon's apartment who killed Felton, right? And Mrs. Sanders saw someone who looked like Sharon running away from the body afterwards, right? So let's assume this mystery woman killed Felton, okay?"

She nodded. "Okay. Her motive?"

"Most likely jealousy if Felton was dumping her to go back to Sharon."

"Plausible," she agreed. "And we can also assume she killed Ray Mize because he took the tapes from Felton's house and tried to blackmail her, right?"

Dean nodded. "It only follows that if Mize took the tapes and attempted to blackmail this mystery woman for sexual favors, she would blast him too."

"But what about Al Roberts who the anonymous caller tagged as Ray Mize's killer?" she demanded. "Are you eliminating him as a suspect?"

"The one witness who saw a woman running from Felton's body and the other who gave a sworn statement implicating a similar woman in a white Ford Bronco virtually eliminates Roberts as a suspect in Felton's murder, wouldn't you say?"

She hesitated. "I suppose it does, but not necessarily in the others. He certainly has a strong motive in the Mize murder if he knew Becky was being blackmailed by him."

"Okay, I'll grant you that, but let's focus on the mystery woman for now. She could have killed Mize because he attempted to blackmail her for sex, and she may have had a motive to kill Sharon because Sharon could identify her as Felton's killer. It makes sense if you consider she struck the first night Sharon got out of jail because she couldn't get at Sharon while she was locked up. She may have even planned to kill Sharon the same night she killed Felton, which would explain her running towards Sharon's door, but couldn't get at her because the door was locked, so she wiped her prints off the gun and dumped it in the shrubbery to frame Sharon."

"But if Sharon could identify her, why didn't she?" Lisa demanded. "It's unlikely Sharon would sit in jail facing a murder rap and let her off the hook. It only makes sense if Sharon was protecting her for some reason. So who was she trying to protect, and why would this woman kill Sharon if she was protecting her?"

Dean leaned against the counter and crossed his arms. "Another puzzling question is why Felton went to Sharon's house on the night he was murdered when he wouldn't take her calls earlier. We now know based on what Jenkins saw that he had his pistol on him when he struggled with the mystery woman in the parking lot, so why did he feel the need to be armed?"

"If Kenny was blackmailing Sharon with his home movies, which made her so desperate when she called him on the day he was murdered, I think it's highly unlikely he would expect her to make up with him, as Sharon claimed," Lisa insisted. "I think there was another reason he went to her apartment that night and Sharon lied to us about it."

Dean clasped his hands behind his head and stared up at the ceiling, befuddled. "That's possible, and if the mystery woman misread his purpose for going to Sharon's house and thought he was trying to make up with her, became crazy jealous, confronted him and killed him, it still makes sense. It even makes sense if the mystery woman then killed Mize after he got the tapes on the second break-in at Felton's house if he tried to blackmail her for sexual favors. I'll even allow this mystery woman may have killed Sharon when she got out of jail because she knew Sharon could identify her, and then killed Carlson Jenkins because he could identify her. But if this mystery woman killed Felton because she was jealous of him for going back to Sharon and Jenkins did recognize her, why would he keep quiet about it?"

"Maybe he didn't recognize her when she killed Kenny," she offered. "But he *did* recognize her when she killed Sharon."

"Then why not inform the police the night Sharon was killed? It still doesn't add up."

"So how do we find this mystery woman?"

"That's easy. We find a cold-hearted crazy bitch that was having an affair with Felton who looks like Sharon from the back and drives a white Ford Bronco."

"I think you're leading me down Primrose Lane, Sherlock," she insisted as the phone rang. "I'll get it." She came back into the kitchen. "It's for you."

"Who is it?"

"Paul Miller."

"Who is Paul Miller?"

"From the sheriff's department."

"You mean *Deputy* Miller? When did he become *Paul*?"

"Just now when he asked to speak to you," she replied smugly.

He went into the living room and picked up the phone. "Dean Davis here?"

"Mr. Davis, I don't need to get my tail in a bind with my boss, so I'd appreciate it if you'd keep this between us like before, you know, cop to cop?"

"Okay, cop to cop," Dean agreed.

"Sheriff Parsons has a press conference this afternoon, so consider this a courtesy call."

"What kind of press conference?"

"We're in hot water up to our ears over that damned press leak concerning the Jenkins scandal so I don't have a lot of time, but we got the film back from Carlson Jenkins' camera this morning. The roll contained pictures of the vehicle and the woman in the parking lot at the Felton murder scene, along with ones he took of the Lucas girl and Felton in her bedroom, which he obviously couldn't tell us about without tipping us off he was a sleaze-ball. We had the photos enhanced and it clearly shows Mrs. Bernice Peters confronting Kenny Felton outside of the Lucas girl's apartment. We also traced a white Ford Bronco registered to Mrs. Peters and matched it to the one in the photo by the distinct rust spots."

"*Mrs. Peters* killed Felton?"

"We picked her up earlier this morning, and according to her preliminary statement, the Lucas girl called her that evening crying and told her Felton was furious about something of hers she had taken from his home and was on his way over to get it back. Mrs. Peters says when she arrived at the Lucas girl's residence she met Felton coming out of the Lucas girl's door with a sack in his hand. Mrs. Peters claims she struggled with him over the sack and his gun fell out of his waistband and discharged when it hit the ground, which explains the scratches on the grip and hammer as well as the trajectory of the bullet entering his lower abdomen and traveling upwards at a sharp angle to strike him in the heart. According to her statement, Mrs. Peters then picked up the gun and the sack and ran to the Lucas girl's door, where the Lucas girl took the items and told her to leave immediately. Apparently, the Lucas girl then wiped her grandmother's prints off the gun and tossed it in the shrubbery beside her door to get rid of it. We conducted a search of the Lucas girl's apartment and found the sack in her closet, which contained four videos of her and Felton, along with other women, having sex in Felton's bedroom."

"That's simply amazing," Dean replied, somewhat dazed.

"There's more, Mr. Davis," Deputy Miller continued. "Al Roberts just signed a confession to the murder of Ray Mize."

"So Roberts *did* kill Mize?"

"His buddy Clyde Hawkins admitted he was your anonymous caller. It seems he wanted to keep a distance from the case because he was having an affair with Mrs. Roberts and thought you would be a buffer. We found the .357 magnum in the glove box of Roberts' truck and matched it to one of the bullets taken out of the wall of the motel room. Hawkins says he followed Mrs. Roberts that afternoon, saw her go into the motel room with Mize, and called his buddy Al."

"I trust your good sheriff will give us the lion's share of the credit for solving those two cases at his press conference since we found the film *and* put him on to Roberts?"

Deputy Miller chuckled softly. "In any case, the sheriff expects Roberts to eventually confess to the remaining two murders as well."

"Why does he think Roberts killed Sharon Lucas and Jenkins?"

"We found the other missing tapes in Roberts' attic, which he admits taking from Mize's car after killing him at the motel. Several of them shows Mrs. Roberts and the Lucas girl having sex with Felton in his bedroom. Sheriff Parsons feels Roberts blamed the Lucas girl for her trysts with his wife, as well as involving Felton in her sex triangle."

"And Jenkins?"

"He figures Jenkins saw Roberts walk up to the Lucas girl's door and shoot her, the same as he saw Mrs. Peters and Felton the night he was killed."

"Then why didn't Jenkins report it the night Sharon was killed, and why would Roberts make Jenkins pull his pants off before he shot him?"

"I'm just the messenger here, Mr. Davis."

"Right, I owe you one. I don't guess you found the 9 millimeter involved in those two deaths in Roberts' glove compartment along with the 357 magnum?"

"No, we haven't located that weapon yet. Um, can I ask you a personal question, Mr. Davis?"

"Go for it, Deputy."

"Do you and Miss Bryant have a personal relationship, or just a business one?"

"You'll need to have Miss Bryant clarify that issue for you, Deputy."

"Please give her my regards."

Dean hung up the phone and returned to the kitchen.

"What did he want?" Lisa asked as she refilled his cup and sat down at the table across from him.

"He wanted to know if you and I had a personal relationship or just a professional one."

"What did you tell him?"

"To ask you."

"Was that all he wanted?"

"No, and gee, do *I* feel *stupid*!" When he finished he heaved a sigh and shook his head. "But it just doesn't feel right. I think there's still a missing piece."

"You're the one who was so sure there was just *one* killer, and surely you didn't expect Sharon to turn in her grandmother for killing Kenny?" Lisa argued.

"I'm still not buying Roberts killing Sharon and Jenkins. The 'leading his little wife astray' theory just doesn't make sense."

"Sharon *was* part of the sex triangle Becky was involved in, Dean, and Al Roberts *is* an insanely jealous redneck—what doesn't make sense about it? And it certainly makes sense for him to kill Jenkins if he could identify him as Sharon's killer."

"Then why make him undress beforehand?" he challenged as the telephone rang and she rose to answer it.

"It's for you," she said when she returned.

"Who is it this time?"

"Charlene Lucas."

"What does she want?"

"Surely *that's* not a mystery to you as well?"

"Damn!" he swore as he went into the living room and picked up the phone. "Hello?"

"*Dean, why haven't you called?*"

"Uh, hang up and I'll call you right back."

She chortled in a low, sexy voice. "*You always were a smart-ass.*"

"I guess you can't change basic nature."

"*Have you heard they just arrested my grandmother for the murder of Kenny Felton?*"

"Um, your grandmother?"

"*And somebody else just confessed to murdering that dry cleaners guy.*"

"Sounds like the sheriff's had a busy day."

"*And have you seen that horrid story about Sharon in the paper?*"

"Shocking, wasn't it?" he replied, thankful the sheriff hadn't given them any credit for turning up the evidence.

"*I don't know why they want to ruin Sharon's reputation. I mean, she's gone now, so what's the purpose?*"

He turned his back to Lisa as she tried to snuggle up to him and put her head against the phone to listen. "It sells papers, I guess."

"*Dean, can we get together this evening?*"

He shook Lisa off as she slipped around him and again pressed her ear to the phone. "Get together for what?"

"*To discuss all that has happened.*"

He stiff-armed Lisa away. "You know as much about things as I do," he hedged.

Lisa glared and punched him in his sore ribs, doubling him over in pain as she moved in quickly and pressed her ear to the receiver.

"*Will you meet me somewhere? I have a business proposition I'd like to discuss with you. I'll treat you to a Texas-sized steak at Big Jim's tonight. Say around five-ish? That'll give us plenty of time to get reacquainted.*"

"*Umm,*" he hedged.

"*And, Dean, I'd prefer your little assistant didn't tag along.*"

Lisa's mouth flew open indignantly as she pulled back from the phone.

Dean hooked his arm around her head and clamped his palm over her lips as he gasped for breath. "I'll see you there!"

Lisa turned on him as he hung up, eyes blazing, and punched his sore ribs again. "*That little*—"

He shuffled away from her. "*Ouch!* Why are you hitting *me?*"

"You *should* have told her I'm your *partner*, not your *little assistant!* And why doesn't she want *me* to be there?"

He warded off another blow. "How the hell do I know?"

"Because I'd only be in the way when she makes a play for you, *that's* why she doesn't want me *tagging along!* I swear you're so dumb where women are concerned!"

He backed away from her flurry of jabs. "So let her make a play for me! It's no big deal, women hit on me all the time—no pun intended! *Ouch! Quit that!*"

"And just what am *I* supposed to do while you're being *wined* and *dined* at Big Jim's Steakhouse?"

He dodged another blow. "Have a bowl of porridge and wait by the hearth for me to return?"

"You *wish!*"

"*Ouch!* That's my sore ribs!"

"You *deserve* it!"

"Ouch! You're *hurting* me! Why do I deserve it?"

"For taking advantage of me last night!"

He dodged a roundhouse right and sucked in the pain when she connected with his ribs with a left uppercut. "I thought we agreed it doesn't count if you can't remember! Besides, she says she has a business proposition for me. I'm almost broke! What do you expect me to do?"

"Quit leading her on and let her know you're not available!"

The ringing of the telephone saved him from further physical abuse as she snatched it up from its cradle. "*Hello!*" She composed herself. "Yes, this is Lisa Bryant of the D and B Detective Agency. How may I help you? I see. You've been very helpful. Thank you. Goodbye." She turned to him. "That was the telephone company. The call Carlson Jenkins placed on the night he was murdered was to Bernice Peters."

Dean blinked. "Now *that* doesn't make a *lick* of sense!"

"It makes as much sense as you taking Charlene Lucas out to dinner!"

"I'm not taking *her* out, she's taking *me* out on business!"

Her eyes narrowed. "Don't play me for a fool, Dean, or *act* like one either!"

"Look, I'm tired of dodging her, so I'll listen to her proposal and subtly ensure she clearly understands I have no personal interest in her in the process."

"You could have told her that over the phone!"

"How could I with you acting like a lunatic? Besides, it's best if I do it in person in a nice way."

"Great, so go then!" she ordered, turning to answer the phone.

With her distracted, he limped up the stairs to get dressed. When he came down wearing his new tan jacket, she appraised him critically.

"Why aren't you wearing the tie I picked out to go with that shirt?"

"My new creed is to wear ties only to weddings and funerals. So, are you okay with me meeting Charlene now?"

"Oh, I'm fine, you jackass! I'll just spend some quality time plotting my revenge while you're gone. I hope you choke on your steak and ale—and for the record, if you want Charlene Lucas, you can *damn* well *have* her!"

He pulled her to him. "*For the record*, I have no interest in Charlene Lucas and you damn well know it." He brushed his lips against hers. "In fact, I plan to eat her free steak while I listen to her pitch, and then blow her off so I can hurry on back home for dessert."

She shoved away from him. "I'm not into bribery, thank you!"

He pulled her back and kissed her sensuously.

She softened. "Umm, hurry back and I'll consider making dessert worth your while," she teased against his lips.

"I should make dinner dates with gorgeous women more often," he whispered as he nibbled her ear.

She stiffened and pushed him back. "Jackass!"

He turned to the door and paused. "On second thought, come with me."

"She specifically excluded me, remember?"

"To hell with her, we're a team and make our own rules."

"Is that another attempt at bribery?"

"In fact, to hell with Charlene—some might consider you attractive in the right light. If you'll ease up on the attitude, I'll let *you* treat me to a steak dinner."

She shoved him out the door. "One of these days, Dean! And be careful, I get bad vibes around Charlene."

He winked at her. "There's not much that can happen in the dining room of Big Jim's. See you in a couple of hours."

"Oh, I almost forgot," she called after him. "That was Mrs. Jenkins who called. She's still furious with Sheriff Parsons about the article in the paper, but said that perhaps she overreacted when she blamed you for it. She wants to keep our retainer in place."

"Did you tell her Sheriff Parsons has all but solved the case?"

"Are you crazy? He hasn't solved it *yet*, and she even offered us a bonus for being so rude when she fired us this morning."

"*Lisa!*"

She closed the door.

Chapter 24

When Dean arrived at Big Jim's the hostess directed him to a table in the back of the main dining room where Charlene waited.

"Dean!" She rose as he approached, eyes shining, and pecked at his cheek. "You're perfectly on time. I admire that in a man."

He reseated her and sat down covertly appraising her low cut white dress, single strand of pearls, flawless makeup, and hair all done up in a bun, finding her resemblance to Sharon haunting, but with none of Sharon's titillating vitality.

"You look lovely tonight," he praised in an obligatory lie.

She beamed. "Well thank you, kind sir. You look rather dashing yourself. Would you like a cocktail before dinner?"

"A beer, please," he directed as the waiter handed them menus.

"I'll have a whisky sour," she ordered.

"In view of all that's happened, how are you holding up?" he inquired politely.

"I'm confident things will turn out for the best," she replied as the server set their drinks before them. After they placed their orders, she smiled and lifted her glass. "To our future."

He tipped his beer in her general direction and sipped amid growing irritation. "You wanted to discuss a proposition of some sort with me?"

"You always did get right to the point. Don't you ever relax?"

"I'm about as laid-back as it gets right now." He sipped his beer as she studied him with a steady stare.

"Actually, I'm concerned about the farm since I seem to have the whole place to myself now. I could use a good, strong man like you to handle things for me."

"Thanks, but I'm afraid I'm not much of a farmer," he replied, puzzled by her mercenary attitude following the double tragedies of Sharon and her grandmother.

She assumed a calculating, sultry look and took his hand. "I could make the job intriguing for you. In fact, you could concentrate on the fringe benefits—like me and that pond you were so fond of out there in the willow trees."

The server appeared with their orders and he took the opportunity to remove his hand from hers as her eyes bore into his. "I don't suppose farming is as exciting as being a private detective, but surely you don't expect to make a living doing that in this small town? What are you going to do when the funds my grandmother paid you run out?"

"I've recently been retained to work on the Carlson Jenkins murder," he replied, omitting he'd been rehired after getting canned earlier over the article in the paper.

"Does it really matter who killed that depraved son of a bitch?" she replied blithely.

He blinked. "It seems to matter to his wife."

"Let's talk about something pleasant—I don't want to spoil our evening now that I've finally got you all to myself." She sliced off a small piece of steak. "Umm, this is good."

"So the farm was the reason you wanted to meet with me?" he asked as he sawed at his steak.

"Partly," she replied. "But mostly, I just wanted to enjoy your company."

"That's a change from when we were kids. You hated me then, as I recall."

She flashed a provocative smile. "That's how little girls flirt. They beat up on guys they're in love with. Don't you know that?"

I know to run for the hills when girls use the dreaded 'L' word, he thought darkly. "Oh," was all he could manage as he busied himself with his steak.

She set her knife and fork aside. "I was *so* in love with you back then, Dean. Surely you knew that?"

He also knew enough about girls to know when *not* to make meaningful eye contact, and that this was one of those poignant moments.

"I'm *still* in love with you, Dean—I realized that the moment I saw you again."

The familiar waves of panic rose as he lofted a hunk of steak into his mouth, thinking this poignant moment wasn't getting any better, and concentrated on chewing since he couldn't seem to swallow.

She leaned forward. "Do you understand what I'm saying, Dean?"

He forced the glob of meat down and took a swallow of beer to chase it. "Charlene, we haven't seen each other in years. You were just a child then and I was only half grown myself."

"It doesn't matter, Dean, I've had you in my heart every single minute of those years! Don't you understand? Now that Sharon is gone, there's nothing to stop us!"

He risked a glance at her. "Your steak is getting cold."

She stiffened. "It's that little tramp, Lisa Bryant, isn't it? You're *sleeping* with her! Admit it!"

He set his knife and fork down. "That's really none of your damned business."

"Okay, let's talk about *us* then!"

"That's an even shorter subject," he snapped, his patience coming to an abrupt end. "There *is* no *us,* so there's nothing to talk about."

She shoved her plate away, upsetting his glass of beer and her bowl of salad in the process. "*Like hell there isn't*! *I've waited seven goddamn years to say this, and now you want to pretend you don't understand me*! This isn't about the goddamned farm! This is about us! We can sell the damned thing for all I care. I hate that place anyway!"

"Calm down, Charlene, you're not making sense," he urged as he wiped at his jacket and pants with a napkin to soak up the beer, aware of everyone in the dining room now focused on them. "You're making us look foolish."

"*I'm not good enough for you, am I?* Only sweet little Sharon was good enough for you! *Well sweet little Sharon is dead now so you damn well need to get over her*!"

He stood up, dug a wad of bills out of his wallet, and tossed them on the table. "Enjoy your dinner, Charlene. Goodnight."

"Where are you going?" she called as he hurried away. "*Come back here, goddamn it*!"

She caught up with him in the parking lot as he snatched opened the door to his Mustang and threw herself against it to force it shut. "*Please*! I'm sorry, Dean! Don't just walk away like this. I *love* you. I don't care about Lisa Bryant. I forgive you!"

He glared at the curious faces watching them through the wide windows of Big Jim's steak house, which was fast becoming one of his least favorite places. "*Forgive me for what?* You need professional help, Lady!"

She drew back. "W-What do you mean?"

"Look, I don't know what's going on in that crazy little mind of yours, but you can leave me to hell out of it!" He turned back to the car and snatched open the door.

"*Wait, Dean! I'll show you what's going on in my crazy little mind!*" She flung her arms around his neck and surged hard against him, her lips covering his in desperate swirls.

He jerked her arms from around his neck and pushed her back. "*Enough, Charlene!*"

"Am I intruding?" a cool voice inquired as Charlene stumbled back from him.

Dean turned in surprise. "Lisa?"

"Sorry I'm running late," she replied, her eyes fixed on the panting Charlene. "I hope I haven't kept you waiting."

"You were *supposed* to come *alone*!" Charlene yelled before hurrying to a parked car several spaces down.

"What are you doing here?" Dean demanded as Charlene's car tore furiously out of the parking lot.

"You invited me, remember? Looks like I arrived just in time too."

"I had the situation under control," he insisted.

She smiled sweetly. "I could see that."

"You were jealous."

She rolled her eyes. "You're so full of yourself."

"Where were you hiding?"

"I wasn't *hiding*, I was sitting in my car when you came charging out with Charlene chasing after you. From all the stares, it appears you two made quite a scene in there. If you don't start behaving yourself Big Jim's might put you off limits."

"Why were you sitting in your car?"

"I was trying to decide if I wanted to come in or not."

"You *were* jealous!"

"I was *concerned*, and lucky for you I was."

"You were *jealous*, admit it."

"Do you want me to punch you in your ribs again with all these people watching?"

"I'd prefer you take me somewhere and feed me. I only got one tiny bite before Charlene starting acting like a damned fool."

"What happened?"

"I'll tell you over dinner."

"I'm thinking I've earned another high class meal at that fancy steak house on the south side of town for rescuing you," she suggested.

"I'm thinking you can pick up the tab then since I'm already out the price of one fancy meal tonight," he retorted.

"Oh, lucky me!" she grumped as she slid into his passenger seat. "Then I'm thinking the rib joint on the north side of town!"

✲ ✲ ✲

"I caught Sheriff Parson's press conference on TV after you left to meet Charlene," Lisa chided as she speared another rib. "His dog and pony show was capped off with the news anchor's high praise of him for solving Ray and Kenny's murders."

"Did he give us credit for tagging Al Roberts for him or finding the film that implicated Mrs. Peters in Felton's death?" Dean asked.

"Not even an honorable mention."

"That's a shocker," he allowed dryly. "Did he mention the other two homicides?"

"Only to imply he was close to solving those as well. So where do we go from here on the Jenkins case?"

"Damned if I know," he replied sourly as he wiped his hands and picked up the dessert menu, graciously signaling she could have the remaining rib on the platter. "How does apple pie a-la-mode sound for dessert?"

She rested her elbows on the table delicately balancing the last rib in her fingers. "I thought you were having dessert at home."

He held her stare. "Is that an open invitation into the innermost sanctums of your *boudoir*?"

"It might be."

"And to what do I owe the honor?"

She shrugged. "Maybe I find you worthy now since you repulsed the advances of a gorgeous female in front of scores of people, which is undoubtedly a *first* in your life."

"Is this a trick to get me to pick up the check?"

"Don't push your luck."

✵ ✵ ✵

He used her key to unlock the door and pulled her against him in the darkened foyer as he devoured her lips. She pushed him back into the living room as he worked feverishly on the buttons of her blouse, her breath hot against his neck in eager gasps as he unhooked her skirt. She drew back and stepped out of it as he pulled his shirt over his head. Both froze when the lamp beside the easy chair bathed them in dim light.

"Welcome home," Charlene greeted.

"How did you get in here?" Lisa demanded as she clutched her blouse together.

"This is getting ridiculous!" Dean moaned despairingly as he lowered his shirt.

Charlene surveyed Lisa's bare legs coolly. "The back door was open, so I invited myself in to wait."

"Well you can damned well invite yourself back out!" Dean allowed.

"I *knew* you two had something going on," she accused bitterly.

"Get out or I'll throw you out!" he threatened.

Her hand lifted with a small pistol in it. "This says differently."

"Hey, easy now, put that thing away," he soothed. "Are you *crazy*?"

She smiled wickedly. "That's the second time tonight you've suggested as much. The truth is some seem to think so. You could have had it all, Dean! You could have had me, the farm, my grandmother's money, everything! But you just couldn't see it!"

"See what?" he asked, keeping his voice calm as he edged a step closer.

"Why are you here?" Lisa asked, taking his cue and easing to her right.

"You had your chance with Dean, you dimwit, just like Sharon!" Charlene yelled. "You have no more right to him now than she did!"

"*Now* it all makes *perfect* sense," Lisa exclaimed as she edged another step to her right.

"*What* makes perfect sense?" Dean demanded, eyeing the gun in Charlene's hand and estimating it to be a nine millimeter.

"*Jenkins!*" Lisa snapped impatiently. "He didn't call Mrs. Peters, he called *Charlene*! Why didn't we see this before?"

"Probably because *I* still don't see it now," Dean allowed dubiously.

"It was right in front of us the whole time. Sharon found out Kenny was seeing *her own sister*! Nothing else makes sense about her breaking off their engagement."

"Is that *really* relevant in the current scheme of things?" Dean demanded, keeping his attention riveted on Charlene.

"Don't you see, little sister came home, wanted big sister's millionaire boyfriend, and went after him. When big sister found out, she dumped him."

"Lisa, under the circumstance, I fail to see the significance—"

"The *significance* is Sharon was killed over *you,* Dean!"

"Over *me*! Are you as loony as this nut case pointing a gun at us?"

"*Bravo!*" Charlene injected as she rose to her feet. "My, my, but aren't you quite the little detective?"

"Please feel free to fill in the gaps," Lisa challenged.

"My pleasure," Charlene offered. "When grandmother picked Sharon up from jail all she could talk about was getting Dean back. She insisted that with one phone call she could have him crawling back to her on his hands and knees. She's *always* had everything she wanted! When I told her Dean was taking me out to dinner, she laughed at me. *Laughed* at me! She said I'd *never* have him, especially when he found out about that horrible place my grandmother sent me to. But she's not laughing *now*, is she?"

"And Carlson Jenkins?" Lisa baited as she took another step to her right.

"He was an *evil* man! He said he *owned* me and that I'd do *anything* he wanted or he'd go to the police!"

"So Carlson Jenkins saw you go to Sharon's door and then run," Lisa continued as Dean eased another step forward with Charlene's attention focused on her. "He sensed something bad had happened, rushed out, saw Sharon's body, and rushed back home, just as his wife described. Later he called you with his demands and you agreed to meet him. And now you're here to prevent *me* from taking Dean from you as well."

"You have no right!" Charlene wailed as she swung the pistol in Lisa's direction. "*You have no right to him now!*"

"*NO!*" Dean yelled as he lunged.

Chapter 25

When the lights came on, they were indistinct. Dean's blurred vision took in the ceiling of a room. He turned his head and saw an IV in his arm. A clear, liquid filled bottle hung on a metal pole beside his white-sheeted bed in the darkened room. Beyond the IV bottle, he saw through a window it was dark outside. He turned his head and saw Lisa asleep in a chair beside his bed, her left arm in a sling, looking haggard and worried, even in her sleep. He lay watching her, taking comfort in the fact she was there. The hazy memory of lunging at Charlene as she swung her pistol at Lisa came back to him as he slid back into darkness.

When he opened his eyes again sunlight flooded the room and Lisa sat in her chair reading a woman's magazine.

"That girlie stuff ... will rot your mind," he croaked, surprised at how feeble his voice sounded.

She threw the magazine aside and rushed to him. "*Dean*!"

He looked at her arm in the sling. "What ... happened?"

"I'll get someone!" She ran out of the room and returned with a nurse.

"How was your little nap, Mr. Davis?"

He worked his parched lips to conjure up a coarse whisper. "How long have I ... been here?"

"They brought you in last night. I'll have the doctor pop in to have a look at you." She disappeared down the hall as Lisa moved back to the edge of the bed sniffing and trying to smile at the same time, her features undergoing hideous gyrations.

"What ... happened?"

She sobbed and half laughed, filled with tenderness. "You jumped in front of me and got shot, you dumb jackass."

"Did Charlene ... shoot you too?"

She wiped at tears trickling down her cheeks. "I sprained my shoulder when I tackled her. Dumb, huh?"

"I don't think the ... Dallas Cowboys ... will be scouting you anytime soon. Where is that ... crazy bitch?"

She snatched a Kleenex from a box on the table beside his bed with her good hand and blew her nose. "She's in jail where she belongs. You're lucky to be alive, Dean. The bullet ricocheted off your thick skull and only gave you a concussion, but it took twelve stitches to close the wound."

"How did you ... manage to subdue her?"

"She cracked her head on the end table when I tackled her and I tied her up with the lamp cord until Deputy Miller got there."

"Deputy Miller ... how convenient ... did you remember to ... put your skirt back on before he arrived?"

"You're jealous!"

"You're as crazy as ... Charlene. Can I have ... some water?"

She filled a glass from a container on the table beside him, stuck a straw in it, and held it for him as he drank the cool liquid, which spread through his insides like a soothing wind to free up his constricted throat.

"Thanks."

"Oh, Dean, I could just kill you!"

"I *do* seem to have that effect on women lately," he whispered.

The doctor came into the room with the nurse dogging his heels and Lisa stepped back so he could lean over Dean.

"Let's have a look at you, Mr. Davis. How do you feel?"

"Rotten," Dean mumbled.

He flicked a light in Dean's eyes and grunted. "You're a lucky man, a very lucky man indeed."

"That depends on your perspective, Doc," Dean wheezed. "How long will I be here?"

"A couple of days. I'll give you something to help you rest." He squirted a needle into the IV tube in Dean's arm. "I'll be back to check on you in a couple of hours." He hurried out of the room followed by the nurse.

"Some more water please," Dean begged as Lisa stepped back to the edge of the bed.

She faded into darkness before she could pour it.

✼ ✼ ✼

His mother's image sitting quietly in a chair beside his bed reading a paperback book slowly evolved into focus.

"Hi, Mom," he whispered.

She stood and put the book aside. "Dean! I've been so worried! How do you feel?"

"Like I've been shot."

She kissed his bandaged forehead. "That's not funny, young man! Lisa ran home to shower and change clothes. How long have you two been together?"

"She's my partner."

Her eyes danced in amusement. "Oh, I think she's a little more than your *partner*, young man. This is the first time she's left your side in two days. She seems very devoted to you."

"Don't start, Mom."

"There's a big article in the paper about all this. You're lucky that Lucas girl didn't kill you. You need to get into a different profession."

"I'm starving. Can you get me something to eat?"

"I don't think you're allowed solid foods yet."

A nurse entered the room. "How are we feeling this morning?"

Dean grimaced. "Better—so don't go putting me back to sleep again, damn it."

"We *are* feeling better, and getting bossy, too. Mrs. Davis, I need to change his bandages now that he's awake. Would you like to wait out in the lobby?"

His mother smiled. "It can't be any worse than when I changed his diapers."

The nurse stuck a thermometer in his mouth, lifted his head at the neck with her left hand and began unwinding the bandage with her right. She efficiently inspected the inflamed area, applied medicated salve, redressed the wound, took his blood pressure, checked his temperature, and wrote on her chart before giving him two tablets and holding a glass while he drank some water from a straw to wash them down.

"Can I have something to eat?" he begged.

"Perhaps some soup at the noon meal," she advised as she hurried out. "Press the button on the headboard if you need anything."

"I had something more like a cheeseburger in mind," he called after her.

His mother reappeared at his side. "We were talking about Lisa, Dean."

"We were *talking* about me getting something to eat, Momma."

"She seems quite taken with you."

"Mom, I'm famished. Please get me something to eat."

"Not until the doctor says so."

"That just proves it," he sulked.

"Proves what, dear?"

"Butch claims you like him best."

A gleam appeared in her eye. "Well, your brother *is* married and *has* got me a grandchild on the way."

"That's really cold, Mom. I bet if Butch was laying here starving to death you'd get *him* a cheeseburger."

"Oh, for goodness sake!" she chided as she settled back in her chair and picked up her book.

☆ ☆ ☆

Lisa returned looking refreshed, but the pills made him so dopey he dozed and starved while she and his mother sat chatting. He didn't get his soup until the evening meal, and then it was merely chicken broth. The nurse returned to change his dressings and gave him some painkillers, after which he slept the night through and awoke to an empty room. He got a small, lukewarm bowl of oatmeal for breakfast, with no toast or coffee, and morosely began planning his escape.

After the nurse changed his dressings and took his temperature, Lisa came in still wearing the sling on her left arm, but otherwise looking her old self.

"How are you feeling, Dean?"

"I want food, damn it."

"Much better, I see."

"Get me something to eat or we're through!"

"Who will cover your back if I'm not around?"

John W. Huffman

He glanced at the sling on her arm. "How's the shoulder?"

"It hurts."

"Next time, butt them with your head—that shouldn't cause you any damage."

"There better not be a next time."

"So bring me up to speed."

"If seems we're the heroes of the day for solving the murders of Sharon and Carlson Jenkins. Sheriff Parsons isn't too happy about it. He came by to see you yesterday but you were asleep. He specifically emphasized that per our agreement we were not to talk to the press until he's completed his investigation." She sat down in the chair beside the bed and adjusted her injured arm to a comfortable position. "He also confided that it's doubtful they're going to prosecute Mrs. Peters for Kenny's death or Charlene for Sharon's, Carlson Jenkins, or even for shooting you."

"You're kidding?"

"He says it's not official yet, but he believes the DA is going to call Kenny's death accidental."

"I can see them not prosecuting Mrs. Peters, but what's the deal with that crazy fruitcake that murdered Sharon and Jenkins and almost killed me?"

"You're going to love this part. It seems Charlene was in a mental institution for the last couple of years diagnosed as paranoid schizophrenic. Apparently, several years ago she had a nervous breakdown and tried to kill Sharon with a butcher knife. She was released six weeks ago."

"So the old girl really *is* crazy!"

"You're lucky you evaded her advances."

"Lucky hell, it got me shot in the head! So what's the good Sheriff doing about the sex tapes?"

"Sheriff Parsons took charge of the tapes personally after the fiasco with Carlson Jenkins and his dirty pictures. He met with the district attorney and they determined that only Sharon and Becky Roberts' tapes were evidence. They plan to destroy the remainder."

He sighed. "Do you really think Charlene killed Sharon because of me?"

"Don't go feeling all guilty about that. Sharon knew Charlene was crazy from the start and shouldn't have taunted her about you."

"It's all so mind-boggling," he allowed sadly.

"So, now that everything is all wrapped up, where does it leave us? Are you going to take that undercover job in Houston?"

"I wouldn't exactly call us the most astute detectives in the world."

"We were right about Al Roberts and we discovered the main evidence in Kenny's death."

"That roughly translates to us being half-assed detectives, especially considering we missed the half that damned near got us both killed. Oh, and we're almost broke."

"We're getting a lot of coverage in the papers which should bring us new business, and if you would agree to pool our resources we could last a couple of months."

"Actually, I've been kicking things around in my head while I've been laying here all doped up and I've come up with a proposition."

"And that is?"

"If you'll get me a cheeseburger, I'll tell you."

Her eyes narrowed. "I'll get you a cheeseburger only if I find your proposition deserving."

"*After* I eat my cheeseburger. I'm too famished to go into the details at the moment."

✲ ✲ ✲

Dean finished his cheeseburger as Lisa watched. "Delicious. You've saved my life."

"It'll be the last time I bother if you don't start talking," she threatened.

"Okay, here's the deal. I'm willing to keep our partnership intact for another three months *if* I get at least *one* uninterrupted night in bed with you wearing that slinky black thing. We'll see how things look after that, but no promises. Deal?"

She burst out laughing. "You *jackass!*"

"I believe that's *certified* jackass, thank you."

✧ ✧ ✧

Late that evening Lisa breezed into the room carrying a sack in the crook of her injured arm and waving a check. "Mrs. Jenkins gave us a ten thousand dollar bonus for solving the case! Apparently, she's coming into a bundle from her husband's insurance and feels responsible for you getting shot."

"You're kidding? So what's in the sack?"

She extracted her black nightgown. "The late shift has settled in for the night and shouldn't disturb us, so turn your head and I'll just slip into this."

"Uh ... that's not exactly what I had in mind."

She cocked her head. "I don't understand—that was the deal wasn't it, one undisturbed night in bed with me wearing my slinky black thing for another three months of partnership? I'm prepared to live up to my end of the deal."

"Well, yeah, but ... I'm immobile here ... and you're injured as well. I mean, I can't even move, much less... and ... and they just gave me a *sleeping* pill ..."

She grinned evilly. "*Ooooh, poooooor, pooooor baby!*"

7664318R0

Made in the USA
Lexington, KY
07 December 2010